Did Not Survive

Books by Ann Littlewood

Night Kill
Did Not Survive

Did Not Survive

Survive

A Zoo Mystery

Ann Littlewood

Poisoned Pen Press

Poisoned Pen Press
6962 E. First Ave., Ste. 103
Scottsdale, AZ 85251
www.poisonedpenpress.com
info@poisonedpenpress.com

Printed in the United States of America

Dedicated to Elmer Aldrich, family friend of my childhood, noted California conservationist, and the first to show me that sometimes magic wears feathers.

Acknowledgments

I'd like to thank several animal management and zoo professionals for their invaluable advice on elephants and other topics included in this book. Mike Keele of Oregon Zoo generously helped with the basic plot, Dr. Jill Mellen contacted Dr. Eduardo Valdes who suggested a realistic study that would put Iris in the elephant barn, Surendra Varma of the Asian Elephant Research and Conservation Centre in Bangalore, South India, provided details of Asian elephant behavior. Penny Jolly, American Association of Zoo Keepers Board Member, kindly read through the manuscript and pointed out omissions, misstatements, and the like. Cynthia Cheney proofread the manuscript with not only her keen editorial eye, but also from the perspective of her years as a zoo keeper and as the publisher of *Penguin Conservation*. There were others as well whom I must acknowledge without naming, as they are weary from the conflicts over elephants that form part of the story within.

Thanks also to the Vancouver, Washington, Police Department for their assistance on police procedures and to an Assistant Special Agent in Charge with the U.S. Fish and Wildlife Service who asked to remain anonymous.

An author reserves the right to err regardless of the advice of experts as well as to bend reality to the service of fiction. I take full responsibility for any and all mistakes and improbabilities that reside within.

Several other writers were kind enough to review and comment constructively on drafts. I owe a considerable authorial debt to my writing group, Nancy LaPaglia, Evan (Dave) Lewis, Marilyn McFarlane, Angie Sanders, Doug Levin, and Christine Finlayson, as well as to Becky Kjelstrom and Elizabeth Voss. Thanks also to Phyllis Gonigam for naming Nimbus.

Chapter One

Finley Memorial Zoo is a small zoo near Vancouver, Washington, and it should have been a quiet one this early in the morning. Damrey and Nakri, the two Asian elephant cows, should have been dozing in their stalls, not trumpeting loud enough for me to notice on the other side of the grounds. Slow-witted and gritty-eyed from lack of sleep, I walked on toward the Commissary, intending to clock in a little early after my night volunteer shift. That brought me closer to the elephant barn. The ruckus continued, and I stopped to puzzle it out. At seven in the morning, I was possibly the only human on the grounds. The night keeper went off duty at two in the morning. The night security guard was on his way home. Neither the day shift keepers nor any other staff had arrived yet, although they would soon.

I wasn't sure what I had to offer to elephants in a dither. I'm a bird keeper and an ex-feline keeper, not trained on elephants. Elephant handling requires special expertise, lots of it. But duty and curiosity called. I abandoned plans for coffee and a scone at the Penguinarium kitchen and jogged off, one hand stabilizing my six-months pregnant belly, to see what was up. At least I could phone Sam Bates, the senior elephant keeper, and tell him what to expect when he arrived.

Wide awake, I would have enjoyed a fine June morning after the dark Northwest winter. Leafed-out dogwoods and ornamental cherries lined the asphalt paths, beds of white and purple petunias contributed perfume, and passionate song sparrows hollered in the bushes. But the path was uneven, my balance and wind were not at their best, and I plowed forward without enjoying the journey.

Out of breath, I slowed to a walk as I passed the giraffe barn and entered the covered visitor area at the elephant exhibit. Through the viewing window I saw Damrey, the older cow, in the front stall. I had never worked this area and was secretly grateful for the pink blotch halfway down her trunk that instantly identified her. Nakri, the younger cow, was shut into the back stall, but the concrete door between the stalls was fixed open a little, leaving a vertical slit several inches wide. Nakri was waving her trunk through this gap, and I could see pink inside her mouth as she roared. What had got them so stirred up?

The elephant barn was a huge concrete box divided into the two stalls and an L shaped work area with hay storage at the rear. The front stall had a massive hay rack at the end to my left and to my right a sliding door, now closed, that gave the elephants access to the outside yard. Damrey circled by this door as though she wanted outside, ears out and flapping. She stopped and leaned her head on the door, banging it in a rapid vibration. The concrete slab rang like the drum of doom. She stepped away, her trunk in constant motion—curling under her chin, searching ahead and alongside her, reaching down to the floor. As I scanned for the source of her troubles, she wheeled and strode toward the other end of the stall.

On the floor by the hay rack, in the stall with the elephant, a person in a brown jacket lay face down in blood-stained straw. Damrey fumbled at the jacket with her trunk tip, then set a giant forefoot on the person's back and began rocking the body back and forth. I bolted for the staff door, fumbling to find the correct key. Inside, as close as I dared to the bars, I screamed at Damrey, "Get away! Get the hell off him!" She paced away from me, striding in a big circle around the stall, coming back to pluck at the body with her trunk and shove at it with a forefoot. Nakri roared again from the back stall and went down on her knees with her trunk outstretched through the gap in the door, reaching ineffectively for his arm.

A man. It looked like a man. Was he alive? Blood smeared the straw beneath and around him, with a dark, thick dribble on his head and down his face. I had to get him out of there before they killed him. If he weren't already dead.

Hyperventilating on air redolent with elephant and hay, I grabbed the radio bouncing at my belt and broadcast a human medical emergency at Elephants. I had no idea who might hear it, if anyone. I clawed my cell phone out of a pocket and searched for Sam's cell number, pressed the button to dial, and yelled at Damrey to leave him alone. Phone to my ear, I ran to the rack where the ankuses—elephant guides—were hanging. I grabbed one, a two-foot wooden handle with a metal tip that was both point and hook, and trotted back to the bars. I waved it at Damrey, yelling "Back off!" She strode away, huge and uncontrollable. Deadly.

She was behind a wall of bars, but I knew she could grab me through them if I got too close. Only the area near the hay rack and the body was safe. There, the bars were spaced too close for her to get more than the tip of her trunk through. I stood by the hay rack, the body a few feet from me, waved the ankus, and felt my heart pound. I couldn't reach him without moving to where Damrey could reach me. It made no sense to risk my own life, and I couldn't risk my internal passenger.

Sam answered after an eternity, and I gasped out the situation. He was wonderfully calm. "I'll be right there, Iris. Keep her away from him."

"I can't. She backed off when I got here, but now she's all over him. He's still alive—I saw him move. She's mauling him. I've got to get her shut away. You live too far."

"I'm at the gym. Fifteen minutes."

"Sam, that's not fast enough." I couldn't keep my voice from rising.

A pause. "Iris, here's what you do."

In the background, Sam's partner said, "Who is it? Tell them to call back later." Sam's voice, turned away from the phone, said, "Shut up, Brent." "Shut up" was something Sam would never say, last of all to Brent.

Sam told me what to do.

Phone clutched the way a diver in trouble clutches an air nozzle, I ran to the door to the keeper work room, through it, and toward the back of the barn. I found the set of levers that operated the hydraulic doors. The massive elephant-proof concrete slabs slid sideways to allow the animals to move between the two stalls and outside to the yard. Small safety windows in the concrete let me see what was happening.

Sam walked me through it, his voice dead steady. With shaking hands, I pulled the left lever to let Damrey into the outside yard. The door creaked wide, admitting sun and cool air, and she strode out. But as I pushed the lever and the heavy door slowly closed, she thundered back in. I could feel her steps through my boots. We waited and hoped, but she didn't go out again. I glimpsed her pacing gray body through the little window, agile and swift, and heard gusty rumbles vibrate down her trunk.

"She knows what you're trying to do," Sam finally said, "and she doesn't like it. We'll try something else." A few seconds of silence. "We need to get her in with Nakri. We want both of them in the back stall." He continued calmly, as though it was high time I learned how to do this ordinary task.

I hastened back to the work room, set the phone on the counter, and ripped open cardboard boxes of apples and carrots and lettuce. I threw a random assortment into a five gallon bucket, grabbed up the little phone, and ran to the back side of Nakri's hay rack, near the door levers. Phone squeezed precariously between my ear and shoulder, I dumped the produce into the chute above the hay rack in the second stall.

"Here, girl," I said, my voice shaky, and Nakri hustled over and tossed the food around, ears flapping, not really eating.

"Now for the tricky part," Sam said. "Open the door between the two stalls."

"Sam, can't I try shutting Nakri in the outside yard first?"

"No, you can't. The door from the back stall to the yard quit working twenty years ago when the building settled. You have to open the door between the two stalls. Be calm. You have to be calm, or they can't be."

I wasn't an elephant keeper. I couldn't read their body language or their vocalizations. Hell, I couldn't even *hear* many of their vocalizations—they were at too low a frequency for human ears. I didn't know these animals, and they didn't know me. Only Sam could have gotten me to open that door, the door left partly open. I could see the front stall through the little safety window as the big door edged sideways. Damrey stood back and swayed and watched it. As soon as it moved far enough, Nakri abandoned breakfast and rushed through, straight to the body. I'd let a second elephant at him. She snuffled her trunk tip all over him, pulling at arms and legs. At Wallace. It had to be Wallace, the foreman. Our boss. Zoo jacket, receding dark hair, bulky. She dragged him a few inches this way and that.

"Iris, say, 'Breakfast, girls. Hurry it up!' Say it loud and give the door a little jolt."

I said it as commandingly as I could and gave the lever a tug. The door between the two stalls closed up a bit. The elephants swung their trunks at it. Nakri blew a long snort.

Flashing lights through the little window caught my eye. A police car pulled up to the visitor area. Someone *had* heard the code I'd radioed in. I was thankful they hadn't used the siren and agitated the elephants even more.

Where was Ian Sullivan, the junior elephant keeper? Or Dr. Reynolds, our new veterinarian? Instead, Hap Ricketts, the Commissary manager, arrived at a run. There was only one reason for Hap to come—as a member of the shooter team, trained for emergencies when human life was at risk. I held up a hand for him to give me a few seconds, but he couldn't see me from where I was, behind the feed room, deep in the barn. I knew what came next if I couldn't get the elephants shut away, and it had to do with the big rifle in a locked case in the kitchen.

"Sam. They won't shift for me. Hap's getting the rifle, and they're both messing around with the body. *They won't shift.*"

"Well, *you're* perfectly safe, so just cool it."

He said it snarky, and in one seamless ripple of emotion I was shamed and then angry, and the anger drove out panic, and I realized this was Sam's exact intent.

Hap spoke briefly to the police officers and stepped into the barn. He moved swiftly through the door to the work room.

Sam said, "They will shift. Say it again and bang the ankus on the bars. Say it like you're amused that they're fooling around."

Deep breath. One hand holding the phone, the ankus in the other. Breathe. "Breakfast, girls! Come on now. Hurry it up. I haven't got all day." I banged on the bars.

"Good. Now start closing the door again."

I dropped the ankus. One hand clenched on the lever's round black knob, tendons white, I started the door, the other hand still gripping the cell phone lifeline. Nakri walked to the opening and put her head into her stall. She waited, halfway through, and I jolted it a little more closed. She rumbled and walked into her stall, turned and squeaked at Damrey. Damrey swayed and rumbled, swayed and rumbled, her trunk moving ceaselessly. Two police officers stood outside in the visitor viewing area with eyes riveted on us, one holding a radio to his mouth, the other with a hand resting on her holstered pistol, as if that little gun had any relevance.

Hap came out with the heavy rifle. Poor bastard, I thought with some remote corner of my mind. Damrey, purchased from a circus thirty years ago with pennies from local kids, featured in every zoo fundraising campaign, subject of this year's children's art contest, faced him and the rifle. She stood motionless except for her trunk tip reaching and bobbing, smelling for him. I could see the strain on Hap's face as he raised the rifle to his shoulder and braced for the recoil. "*Wait,*" I called. "*Wait a minute.*" Hap gave no sign of hearing me.

Nakri rumbled. Damrey turned and, in two strides, slipped into the second stall and draped her trunk over Nakri's neck, brushing it down her friend's broad face, the tips of the two trunks twining about each other. The door slowly, slowly grated shut, the lever slippery with my sweat.

Chapter Two

"Hap, it really was Wallace? I never got a good look. He was face down and then the EMTs swarmed all over him. Could the cops be wrong?" The jitters still ruled. Hap's bulk next to me should have been comforting, but the rifle seemed to have left some dark stain on him.

"Iris, they pulled his wallet. You know that."

We sat side by side on folding chairs in the zoo's empty auditorium, waiting while the zoo's director, Mr. Crandall, rounded up the rest of the staff. We had been sent from Elephants once the police were finished with us, and we were the first to arrive for this meeting. The two police officers had spent over an hour photographing the elephant stalls, poking around the barn, bagging up bits of straw, and asking questions. Sam, Ian, and Mr. Crandall had shown up one at a time and endured their own interviews. I looked at the clock. Half past eight. I would be well behind schedule before this meeting was over. I fished out my cell phone and dialed Calvin Lorenz, head keeper and my supervisor at Birds, and told him I was tied up with an emergency and needed help. It was his day off. He didn't ask questions. He said, "I'll be there quick as I can."

Gratitude calmed me for only seconds. I turned the cell over and over in my lap. "I saw blood on the hay. Blood on his head. Did you see if he was injured anywhere else?"

Hap twitched a broad shoulder. "Nope. No idea. All I could see was that elephant's face through the sights. I barely noticed him."

"I saw him jerk his hand once, that was all. I was really bad at shifting them. All that time being mauled. He might die because I couldn't get Damrey to move. I couldn't get her away from him."

Hap focused on me, pale eyes in a broad face, bald on top, a close-cropped beard below. "Iris? Chill. You did good. I didn't have to shoot anything."

"If he dies…" Wallace dead. I couldn't imagine it, couldn't imagine not having him as the foreman. He'd hired me. He'd always been in charge of keepers and animal management. Our schedules, animal acquisitions, exhibit repairs…Crabby, decisive, knowledgeable. "Hap, if he dies…"

Hap slung a thick arm around me. The dark tattoos on his wrist, disappearing up his sleeve, reminded me of powerful gray trunks.

Denny Stellar, reptile keeper, took the seat on my left. "Wow. I just heard. Do you think he had a heart attack? He was a text book case. Type A personality, ate white foods and red meat, had that crease in his ear lobe."

Crease in his ear lobe? "I don't know. He was passed out face down. I saw blood on his head. He lost a bunch of weight lately so maybe not a heart attack."

"Maybe he had a stroke. Maybe he paid too much attention to Nakri and Damrey got jealous. Could be she's got a brain tumor, and we'll have to euthanize her."

"Denny, *we don't know.*" As if anything I could say would stop Denny's ceaseless, off-kilter rummaging for explanations. I relaxed a little. The jitters could not survive the mystification and annoyance that Denny aroused. We weren't quite friends, more like herd members that would fight off the lions together, then kick one another at the water hole.

Keepers clustered near us as they trickled in, the office staff segregating themselves on the other side of the room. I glanced over my shoulder and saw Sam sitting behind us looking haggard. I was surprised he left the barn under Ian's supervision. Civilians in animal areas required constant vigilance, and police would be especially challenging. Ian was hired as the new elephant keeper three months ago. Would Sam already trust him? Perhaps the officers had finished and left.

Dr. Jean Reynolds, the zoo's veterinarian, sat in our group, with Kayla Leadon, the veterinary technician. "Poor Kevin. This totally freaks me out," Kayla said to the vet. "Elephants are supposed to be wise and gentle. I didn't think they killed people, at least not the tame ones."

None of us chose to enlighten her. Elephants in captivity kill a keeper every year or two in the United States or Europe. In India, where more people have contact with the animals, the toll is two hundred people a year or more. When you weigh four tons, a moment's irritation or panic is easily fatal for any human in the way.

With all the on-duty staff present except for Jackie Margulis, the office secretary, the little room was full. Jackie was stuck in the office to deal with the press and public, not to mention the phones. She would expect me to brief her afterward.

Mr. Crandall waited at the podium in front while stragglers seated themselves. The director was tall and silver-haired, erect of posture, usually benign and confident, a white beard confirming his silverback status. His age was a closely held secret, and the word "retirement" was not to be spoken in his hearing. Today he looked grim and preoccupied. I had a brief flare of hope that he would know something I didn't, something to make sense of this dreadful morning.

Only last week, Wallace stood at that same podium to run the keeper meeting, reporting the zoo's slow progress toward accreditation by the National Association of Zoos, urging us to chat nicely with visitors at every opportunity, announcing that he had tentatively found a pair of orangutans available for breeding loan.

Mr. Crandall stiffened to attention and muted conversation ceased. "We've had a serious accident here at the zoo today, and I want you all to have the facts, to the extent they are known. Kevin Wallace was found early this morning unconscious in the front elephant stall with Damrey. We do not know his medical condition at this time except to say that it seems serious. It appears that Damrey attacked him. He is receiving the best medical care, and I will keep you apprised of his condition to the extent possible."

By the muttered exclamations, I gathered that Wallace's calamity was news to some.

Mr. Crandall waited for the murmurs to die down. "We will take all precautions to prevent any additional accidents. From now on, our elephant management is changed to protected-contact. No one will go in with either elephant under any circumstances. They will be managed entirely by remote procedures. Under the circumstances, Damrey must be considered an extremely dangerous animal."

This was greeted with silence. I half-expected Sam to protest and glanced back at him. He sat with his back stiff and said nothing.

Mr. Crandall had more. "Please understand the seriousness of this incident. If it weren't for fast action by Iris Oakley, who happened to be on the grounds, Kevin Wallace could well have been killed outright, and certainly Damrey would have been shot to allow emergency personnel to reach him."

"Sam did it," I protested. "He walked me through it on the phone. I didn't know what to do."

Mr. Crandall's gaze shifted to me, but his expression did not flicker. "I appreciate that you worked well together. It is what I expect of our staff and what you always deliver. I could not ask for more." This was a stock compliment, worn thin. He looked over his audience. "I will be acting foreman at least until we understand the situation better. I will request that the National Association of Zoos send a professional committee to investigate. Occupational Safety and Health Administration will no doubt participate, and the police may also, at least until the nature of the accident is clear. I ask that you not discuss this event with the press, but instead refer all inquiries to me. Your assignments remain as before. I will keep you informed. The zoo will be closed today. Thank you."

Sam stood up, tall, lanky, graying, a senior keeper with thirty-five years at this zoo. "If I could say something."

Mr. Crandall nodded warily.

"I'd like to thank Iris for her good work this morning. She got the girls shifted, and it would have been hell to pay if she hadn't. And my personal appreciation to Hap for holding fire and giving it an extra minute." He paused, either to let that sink in or to regain control of his voice. "I'd like to add that Damrey would never have hurt Wallace in a thousand years. I don't know what happened, but she didn't attack him." He sat down.

I understood now why he'd left Ian at the barn and come to the meeting. Damrey would not take the rap if he could help it. He hadn't seen her mauling Wallace, and he wasn't ready to believe it.

Mr. Crandall nodded impassively, said "Thank you," and left us.

We moved out of the room, little wiser than when we entered, and some of us paused outside under the roof overhang. Not Sam—he headed for the elephant barn with his long stride, no word to anyone. This was a terrible situation for him, and it wouldn't end any time soon.

Hap biffed me on the shoulder and took off for the Commissary.

Dr. Reynolds stood a little apart in her white lab coat, staring into space. She was tall, almost my height, slender without looking frail, attractive in an understated, sober way. Long, loose brown hair framed a narrow, serious face. Her "uniform" consisted of brown twill pants, a gray turtleneck sweater, and a short white lab coat. Never any makeup or jewelry. She'd had a few years of experience, including working with wildlife in Africa, but this was her first job as the sole veterinarian at a zoo. She'd been with Finley Memorial only a few months. Today her customary professionalism was out of focus. She looked as though she'd lost track of what to do next.

Kayla, the vet technician, waited pale and patient beside her. When Dr. Reynolds was hired, somehow the deal included hiring Kayla as well. Kayla had worked in small-animal clinics, but she was new to the zoo world. The gossip machine claimed they had been college roommates. Nobody cared much about the favoritism because, on a normal day, Kayla was a kick to have around. Shiny brown hair bouncing down her back, brown eyes enhanced with careful makeup, a tattooed garland around each wrist. Today she wore a pink, v-necked little shirt over tight jeans and earrings of pink gems. Her white lab coat was slung over an arm. The vitality and good humor had gone missing this morning.

Linda, feline keeper and good friend, stood with me. Linda's face was pale beneath the freckles. "Iris, are you all right? What happened?"

Dr. Reynolds came out of her trance and listened. So did Denny, next to us.

I said, "I have no idea. The cows were bellowing, and I walked in to see Wallace face down in Damrey's stall. She was all over him with her feet and her trunk. There was blood. That's it, that's the lot. Except for me having a stroke trying to get those elephants shut away from him. It took forever. They were really messing with him. He might die because I don't know crapola about elephants."

"The docs will know," said Denny, ever helpful. "They can tell when internal injuries and broken bones occurred."

"Stop it," Linda said. "Iris got the job done."

Dr. Reynolds lost interest and walked away, Kayla at heel.

Linda said, "The question is, now what? What if he…doesn't come back as foreman? I mean, it could be months."

"Or never," Denny said. "Crandall can't run the entire zoo. He'll have to hire someone. Maybe get one of the senior keepers to take over temporarily. Who knows—it could end up better."

"Shit, Denny," I said. "You battled with him, and now you're glad he's dying or crippled? And Damrey may have to be euthanized. Congratulations on making lemonade out of *that*."

"I was just saying! I don't want anybody to *die*." Denny looked misunderstood and aggrieved.

Linda curled her lip at him. She grabbed my arm and tugged me away. "Really, are you okay? You need to be careful."

"I'm fine," I said reflexively, then caught her meaning. "I won't tune out like I did…before. I'm good." For weeks after my husband's death six months ago, I'd stumbled through my life and my job. I had been lucky to survive. Elephants aren't the only danger in a zoo.

"Call me and I'll come to Birds whenever you want to talk. Everything's good there?" Linda glanced at my belly.

"Running was not so good, but it feels fine now." I massaged it lightly to be sure.

She gave my arm a little shake. "I've got to get to work."

"And I've got to talk to Jackie," I said, and abandoned Denny while he was still explaining what he'd really meant.

Jackie would be afire with curiosity about the meeting. We kept a balanced information flow: I told her the happenings on the animal side and she leaked as much as she dared about the administration side. I'd have to keep it short today.

In the office, Mr. Crandall's door was closed, as was Wallace's. Jackie was on the phone saying that all she could do was take a message. She hung up and made a face. "I've got to get out of here before I kill someone." She did something complicated to the phone system, rummaged for her smokes, yelled "I'm on break" toward the closed doors, and charged outside. I followed, and we ducked around the corner of the Administration building to a spot under an overhang and out of most lines of sight.

Jackie reminded me of crows—black hair, bold features, and thin bones. She was somewhere beyond forty and had been Mr. Crandall's secretary and the office manager for years. Bored by her job and a solitary home life, she had cultivated a talent for infusing drama into any event, and she loved to share the results. Today she looked like she'd already overdosed.

The cigarette wobbled between her lips. "How crazy can this place get? The press is all over us like stink on…well, you know. What did Our Glorious Leader say?" she mumbled as she activated her lighter.

"What *could* he say? Apparently Damrey really flipped out. Wallace is down and out, we don't know how bad. Mr.

Crandall's acting foreman. From now on, no keepers going in with elephants."

"Wallace loved those elephants. Half the time he had that smell on his clothes from hanging out there. Ironic, right?" She took a deep drag and blew noxious vapors toward me.

"Kind of like cigarettes," I said. "Reeks and can be fatal."

After the required dirty look, she said, "Junior's okay?"

"No problem." I automatically wrapped a hand around my bulge.

"I guess you must have been the worst person to find him, right?"

Smoke curled up and around her face as she glanced at me with a delicate intensity, and I recalled the price of being her friend. Never show weakness, never say anything you didn't want circulated. "Just another day at the office," I said. "Sam talked me through it over my cell."

"Yeah, sure." She blew more smoke, aiming it off to the side. "Sorry it had to be you. Must of brought up bad memories."

Still not going there. "I've got to get to work. I'm way behind. Let me know when you hear how Wallace is doing."

"Read the paper instead. The press gets everything before we do. And those picketers are going nuts. They've got bullhorns now."

I'd forgotten about the picketers. Of course they were stirred up. They showed up in front of the zoo a couple times a week, starting a month ago, when a rumor got loose that the zoo was about to start construction on the new elephant exhibit. The good citizens of Vancouver had passed a bond measure almost a year ago to finally, finally bring Finley Memorial Zoo up to modern standards. The Asian Experience complex for orang-utans, clouded leopards, and a few birds and reptiles was well under way. Better, bigger elephant housing was expected to be among the improvements.

No such construction was happening, to Sam's considerable ire, but the rumor lived on. Generally three or four protesters walked in a loose circle outside the front gate carrying signs. I was familiar with the messages: "Zoos are no place for elephants,"

"Elephants deserve better," "Sanctuaries, not prisons." I'd read enough in the papers and online to know that certain animal rights groups were convinced that no zoo could provide a decent home for elephants.

"They already heard about the accident?" I asked.

"See for yourself."

I walked closer to the entrance's locked turnstiles and metal mesh gate. A black van with TV station call letters on the side and a satellite dish on top was illegally parked in front of the entrance. A sleek man in a stripy tie and blue dress shirt held a mic up to a bushy-haired guy in denim coveralls, who was speaking with emphatic head movements. The interviewee had a picket sign slung over his back and a bullhorn dangling low from one hand. The other picketers, a mix of men and women, circulated slowly. Their professionally-printed signs were gone, replaced by ones hastily hand-lettered with colored pens. "Zoo life makes elephants crazy," "Don't blame the elephant," "Already a prisoner—set her free."

Jackie spoke from behind me. "Try to improve the place and the hu-maniacs are all over us. They think we ought to pack up both elephants and send them off to some sanctuary paradise on their say-so instead of building a decent place here." She stubbed out her cigarette and added, "Yesterday, I would have said they were wasting their time."

Chapter Three

I left Jackie and finally showed up for work at the Penguinarium kitchen, the food preparation area for Birds. Calvin had gotten there first and started the daily routine. He was a quiet, stocky guy maybe sixty years old. I'd come to admire his honesty and hard work, his passion for anything in feathers, and he seemed comfortable working with me at last. As senior keeper of Birds, he directed the work, but he listened, and we made a good team. Calvin was a widower with a daughter and some grandkids. Now and then he pulled out pictures to show me a junior high school graduation or vacation shot. He was delighted by my pregnancy and insistent that I avoid many activities he perceived as risky.

I filled him in on the morning's disaster while he rinsed fish in a bucket at the left sink, and I stuffed vitamin pills into their gills at the right sink. The silvery smelt and herring were barely thawed, and yellow rubber gloves did little to protect our hands from the cold. I stacked the supplemented fish into a stainless steel pan on the counter. The rest went into a five gallon bucket.

African penguins hung out by the keeper door that let us access their exhibit. They liked to stand on their island and watch us work. Some of them were willing to waddle into the kitchen and supervise us more closely, so we stretched a baby gate across the door in the morning. We shut the door when the zoo opened and visitors started showing up.

When I'd finished my news bulletin, Calvin asked, "What were you doing here so early?"

I'd skipped that part. "Linda has a night watch going on Losa, the clouded leopard. She's due any day. I took a shift. The camera's set up in the Education office since I'm not allowed in Felines until my baby comes. I mean, I can visit, but I can't hang out."

"I'm surprised you're up to doing that night work, big as you are. Need your sleep."

I tried not to bristle. "I'm fine, and I really want to see those cubs."

Linda and I had watched when Losa was first introduced to Yuri. Clouded leopard boyfriends are prone to domestic violence, sometimes fatal, but Yuri had tolerated a stranger in his space, kept his focus on reproduction, and got the job done, albeit with teeth and claws and yowling, while two nerve-wracked keepers and a veterinarian stood by wondering whether to use the hose to separate them. Now Yuri was safely shut away from Losa for fear he was not up to parental responsibilities, although they stayed acquainted through wire mesh. She was showing a little belly, eating a little more, and pissing out urine that said, yes, yes, babies in progress. Linda and I were ecstatic and had shifted our worries to her mothering skills.

Calvin stepped over the baby gate with the pan of supplemented fish. Penguins crowded around. "What is it, three-four months for them? Must sound like a breeze to you."

That it did. "Thirteen weeks gestation." Whereas I had been gravid for six months and had three left to go.

"Good thing you were here early," he said as he handed out fish to eager beaks. "Be terrible to shoot Damrey. Sam would never get over it. *Wallace* would never get over it."

He seemed to be assuming Wallace would survive.

Calvin shifted his attention to the penguins and chatted with them, calling each by name and admonishing them to be polite. When they were fed, we worked methodically to prepare food for the other birds, without a cross word from him about his beloved penguins breakfasting late or about having to work on his day off.

The zoo was strange without visitors. I'd always thought that it would be wonderful to have the place all to myself without the noise and trash of the great American public, but the silence and empty paths emphasized the day's tragedy.

I hid out at lunch time, avoiding Denny and the rest of the curious, and tried to hold up my end of the work despite a head full of leftover dread. Calvin left two hours before quitting time, when we were caught up. I clocked out the minute my shift ended and fled to my truck.

My new house was a welcome sight, even if it didn't feel quite like a real home. Winnie and Range, my dogs, were world-class therapists. I threw dirty zoo coveralls—Calvin's, since they fit me and mine didn't—into the washer, and we all bolted our dinners. Theirs was expensive kibble, mine was of the previously frozen variety. I managed a stroll around the block so that they could check their smell phone messages and tossed two tennis balls in the back yard for half an hour. Winnie, mostly shepherd, romped after Range, a sturdy black lab mix, but wisely let him collect both balls. Happy dogs goofing around cheered me up and dozing in front of the television set shut off compulsive rehashing of the day's crisis. Nonetheless, I slept badly, dreaming of slithery gray trunks whuffling elephant snot all over me while giant round feet came down way too close. I woke with a pounding heart and got up early rather than risk falling back into it.

I drove to work still unsettled and edgy. Mr. Crandall was waiting at the time clock, which was pretty much unprecedented. Mr. Crandall arrived in his office at eight in the morning. You could set your watch by him, Jackie claimed. It was also Sunday, which was officially a day off for him, along with Mondays. But there he was in his charcoal suit, white shirt, and polished leather shoes at seven thirty at the Commissary where we clocked in. When the roster of brown uniforms was assembled—Denny was five minutes late—Mr. Crandall squared his shoulders and began. "As I said, my intention is to keep you informed during this challenging period. Kevin Wallace remains in critical condition. As you should already know, I have assumed his duties. Are there any concerns over scheduling or your job responsibilities?"

"Could *Nakri* have whacked him?" Denny asked. "Instead of Damrey? I hear the door between the stalls was open a little. Could she get her trunk through?"

Mr. Crandall never allowed himself to look disconcerted or annoyed. Instead, he eyed Denny and paused, as though waiting for him to come to his senses. That wouldn't happen any time soon.

As the closest thing to a witness, I felt obliged to field it. "I don't see how. Nakri couldn't reach him where he'd fallen, and she tried. It would be pretty peculiar for him to walk over to her, get clobbered, and fall so far away."

"He could have staggered around," Denny argued. "Or Damrey dragged him away."

That was remotely possible, but I kept quiet, hoping to hear whatever Mr. Crandall had to say. But before he could reclaim the reins, Arnie Bertram, the bear keeper, said, "Nah. Old Damrey went berserk and smacked him."

Where was Sam to jump to her defense? Ah. Sunday, his day off. Ian was present but silent. Not so Denny. Mr. Crandall opened his mouth, but Denny said, "What did the doctors say about his injuries? Could someone have attacked him? Not an elephant, I mean."

Every now and then, Denny's compulsive hypothesizing came up with something useful, but this was not one of those rare occasions. "*Denny*," I said. "All the indications are that Damrey flipped out for some reason. No conspiracy required."

That earned me a brief, forced smile from Mr. Crandall. "Iris is correct as of our current knowledge. More information may be forthcoming, and I will share that with you as it becomes available." He added, as an aside, "I'm sure you know that medical information is confidential by federal law."

Denny wasn't deterred. "What was he doing there alone? Maybe an experiment on Damrey or he was meeting someone secretly. Maybe it had to do with those animal rights activists. Or blackmail. There's a lot we don't know about Wallace's personal life. Blackmail gone wrong…"

Linda yanked the conversational ball away. "What's going to happen to Damrey? If she's really that dangerous, can we still keep her here? We're not exactly state-of-the-art in elephant facilities."

I checked out Ian and caught a tiny, rigid nod of agreement.

Mr. Crandall took a breath and resumed our regular program. "No decisions have been made in regard to either elephant. I am sure answers about the incident will be forthcoming as a result of the police investigations and the National Association of Zoos committee visit, which is being scheduled. I will keep you informed as I learn more." He picked up steam—a tiny frown and the voice of authority. "I've been assured that with the new protected-contact procedures, no keeper is at risk from the elephants. Please let me know if you have safety concerns. Some of you may be interviewed by the police as well as by the NAZ committee, and I expect you to cooperate fully. The zoo will re-open today with normal hours. Again, please refer all questions to me and avoid speaking with the press." He nodded in farewell, took a step toward the open door, then turned back with an actor's precision. "Be safe out there, all of you." Another nod, this one for emphasis, and he walked to the steps that took him down off the Commissary dock and strode with dignity toward the Administration offices.

He hadn't promised any more early morning updates. Perhaps he had taken away a new understanding of why Wallace was so often irritable after meeting with keepers. I scuttled out quickly, evading the bull session that was sure to follow. No one knew any more than I did, and reliving my experience trying to shift Damrey was the last thing I needed.

Sunday was a day off for Calvin. "Real" weekends off were a prize available only to the most senior keepers. Saturday and Sunday, I normally worked Birds all day alone. On the three days a week that Calvin and I overlapped, we undertook the big jobs, such as draining and cleaning the penguin pool, or, if Calvin didn't need me, I was assigned elsewhere, usually Primates.

Today I wasn't at top efficiency, thanks to a lousy night's sleep, and the extra weight I was packing was starting to slow me down. But without Calvin around, I had nothing to prove and could go at my own pace. I settled into the familiar routine. The kitchen smelled of fish and fishy excrement and the air periodically rang with penguin brays.

I stepped over the baby gate and handfed penguins while I inspected them for lack of appetite, lameness, or any other sign of decline. I checked out Mrs. Green, so named because she had a green wing band for identification and a well-established gender from years of laying eggs. She had become widowed about the same time I had, but was much farther along the path of grief and acceptance. As Calvin had pointed out, she was undeniably putting the moves on Mr. Brown. Despite Mrs. Green's age—advanced for an African penguin—Mr. Brown was responding. Mrs. Brown, on the other hand, apparently held to the "mated for life" rule. I hoped nobody lost an eye.

Zookeeping has its share or more of boring work, and today I was grateful for that. I felt too twitchy and nervous to face any challenges. Wallace and the elephants intruded as I pushed a steel cart loaded with food pans along asphalt paths. He was an experienced elephant person. Damrey had been at the zoo for decades and never hurt anyone. What had gone down? I hoped Sam would figure it out soon. I hoped Wallace was recovering.

The zoo was open, a sliver of normalcy. Visitors arrived and wandered about. Delivering food to the duck pond set off the usual avian food riot and drew a crowd, almost all moms with strollers or toddlers or both. The older kids were fascinated by the mass of wild, uninvited mallards shoving aside the zoo's mandarin ducks, pintails, and wood ducks in a grand display of oafishness. The mute swans rose above the fray, literally. Tall and long necked, they outcompeted the free loaders and scarfed their share.

I checked out the variety of kid carriers, an excellent distraction. Strollers ranged from Porsche to Hummer. How did women get these contraptions in and out of cars? The backpack carriers with sleeping or fussing infants looked good for climbing Mt. Kilimanjaro. Did Goodwill have an infant department or did I need to refinance the house to buy this stuff?

One woman hoisted a toddler, a little boy, up on the guardrail to see the waterfowl better. Her belly bulged even more than mine. The prospect of managing a pregnancy and a kid at the same time made my knees weak. The little boy wiggled and his mother set him down. She missed a grab for his hand and he shot off. She called after him in a voice thick with artificial sweetener, "Cecil, Mommy wants you to stay close. Come back now or Mommy will have to come get you."

This was a world I must master and somehow I would, but no child was ever going to hear me refer to myself in the third person.

Next up was cleaning the owl and hawk exhibits. Usually that was a simple matter of picking out the casts—tidy regurgitated pellets of bones and fur—and raking the wood chips until the droppings were hidden. Today the exhibits were due for a more thorough cleaning. The old spectacled owl was unaggressive. I pulled a little white mask over my nose and started shoveling chips into the wheelbarrow.

Shoveling was mindless work and my brain soon wandered. Wallace on the floor…Damrey rampaging…My heart rate and breathing ramped up. Clutching the shovel, I hoped fervently he wouldn't die because, logical or not, I would feel somehow responsible. I willed away the image of his limp body. His and Rick's, months ago in the lion exhibit…A peacock yelped nearby and startled me out of grief. I straightened and stretched and wrapped an arm under my belly. I couldn't bring back my husband, but our child felt like another chance.

By lunch time, Birds was in decent shape, and I'd eaten all the food I'd brought. Time to forage. Time to see whether more information had come in about Wallace. Maybe connect with Linda and get an update on cats.

As luck would have it, Linda and I converged outside the café, and we walked in together. I played it safe with a beef burrito, and she opted for a turkey sandwich and potato chips. The day was nice enough to sit outside, and we got a good table, one that didn't wobble, with chairs not adorned with peacock droppings. Visitors wandered in and out of the entry gate and the gift shop. They didn't ask us any questions about Wallace or elephants so we didn't send them to Mr. Crandall.

Linda had replaced me as Feline keeper about five months ago. The rough transition was not her fault—I trusted her competence utterly. She was grounded and sensible, although she'd developed a bluntness that was at times unsettling. The Linda I first knew was a little shy, a little cautious about speaking her mind. Maybe it was hanging out with the big cats. Her hair had grown out a couple of inches from the last time she'd whacked it off. The tips were blond and the roots were her natural dark red. She kept adding metal rings to her ear rims, something a cat keeper could afford to do. Anyone who worked Primates was likely to have them yanked off. Linda was average height, a few inches shorter than I, and square shouldered. No one worried about Linda injuring herself picking up a bag of feed.

Denny joined us, and, after hesitating, Ian pulled up a chair as well. We formed a loose circle, with Ian and me facing toward the zoo's entrance.

Denny and Ian shared a lean body type, and that was about it. Denny was blond and lithe with intense gray eyes, radiating energy and—I hated to admit it—a sexuality that I could never quite ignore. That last characteristic had led us to a brief period as a couple, before I met and married Rick Douglas, now deceased. Given a choice, I might have fled permanently from Denny's restless delight in all ideas bizarre, conspiratorial, or both. But we worked together and he was dating, as in "with benefits," my best non-zoo friend, Marcie Altman. Denny had his virtues, but this was a doomed relationship. I regretted introducing them, but neither had any interest in my blessing.

"You know they had the veggie burgers today," Denny said. "That red meat is setting up the kid for obesity and heart disease."

Hang me for eating a burrito. "Denny, zoo burritos have about a teaspoon of real meat. It's 98% beans."

"Here's some goji berries. They'll balance out that stuff. Awesome antioxidants. Are you using the whole salt I got you?"

I stuffed the packet of dried fruit into a pocket and wondered if three more months of Denny's helpfulness would lead to the headline "Woman In Labor Slays Co-Worker With Fetal Monitor."

Ian's was a different style of odd. He was built like a runner or mountain climber, all sinew and bone, strength without bulk. His face was narrow, with a long thin nose that looked as though it had been broken and left to heal at an angle. Murky brown eyes, ordinary brown hair. The peculiar feature was his ears. They were small and round and stuck out from his head at right angles, cupped forward like those of a panda or a baby rhesus monkey. Maybe he could hear better than those of us with flat ears. He was not a talker, and no one had learned much about him in his few months at Finley Memorial. He had thwarted our highly functional gossip machine, and I found that intriguing.

"What do you think happened to Wallace? Why did Damrey go nuts?" Denny asked him.

Ian shook his head. "No idea."

"You must have a theory. You know those animals. You know Wallace," Denny persisted, not yet wound up, asking nicely.

Ian shook his head and kept his eyes on his burger. "Nope."

"Did you know elephants used to be executioners? They called it 'crushing'. Rulers in Asia would train them to kill prisoners. They would—"

"Denny!" "Stop it!" Linda and I spoke on top of one another.

"I'd think you'd want to know," Denny muttered, subsiding. "I also found out that—"

Arnie pulled up a chair, and we all scooted over to make a space. He leaned toward me, beaming. "Hey, Fertile Myrtle. How's your parasite doing? Need any more pickles or ice cream?"

This ragged give-and-take was the reason Linda and I often ate in the Feline kitchen in bygone days. The Feline building was forbidden territory for pregnant people, so we lunched with our co-workers, like it or not. Maybe "annoyed" was a good state of mind. It beat "panic stricken," also "irrationally guilty and anxious."

Arnie was short, even with Western boots adding a couple of inches. His cheap cowboy hat was dark red with a ring of tarnished silver conchos around the brim. His smile was toothy and clueless through a brushy mustache.

"I'm fine." I short-circuited his grilling on the state of my womb by asking Linda about Rajah.

She shrugged. "Some days he eats, some days he doesn't. He's drinking a lot of water. Doesn't move around much."

"That old tiger has a lot of miles on him," Arnie chimed in. "He's what—twenty-five or six?—about at the end of the road."

Linda and I exchanged a look. Raj was a favorite with both of us. It was going to be hard when his time came.

"Losa's in some kind of holding pattern," Linda said, not waiting for my next query. "Nothing happening that I can see. Maybe she reabsorbed all the cubs, and we'll watch and wait for months until we catch on. She's toying with us." She picked at her potato chips.

I'd already inhaled most of my burrito. "Nah, you have to *earn* cubs by suffering. We haven't suffered enough night shifts yet. Who's on watch tonight?" My own belly transmitted a tiny squirm.

"Me. And I am going to be pissed if she doesn't pop."

"I'll let Losa know." I headed back to the cafe for another burrito. I said "hi" to Olivia, the Children's Zoo keeper, settled at another table with her crew of four volunteers. They had their own slice of the zoo and it didn't overlap much with the rest of us.

When I returned, Arnie was expounding on how unreliable elephants could be, interspersed with a lecture from Denny on musth. Since musth applied to male elephants, a condition in which they suffer from self-generated testosterone poisoning and become aggressive, I didn't see the relevance. Ian kept his mouth shut.

"Anyhoo," Arnie said, "I'm sure glad I don't have to work with that Damrey. Once they go rogue, there's no going back."

"She's not a rogue," Ian said softly.

We pricked up our ears, but that seemed to be all he had to contribute.

"Here's what I think happened," Denny said.

"Fasten your seatbelt," I muttered.

Denny didn't notice. He learned forward, jabbing a finger toward the rest of us, all enthusiasm and energy. "Damrey and Nakri have some sort of issue going on, and Wallace tries to break it up. Damrey aims for Nakri, he gets clobbered by mistake. That's one possibility. Another is that those animal rights people broke into the barn and planned to turn both elephants loose. Have them roaming all over the zoo to get a lot of press coverage. Wallace tried to stop them, they hit him and ran away. But it could be that Wallace was involved in some sort of corruption with the bond measure money and got wiped out for a double-cross. The hit man dumped him in with the elephant so that she'd take the blame. I think that's the most likely." Denny paused to lick catsup off his fingers. He'd managed to consume a mushroom burger while free-wheeling. "And," he added pointedly, "I hope he wakes up soon and tells us."

Hearing Wallace's injury processed through Denny's mental cyclone somehow made the accident less the stuff of nightmares, closer to everyday reality. Denny's fantasies aside, wild animals were always dangerous. Accidents happened. I shivered anyway, seeing that hand twitch as Damrey's trunk tip plucked at his jacket.

Ian, by contrast, looked at Denny about the way he might look at a goldfish in a hay bale, but he didn't say anything. Kayla, the veterinary technician, tugged a chair over from another table and perched on the edge of our circle next to him. A lacey lavender shirt contrasted with her lab coat and our dull uniforms. Today's jewelry—her signature—was a necklace of big silver links. "Do you guys know yet what happened with Kevin Wallace and that elephant?" she asked.

"No!" said several voices.

Kayla recoiled. "Just askin'! Good grief! What's up with you guys?"

Denny sat back, already changing channels. "Did you know that humans and elephants can transmit antibiotic-resistant bacteria between each other? That's the kind of superbug that gives you boils and abscesses."

"Still eating," Linda warned.

"What does that have to do with Wallace?" Kayla asked him.

"Nothing," I assured her. "Denny is speed-hypothesizing. Try not to get any on you."

"I want to know," she insisted. "Mr. Crandall won't let me in the barn anymore, keepers only. We need to finish the elephant project. Jean—Dr. Reynolds—is upset about it."

We turned to Ian for elaboration.

"Only keepers in the barn."

"I got that," I said. "Are you and Sam safe? With the new rules?"

Ian chewed the last of his burger, stalling. "Manage behind barriers." He paused, apparently to let a trickle of words refill his verbal well. "I worked places that manage elephants that way. Train them with treats instead. Takes longer at first, but it works. Fewer accidents." He considered for a moment while we waited. "Better to transition gradually. Not in one day." I thought he was done, but he added, "Wallace took chances."

"You mean routinely?" I asked. "He didn't follow his own rules?"

Ian nodded.

Sam's voice startled us. He'd come up behind me, where Ian wouldn't see him either. "Wallace knew elephants. He didn't take chances. Something strange happened the other night, and we'd better figure it out quick. Damrey is getting railroaded. Crandall is riled up and making up rules about stuff he knows nothing about."

I swiveled around. The tall elephant keeper looked tense and miserable. "Pull up a chair. Isn't this your day off?"

Sam shrugged. "Needed to come in." He didn't pull up a chair.

A young man with long dark hair, a visitor, sat down near us. He didn't have any food, just sat facing away from us, close enough to overhear.

"What do you think happened?" I asked Sam, my voice quieter.

"I have no idea. Damrey would never hurt him, but now Mr. Crandall is treating her like a crazy killer."

I spoke as gently as I could. "Sam, it really looked like she was mauling him. If you keep trusting her, you could be next."

He looked grim. "Working Elephants could be a lot more dangerous than it used to be. I'm thinking about carrying my .38 until this is settled. I've got a concealed permit."

In the silence that followed, Arnie said, "A .38 isn't any use against an elephant." We let him figure it out on his own.

Linda said, "The city won't allow it. Not even the security guards have guns. You really think a person hurt Wallace and not Damrey? "

Sam's shoulders twitched, shrugging her off. "The investigation should clear this up, but Crandall's not waiting. He's shoving dolphin training down our throats for elephants. Thousands of years of elephant expertise, all of it full contact. A cow that's been totally reliable for decades. But he's tossing all that out and buying into the latest hippy-dippy theories about love and positive thinking. How am I supposed to manage them when I can't go in with them?" His fierce glance at Ian made it clear who he thought was influencing the director.

Ian evaded his gaze. He took out a pack of Camels and lit one. Linda leaned away from the smoke.

Sam scanned us all. "I would appreciate it if none of you went around blaming Damrey." His gaze lingered on me. "She gets a reputation as a killer, she's going to get shipped off somewhere. That leaves Nakri alone, after almost twenty years together. You can figure out what that'll do to both of them. And it would put the last nail in the coffin of a new exhibit." He looked each of us in the face again, as if searching for the weak link, and walked off toward Elephants. The dark haired visitor got up and walked in the same direction.

Ian looked at his watch and made no move to follow Sam. Probably he had a few minutes left of his half hour lunch period, but it made me realize that the two elephant keepers didn't move as a team.

"*Dolphin* training?" Denny asked.

"Operant conditioning," Linda said. "You've heard of it?"

This was a sneer. The zoo had brought in a consultant to provide a workshop on modern animal training for all the keepers. The method began in psychology labs and was refined in aquariums and sea parks. Most zoos were using the techniques, which turned formerly stressful events such as veterinary examinations and even injections into opportunities for the animals to earn special goodies. It was amazing what animals would volunteer for if they had the right training and the right reward. Wallace said it was revolutionizing animal management in zoos. Finley Zoo had come late to this, but now we were all expected to incorporate "husbandry training" into our daily routine. I'd started with the lions before I left Felines, and now Linda had them opening their mouths for dental inspections, and she could position them wherever she wanted in the den to inspect all body parts. Calvin and I had the penguins trained to step onto a scale one at a time, rather than grabbing them to weigh them.

"Yeah," Denny said, "I have heard of training, believe it or not. It just surprised me to hear him go all traditional and rejective. Sam needs to let go of that negativity and of this gun thing, or he's going to hurt his back again."

I wasn't sure whether this was a non sequitur or actually made sense, aside from "rejective." Sam *was* prone to back trouble. The idea of him packing a pistol was alarming. In our little zoo, full of visitors, most of them children? It was also troubling to hear Sam speak so disparagingly of alternative methods, on top of denying what had happened to Wallace.

"This is all very interesting, but it does not help a bit," Kayla said. "I can't go into the elephant barn anymore, and Dr. Reynolds wants the project completed. How's that going to happen?"

"She'll figure it out," Linda said, getting up to go.

Kayla folded her arms under her breasts. "Yeah, maybe. She's not dealing at all well with this. You'll call me when the kittens come? Please?"

Linda said, "Of course," and headed back to work. Everyone else left, Kayla last, and I sat for a moment gathering my energies.

When they were first hired, Linda had watched Kayla and Dr. Reynolds closely and concluded that they were not a couple. Linda had reason to care. She asked me wistfully whether I thought Kayla dated girls. "I know how to find out," I'd responded. "Ask her." Linda had plenty of guts when it came to her job, but none for dating. The question answered itself when Kayla commenced flirting with any guy who would play. Linda went back to researching lesbian bars she didn't have the nerve to enter. I worried that being around Kayla was tough on her, but if Linda had feelings for the vet's assistant, she kept them well buried.

Denny/Kayla was less complicated. She'd flirted, he'd shared his view that since swine flu was a mix of bird and pig genes, it was an effort by the planet's animal consciousness to combat global warming by killing off most of humanity and that, on the whole, this was not a bad idea. No need after that for me to intervene and keep him safe for Marcie.

"How can any guy that hot be so weird?" Kayla had asked.

"Raised in a yurt by Wiccans," I told her. She'd thought I was kidding.

I got up and tossed my lunch trash into the crocodile-jaw garbage can. Jackie wasn't in today. No Wallace updates available from anyone. I stopped by the tiger exhibit and said "hello" in my best tiger poof-rumble-growl. Raj prüstened back at me, which never failed to delight. He was laid out in a patch of sun, looking bony and faded, but he had his head up and was paying attention. My chest tightened at the thought of losing him.

I ignored the lions in the next exhibit over. I couldn't logically blame them for killing Rick, it's what predators do, but we were hardly friends.

Walking on, I pondered the fragments from lunch. Sam was stressing out, and I didn't envy Ian working under him. Sam was meticulous almost to a fault—my first week, he'd trained me exactly how to coil a hose properly—and he'd been taking care of the two elephants for years. I hadn't thought of him as closed to new ideas, but Ian hadn't sold him on a different style of handling the animals, any more than I convinced him that Damrey was dangerous.

Who did Sam think he needed to defend himself against? My skin prickled.

Soon Wallace would recover enough to tell us what happened. Then this would all make sense, and we could settle down again. I looked forward to that.

Chapter Four

"She's licking it," Linda murmured, to a chorus of soft "ahhs." We spoke in whispers, as though the clouded leopard a city block away behind thick concrete walls might somehow hear us.

It was five in the morning and we were transfixed by the video monitor in the Education office. For an hour, the den camera had showed a restless Losa turning on her straw bed, standing up only to lie down again. Several minutes ago, we'd spotted a small gray lump on the straw. Now Losa was lying curled around the lump, pink tongue at work. The light was too low for details, but it was clear that she was finally delivering her cubs. Or cub.

Linda had phoned me twice. I'd missed the first call and laid in bed half asleep trying to figure out who it could have been and what to do. But she'd dialed again immediately and this time I'd lunged before voice mail kicked in.

"Losa's pacing around. I think this is it. Bye, gotta call Dr. Reynolds." And she'd hung up.

Here we were, heads bumping as we leaned our faces to the monitor—me, Linda, Kayla, and Dr. Reynolds. Dr. Reynolds relaxed on her chair as though this was exactly what she expected. Kayla fidgeted on a stool. Linda and I acted as though this were the first clouded leopard birth in the history of the planet.

After several minutes of watching Losa alternate between licking her offspring and quietly panting, I stood up and started a pot of coffee. I'd brought some bananas and Linda had a bag of vegan oatmeal cookies, so I figured we would survive the morning's drama.

The clouded leopard coat pattern is irregular blotches—"clouds"—outlined in black and tan. They have gorgeous pelts and live in southeast Asia, in forests that are fast succumbing to loggers. It follows that they are at risk of extinction from hunting and habitat loss. They are not all that common in zoos, and it was a tribute to Wallace's wheeling and dealing that we'd gotten a pair.

In the next thirty minutes the cub managed to orient toward its mother's belly and possibly suckled a little. We cheered its success and wondered if this chapter was over. Perhaps one cub was the allotment for this mating and pregnancy. I discovered I was rubbing my belly, unconsciously trying to include my inhabitant in our delight. Losa now knew more than I did about birth and nursing.

Linda gnawed a cookie, never taking her eyes off the monitor.

Kayla stood and stretched. "You guys look like you just won the lottery." She sat back down and sighed.

After a quiet period, I said, "What I keep thinking about is Wallace. Clouded leopards were such a big deal for him."

Linda said, "He asked me about them almost every day."

Dr. Reynolds looked interested.

"He spent most of a year trying to get a pair, while I was feline keeper," I told her. "It was Christmas and Fourth of July when he found out Losa was available. Cubs were huge for him. Is he awake enough that we could tell him? Might cheer him up."

Dr. Reynold's shoulders rounded forward. "I tried to visit him last night—earlier this night. He's in ICU and I couldn't get in. The nurses are circumspect, but my impression is that he's still unconscious."

"Is that another one?" Linda's voice cut through my concern.

We stared even harder and muttered—"Did that dark bit to the left move?" "Is that a head?" "What's that behind her leg?"—until we were all satisfied. Two cubs.

"They are so *cute*," Kayla warbled. She had to be using mostly imagination given the low light level. "Is there anything cuter than baby kittens?"

"Cubs, not kittens," Linda said absently. "Like lions."

Even though clouded leopards are technically "big cats," classified with lions and tigers, they weigh only thirty to fifty pounds. Losa was toward the small end.

Losa focused on the second baby while the first squirmed about randomly. Linda's face looked as though she were about to ascend to a new level of existence well above our ordinary lives. "Two," she breathed. "One more? How about one more?"

I handed out celebratory cookies.

"She'd better not blow it," Linda said. "Not after all this."

Dr. Reynolds shook her head and fingered her hair. "We'll keep the area quiet around her. She's got another den to move them to if she gets nervous. She'll be fine."

"She's a timid cat," Linda fretted.

"Not like she was when she first came," I reminded her. "She settled in a lot."

"Maybe we should have waited to breed her, given her more time…Never mind, I'm wound up," Linda said. "It's just that these cats make every step so hard."

"I've raised house-cat kittens," Kayla said. "It wasn't that hard."

A little silence fell. We all knew that wild felines sometimes kill their young if they're disturbed, sometimes even if they aren't. First-time mothers are especially likely to fail. It happens in the wild, too, not just zoos. All our worries were shifting this direction.

Dr. Reynolds had a small edge to her voice. "We could hand raise them, and we might have to, but I prefer to have her raise them if at all possible. They need to nurse to take in colostrum. That will provide some protection against disease until their own immune systems start to work. They'll also behave more normally if their mother raises them. We'll pull them only as a last resort."

I knew all about colostrum from the pregnancy books my mother had piled on me. It's the first milk a lactating mammal produces, watery and full of antibodies. Eventually I would be churning it out myself.

Kayla persisted. "You're the boss and all that, Jean, but couldn't you let them nurse and then pull them? I mean…what if she freaks out and kills them?"

She didn't seem to realize that she was poking at a sore spot. Linda stayed current on the latest in clouded leopard management, and the latest from other zoos said that hand rearing looked like the best way to go. Aside from protecting them from mommy dearest, hand-rearing resulted in cats that were calmer and more tolerant of changes in their environment. Linda was all for pulling the cubs and Wallace had been amenable, but Dr. Reynolds was firmly on the side of mother rearing. With most mammal species, everyone would have agreed with her. But clouded leopards were a tough species to manage, and conventional methods didn't work as well.

Dr. Reynolds said, "We will start out giving Losa every—"

"Another one!" Linda said. "Three! Three! Hot damn!"

We watched until it was time to start work. Losa behaved perfectly, cleaning the three cubs and lying still for them to nurse. The babies were totally incompetent, inching around in the wrong direction, tangling up with each other and with Losa's legs, exhausting themselves in futile struggles to find sustenance. I wanted to grab them and stick each one on a nipple. It's a wonder that any creature survives without human help. But by the time I had to leave, all three had been attached at least briefly.

I stood up to go, suddenly stiff and aching. Linda practically skipped to the white board on the wall and wrote down the date and time. Underneath, she wrote "0.0.3 *Neofelis nebulosa.*"

"I'll bite," Kayla said. "I know the Latin for clouded leopards, but not the number stuff. We didn't use that in the clinics I've worked in."

"This is the first significant birth or hatchings since we started here," said Dr. Reynolds. "The first number is males in the litter or clutch, if it's birds. The second is females. Since we don't know the sexes yet, we can only put the litter size in the third place."

Linda wrapped her arms around me in a brief hug. "We did it. I am so happy for us," she said in my ear.

I grinned all the way to the Commissary to clock in. No one but Hap was around to hear the news, but he bumped bellies with me. "Congrats! You're on a reproductive roll. Keep them coming!"

I wrote on the whiteboard at the time clock: 0.0.3 *Neofelis nebulosa* and the date. It looked fine in my handwriting, too.

Dr. Reynolds would make the official report to Mr. Crandall, who would report it to the press. He would be delighted to have good news to share with newspapers and television, after the spate of bad publicity about the accident. "Rogue" was the most common adjective for Damrey in the press, and questions were being asked about her future. The parents of the little girl who had won the draw-an-elephant contest were threatening to sue. The zoo had "knowingly" endangered their child by having her picture taken petting Damrey. This was weeks before Wallace's accident and the girl was thrilled, but a TV reporter interviewed the family and got the father worked up. I wished we had more good news in the pipeline.

It was Monday. Calvin had taken the day off since he had come in Saturday to help out after Wallace's injury, and I worked Birds alone. I was still feeding the penguins and still smiling every time I thought about Losa when Jackie called to let me know a police officer was on his way. All too soon, a big old guy with a buzz cut and keen eyes in a sagging face knocked on the door and said, "Ms. Oakley? Detective Quintana. I'd like a few minutes of your time." He wore a black jacket with a white shirt, black pants, and black shoes. He looked like an undertaker. An undertaker with a bulge under his left armpit.

I instructed him on use of the disinfectant footbath, persuaded him to wash his hands, and poured coffee into one of the elegant blue cups Linda had made for me. I shut the keeper door on penguins that wished to observe and critique. He sniffed at bird by-products and fish, winced, and got down to business. Penguins brayed in the background. He set out a tape recorder, and I agreed to its use.

For most of an hour I relived the scene at the elephant barn two mornings previously, demolishing my triple dose of cub-joy. The officers who had responded first had asked innumerable questions right after the incident. This was even more intense—all the details, going through it again and again, backing up to explain how animal management worked, the little I knew of how elephants behaved, why we did things the way we did.

Over and over, I described Wallace lying on the straw, blood on his head, the ankus next to him, elephants milling around and tugging him with their trunks, his body sliding a few inches at a time as Damrey shoved him with her forefoot. I kept good control over my voice and hid my hands in my lap.

"Tell me again why you were here alone before the zoo opened."

"All the keepers come to work before the zoo opens. We have to get the animals fed and cleaned. I was extra early because I had a night shift watching a clouded leopard who was due to give birth." I had to explain that the monitor was in the Education office instead of at Felines for health reasons related to my own reproductive status. "I can't spend much time in the Feline building. I need to wear gloves and a face mask when I do. Cats shed an organism called toxoplasmosis that's harmful to human fetuses." He seemed skeptical, as though I was faking Losa's pregnancy or my own.

"So you were here that night with no one around?" he asked in his deep, flat voice.

I didn't like the implication. "I filled out a behavior log. You can take a look at it. And the vet called me a few minutes before I left."

"On your cell phone?"

"No, on the phone in the Education office."

That seemed to satisfy him.

"Tell me about your relationship with Kevin Wallace."

That was tricky. "He, uh, wasn't long on charm. He could be rough-tongued, although he'd lightened up a lot the last couple of months. He was fair and good at his job."

"Who didn't like him?"

"It was an accident, right? What are you getting at?"

Detective Quintana gave me a mournful look. "Routine. We have to explore all the possibilities. Who didn't much like the guy?"

"I have no idea." I was not going to toss him Denny.

"Your husband died here a few months ago, right? In another animal accident."

"Yeah. It's in the police reports." I was grateful when he decided not to dig further in that particular black hole.

Nonetheless, I felt as if I'd been clear-cut and strip-mined. When he paused to review his notes, I groped for something to salvage from this painful process. "Could he have hit his head on the wall? Maybe had a heart attack?"

Of course he didn't answer.

"Why is this a police investigation?" was my next effort.

"It's a high profile situation." Detective Quintana handed me his card, shook my limp fingers, and said he might need to get back to me later. "Does it smell like this all the time?" he muttered. Wimp.

I held the door for him and went back to hand-feeding the penguins, grateful to be done thinking about elephants. The penguins were upset that I was late with the rest of breakfast after excluding them from an interesting visitor. Some were pushy and some were standoffish, and I was even more behind schedule when all had eaten whatever they were willing to. Mrs. Brown ate little, while her faithless ex and Mrs. Green were relaxed and hungry.

A hasty feed-run to the aviary and pond, and it was past my lunch time. I'd missed my fellow keepers, perhaps just as well. But Jackie stepped out of the café and wanted to know how my inquisition went. I shrugged. She told me that Sam and Ian were still on the hot seat.

"I wish we knew how badly he's hurt," I said.

"'Head trauma' is all I can find out. Which means, like, nothing. No details available. And Mr. Crandall is driving me crazy. He's coming in early and messing with everything. If Wallace doesn't come back soon, I'm going to lose my mind. I never thought I'd long to have Kevin Wallace at his desk."

"Kevin Wallace: competent and crucial," I suggested as a tag line. He *had* changed for the better, and I'd been slow to re-evaluate my old insecurity and aversion to authority.

She shrugged. "Cranky, constipated, and conspicuously absent." She smiled at her own wit. Sentimentality was not Jackie's thing. "I have to get back to work. Come on by when you can and tell me what that old cop wanted to know."

"Will do," I lied. I bought a veggie burger to go and met Linda halfway back to the Penguinarium. She was even later to lunch than I was. "How's it going?" I asked.

"Still three, all nursing. Losa looks pooped. She's sleeping. You look wrecked."

"You, too. You won't forget to tell everyone to keep the activity down near her den? Maintenance, too?"

"Nope. I won't forget. If I hear so much as a nail drop, blood will be spilled."

Satisfied, I hiked back to my herring-perfumed refuge and settled in for a cold pseudoburger in solitude.

I sat alone at the little table and chewed and stared into space, trying to recapture the elation from seeing those shapeless little cubs, trying to override the scene the police officer had made me reconstruct so thoroughly. Lack of sleep, the grueling interview, pregnancy hormones—for whatever reason, my defenses failed. I was back in the elephant barn trying to get Damrey away from Wallace. The elephant barn morphed into the outside lion exhibit, Wallace's limp body merged into Rick's...A different police interview, that one from a woman. Going home to a house that I would never share with him again. Rick gone forever, maybe because we'd quarreled and so I wasn't with him that night.

I lived in a new house now, one I'd bought with Rick's life insurance, but I perched uneasily in it, unable to turn it into a nest. We are a species that pair bonds and I was a female with no mate. All I had left of Rick were a few possessions, his big-hearted dog, and our last tangible connection—a flutter in my belly. Those, and shards of guilt that sometimes didn't stay buried.

The kitchen door opened, and I lurched back to the present. Dr. Reynolds squished through the foot bath. "Hi, Iris. Could we talk for a minute?"

In my experience, zoo vets didn't ask to "talk" to keepers. They requested information and gave instructions. I got her a cup of coffee in the guest cup and sat back down, wondering what was on her mind. I offered her an orange and peeled one for myself.

Today she seemed uncharacteristically hesitant. I broke the awkward silence. "I saw Linda a few minutes ago. She said Losa was doing fine with the cubs."

"Yes. It looks good so far." Short finger nails carefully stripped the rind from the orange. "These cups are lovely." She broke off a segment and ate it.

"Linda's a potter on the side." I chewed on my own orange and tried to guess her mission. Second thoughts about hand rearing the cubs? She would talk to Linda, not me. Changes to bird management? That would be Calvin.

Her fingers methodically tore the rind into small squares. She shifted in her chair. "The accident—Kevin Wallace's accident—has caused some disruption. Mr. Crandall has banned non-keepers from the elephant barn. It has to do with the zoo's insurance policies. Kayla can't collect urine samples for a research project."

"She mentioned that at lunch yesterday. She's worried about the project." Why couldn't I escape talking about Wallace and elephants for one little lunch break?

Dr. Reynolds pushed a strand of long brown hair back over her shoulder and stacked up the bits of orange peel. "This study is our first significant collaborative research with other zoos. I think we have useful data to contribute, and a research program is required for the National Association of Zoos to give us accreditation. This project started with antelope, looking at nutrition and phosphorus levels. The project head recently added elephants and asked us to participate, along with about a dozen other zoos that hold elephants. Kayla has good experience with domestic animals, but Mr. Crandall perceives her as inexperienced with exotics."

I nodded, wondering why she was explaining this to a bird keeper. The orange scent masked the fishiness. Maybe I should ask Calvin about trying a citrus-oil cleaner.

"I'd like to ask you to collect the samples until the incident is resolved or until the study ends next month. Mr. Crandall has approved it."

"Me?" I hadn't seen it coming. "I'm not good with elephants. I don't know anything about them." And I didn't want to go back there. Not even a little bit.

"It's not at all difficult. You were Sam's first choice."

"I see."

Dr. Reynolds relaxed and smiled a little as though I'd agreed. "Ian trained the elephants effectively, and they urinate on command. You reach through the bars with a cup on a stick, collect a sample, and refrigerate it. I pick it up later. That's all there is to it. It's only on your regular work days. If you could start tomorrow…"

"Why don't the elephant keepers do this?"

The vet spoke with a careful absence of emotion. "Sam says that they don't have the time, especially since he is helping design the new exhibits for Asian antelope and deer. He says that elephants plus the zebras, giraffes, and other animals that he and Ian are also responsible for don't leave time for sample collection. I agree that the staffing level is too low."

"Kayla was the logical person to do it."

Dr. Reynolds nodded, her face still carefully neutral. "Kevin said Kayla could do it if a keeper were present at all times, and Mr. Crandall agreed." She pushed the bits of peel aside. "Kevin Wallace said that if we want to breed Nakri, we must track her cycle. Sam accepted that the training was a reasonable investment of Ian's time." She let her frustration show. "For a simple procedure, I've invested hours in setting this up. It would be quicker to do it myself, but I need to set the precedent for future research projects. I can't do it all."

"So you need some keeper to show up and do what Sam won't do himself or let Ian do."

"That's the size of it. Sam prefers that it be you. He assures me that whatever happened with Kevin was a fluke and that Damrey is acting normally. I don't see any risk to you as long as one of the keepers is present, and you follow the procedure. Otherwise of course I wouldn't request this. Would you rather not because of your pregnancy?"

"No, that's not a problem." I was pregnant, not disabled. "It would put me behind on work here at Birds, though. I've had a lot of disruptions lately."

"The procedure takes only a few minutes, but I'll get an authorization for overtime. Mr. Crandall is quite supportive of this study."

Being paid overtime generally required Congressional intervention. This was compelling evidence that the veterinarian and director were serious about the study. Sam had tagged me. Refusing without a persuasive reason was unwise. Why couldn't elephants carry some disease pregnant humans were required to avoid? The flesh-eating bacteria Denny talked about…No, for now I had to go along. "Um, afterward, could you maybe put a little note in my personnel file? I kind of need to balance out some…stuff…that happened a while ago?"

"Of course. I would do that anyway. Your help is greatly appreciated."

So it was settled.

I circled back to something she'd said before. "You're thinking about breeding Nakri? Artificial insemination? I know we can't keep a bull."

"Perhaps. Assuming a new exhibit is constructed, one big enough for a calf and, of course, a modern elephant restraint chute and a scale."

"I don't understand why it's been delayed."

The vet shrugged. "We may be out of the elephant business anyway, depending on the NAZ committee investigation. I hope they can figure out what happened and why."

I hesitated. "When Wallace wakes up, he can tell us, right?"

After a little silence, she answered quietly. "I don't think that is going to happen." She looked away, the corners of her mouth pulled down.

Kevin Wallace was more than her coworker.

Pieces came together. He'd lost much of his excess weight in the last several months. We thought he'd had a health scare. He'd been unusually cheerful. I'd thought it was due to the new exhibits going up. He and Dr. Reynolds held regular meetings in his office. We thought it was because she'd been hired only a few months before. Wallace in a relationship with a woman fifteen years younger? I was pretty sure no one else had put two and two together either, or the gossip mill would have been red-lined.

"I'm sorry to hear he's in such bad shape. I didn't realize."

Dr. Reynolds didn't say anything.

She flipped her hair back again. I pulled the Styrofoam cups containing routine penguin fecal samples out of the fridge. She took them, thanked me for the coffee and orange, and left to finish her rounds.

I started toward the aviary, late again. I picked up litter, examined the birds, and pondered. The vet thought Wallace was going to die or stay in a coma forever. The police were conducting a serious investigation. Sam wanted me to go back into the barn and work with the elephants. I didn't like any of it.

Chapter Five

My hand shook a little as I put the key in the door to the elephant barn, adrenaline detritus from my last way-too-dramatic visit. This morning, however, the morning after Dr. Reynolds' request, I found Peaceable Kingdom. Damrey rocked gently at her hay rack masticating a big wad of hay. Nakri's rump was visible through the gap in the door to the back stall. No roaring, no trumpeting, no limp body. The work day had barely begun, the stalls hadn't been cleaned yet, and the atmosphere declared the barn was full of herbivore—strong, warm, and humid. Science must march on, and so I marched in.

Ian nodded "hello" as he stretched a fire hose down the keeper alley toward the elephant door to the outside yard. He was careful to keep the hose close along the visitor window. I knew why after more episodes than I cared to remember of cougars chewing on hoses I'd left within reach. "The girls" would love to entertain themselves by snagging the hose with their trunks.

Through the open keeper door, I spotted Sam standing at a counter in the work room. Like Ian, he wore a green polo shirt with the Finley Memorial Zoo logo. A thick twist of red twine cut from hay bales stuck out of the rear pocket of his brown uniform pants. No shoulder holster, no bulge at an ankle. I relaxed a little.

I wouldn't be back in zoo pants for months. It was baggy brown coveralls until the baby came, with the name of someone built thick sewn on the pocket, like "Calvin." I peeled off my zoo jacket, also brown, and draped it over a chair in the little office area. "Hi. I'll be your Kayla today," I told Sam. "Today's breakfast special is warm piss." Nothing like smart-mouthing to cover up the jitters.

Sam handed me a five-foot broomstick with a funky wire loop in one end and two unused paper coffee cups. "Here." He demonstrated how a cup fit in the loop. "This is the official scientific pee collector. Ian will demonstrate the technicalities of operating it. Thanks for doing this." He handed me a pair of disposable white gloves and waited for me to leave and get started.

Sam was sensible and careful and had mentored me kindly when I was new. It was Sam who taught me to be aware of each animal's agenda and not just my own, Sam who told me not to take Wallace's growling personally, Sam who first welcomed me to the lunch gatherings. He was an old friend, and nothing bad would happen while he was in charge. I swallowed and walked through the door and toward the front stall.

Ian was waiting near Damrey's hay rack. He held out a hand to show me a fistful of raisins mashed together to make a lump. "Stand here. Watch her. Don't be where she can grab at the stick." He studied me to make sure I was digesting this. I nodded obediently. He added a final precaution that sounded as though someone once said it to him and he had memorized it: "Most dangerous time is when you know the routine and it's all working good. People get careless."

I nodded several times. No carelessness. Not me.

"Damrey," he called.

Damrey wheeled to face us. The bars near the hay rack were too close for her to reach her trunk through, but she tried. A little pointed beard of long hair hung from her lower lip. "Pee," Ian said quietly. The elephant rocked from side to side, ears flapping gently, as she sniffed in my direction, then the trunk swung toward Ian's hand with the raisins. She turned away and walked toward the other end of the stall and circled back. Her footsteps were almost silent, only a shushing noise as her feet scuffed straw and wood chips out of the way. Each step seemed deliberate, not like the nervous tapping of a blackbuck antelope or a deer. I wondered how many ribs those feet had broken when she was mauling Wallace.

"Has to get her mojo working," Ian said, which was the liveliest thing I'd ever heard out of him. He seemed almost relaxed around the animals, and his words flowed more easily.

Damrey circled back toward us, checked again that Ian really did have raisins, and turned around to present her butt to the bars. Ian took the stick from me and waited. Instead of urinating, she turned around and sniffed at us again with her gray and pink trunk tip, the wet little finger on the end working. She blew a long snort, picked up some straw, and threw it on her back. She walked to the far end of the stall, rubbed her side against the rough wall a bit, and then stood rocking from side to side with her back to us. Ian didn't say or do a thing.

I felt as though I were deaf. Damrey was fairly shouting at me with body language, and I had no idea what she was saying, except that she didn't feel like standing near me and emitting bodily fluids.

After a minute or so, Damrey walked to the door to Nakri's stall and squeaked. Nakri squeaked back. Damrey ignored us some more.

"Come on," Ian said to me. "Time out."

Damrey wasn't cooperating, and he was withdrawing his offer to trade a treat for pee. We walked into the work area, where Sam was measuring quarts of grain into five gallon buckets.

"No pee?" Sam asked. "We haven't got all day."

Ian didn't say anything.

We stood around for three or four minutes watching Sam work and went back out. Damrey stood at the far end of the stall next to the bars with one hind leg stretched behind her and rocked, shifting her weight from front to back. "What's she doing?" I asked.

Sam answered from the doorway behind us. "She does that when she's upset. She spent years in a circus, and they chain their elephants most of the time when they're on the road. She's pretending she's chained by that leg."

It was weird, watching her tug on that invisible chain over and over. For the first time, I noticed the faint pink line circling her ankle. An old scar.

Ian said, "Damrey. Pee." Damrey stopped her repetitive motion, came right on over, and started in with the smelling again. Her deep-set little eyes seemed filled with suspicion, the long, sparse lashes waving as the wrinkled gray eyelid moved. Sam stepped up to the bars to our right, where they were wide enough apart for a person to slip through sideways.

"It's me, isn't it?" I said.

"She doesn't know you yet," Sam said.

"And I'm associated with Wallace's body."

Neither elephant keeper said anything.

Damrey turned toward Sam and draped her trunk over his shoulder. He rubbed the trunk, his hand moving firmly over the rough, wrinkled hide. It looked like old friends comforting one another in a tough time, trying to get each other through. Would she really turn on a person she knew, who'd been careful and gentle with her? It could happen, I knew it could happen. But this particular elephant? "See?" Sam said. "She hasn't got a mean bone in her body. Wait till you get to know her."

Huh. So that was why Sam tagged me for this job. I was the chief witness against her, and he wanted a chance to show me the Damrey he knew. I didn't like being manipulated, but I wasn't going to hold it against him. The facts would speak for themselves. But I wished he'd get out of her reach. Hadn't Mr. Crandall forbidden physical contact? Had I misunderstood that?

"Pee," Ian said quietly, holding out the raisins for her to smell again.

"Have Iris give her the raisins, and we'll try again tomorrow," Sam said, still touching the elephant.

Ian ignored him.

I kept my eyes on Damrey, trying not to feel the tension between the men, trying to conceal my uneasiness.

Sam stepped back out of her reach, and I relaxed a little. After a few more moments of watching the swaying and tail swinging, he commanded, "Enough. Drop it. We need to get this place cleaned up." He was talking to us, not Damrey.

Ian didn't move. I glanced nervously at Sam and, while I focused elsewhere, Damrey swung her rear toward us and unleashed a flood of pee. Ian stuck the stick through the bars into the deluge and pulled it back. He blew a toot on the whistle he had on a string around his neck and handed the raisins to me. Damrey stepped away from the puddle and stuck her trunk in the bottom of the hay rack, fishing around. "Toss them in," he said. I calculated the trajectory through the bars and tossed. And missed. The clot of raisins hit the floor. Damrey searched the hay rack thoroughly while I winced. She gave up on that, swept her trunk over the floor beneath it, and soon sucked them up. She stuffed the lump in her mouth and chewed it with huge teeth.

Sam said, "If Nakri gives you any trouble, cut it short. I mean it. This has got to be quick or not at all."

Ian carried the stick and cup to the work area, put a standard plastic coffee lid on the cup, pulled it out of the wire loop, wiped it off with a paper towel, and pressed a piece of tape over the sippy opening. He handed me a pen. I wrote "Damrey" and the date on the cup. He nodded and pointed with his chin toward the fridge.

On to Nakri. I pushed a fresh cup into the wire loop. "Dried mango slices," Ian said. "You use the pole." We walked through the work area to come up on her stall from the back. The hay rack in the back stall was similar, also with closely-spaced bars, and Nakri seemed ready for business.

"Nakri, pee time," Ian said.

Nakri didn't waste any time checking me out or working through performance anxiety. She swung her rear around and let go. I wasn't expecting such rapid production and was lucky to catch the last of it. Ian tooted and handed me a big sticky slice of dried mango. I flicked it into her hay rack, spilling some of the urine in the process. About an inch was left in the cup. We looked at it and shrugged. Nakri chewed her treat and scratched an eyelid with her trunk tip.

"As good as we're going to get," I said, and carried the cup into the kitchen to process like Damrey's.

I heard the squeal and grate of the big doors operating. Sam was opening Nakri's door so that she could join Damrey and also opening the outside door. The two buddies greeted one another and ambled outside. Sam shut the door to lock them out so the keepers could clean the stalls.

"Be consistent with Damrey," Ian said quietly. "Routine-bound. May take a week to get used to you, like with Kayla. Faster if you do everything the exact way I do. Nakri's not so fussy."

"Will you walk me through it again tomorrow?"

Ian nodded. "They'll be together."

That should make my task even more interesting. I was late to my real job, stressed out from close contact with an animal I'd seen almost kill someone, and tomorrow I'd need to avoid getting swatted by both elephants at the same time. "Why back together?" I asked.

Ian looked surprised. "Nakri had an abscess on her hip. Damrey messed with it at night. Healed up now."

Of course. The elephants would want to be together. They were herd animals, social, and were separated only for a medical reason. That was why the door between was left a little ajar at night, so they could visit with one another.

Sam caught me as I was on my way out. "Iris, this situation with Wallace is a misunderstanding as far as Damrey goes. You'll see when the committee gets here, and we have all the facts. Just don't go calling her a rogue, okay?"

"Of course I won't call her that. But come on, Sam!" I softened my voice. "No wild animal is totally reliable. You taught me that. They have their bad days and pet peeves like we do, except that when an elephant gets crabby, somebody ends up smashed flat because humans are small and breakable. You know that way better than I do. Everyone wants the real story, everyone wants the best for Damrey. And there isn't much you can do to steer this."

"All I'm asking for is an open mind," he said, not quite snapping at me. "I'm not asking for the moon, only a little help saving an animal's life. She didn't attack Wallace."

"Sam, if you're wrong and you keep giving her the chance, she might kill *you*."

Sam's shoulders sagged. "Iris, you're not hearing me. You are *not* hearing me."

This was so not worth Dr. Reynolds' gratitude.

Outside the barn, I stopped to view the yard where the two cows he cared so much about were enjoying the morning. The pink tops of their ears glowed from the low sun shining through, a benign contrast to their other-worldly silhouettes. They really were something else. Strong, smart, sociable, complicated. I loved big cats, which were at least as dangerous. I could appreciate elephants as well.

Wallace might wake up. The NAZ committee would figure out what happened. Sam would be proved right or not, and we would all cope. Calvin must be wondering what was taking me so long.

"Don't you wish you could do better than this?"

My head jerked around. Two scruffy men, both with picket signs, stood near me. The one that had challenged me said, "Every day you work here is a day these elephants suffer. Isn't it time you took a stand for better living conditions?"

He spoke from a thicket of beard, another bush radiating out from his head. He was a little shorter than I. Whether that was fat or muscle filling out the denim overalls and dark red jersey shirt, I couldn't tell. His sign said, "Sanctuary from Suffering," and a blue and gray backpack sagged on his shoulders. The other man was a boy, maybe eighteen, in regulation jeans, dark sweatshirt, and muddy running shoes. His black hair was too straight to make a good bush, but he was trying hard by leaving it long and not combing it. "Prisons drive animals Insane" proclaimed his sign. He looked familiar.

"How did you get in? The zoo's not open yet."

Bushy Hair said, "The front gate's unlocked. I know you're not an elephant keeper, so maybe you can be objective. Is this any way to keep those majestic animals?" His arm sweep took in Damrey and Nakri minding their own business, idling about the yard. "Wouldn't you rather see them roaming grassy hillsides?"

"I assume you mean an unaccredited sanctuary with no oversight, where the public has no idea what's going on. No, that doesn't sound all that wonderful."

"I could show you pictures. It *is* wonderful," he said.

"Why don't you put your energy into saving elephants in the wild? Do you realize how endangered Asian elephants are?" Mr. Crandall had forbidden us to get sucked into this debate, but still…somebody had to push back.

"It's irresponsible to keep two elephants in an exhibit this size. They're meant to roam miles every day, not hang out in a space the size of a backyard."

The younger one nodded and scowled.

I said, "That's why we passed the bond measure to build them a bigger, better exhibit. Why is it I don't see you demanding that construction get started?"

"Because there is no way you can build an exhibit large enough to keep them healthy and happy. They're sure to get foot and leg problems, and there isn't room for a normal size herd." He'd had this debate before, and he was enjoying it.

I wasn't. I was getting pissed off. "People work night and day to keep them healthy and happy." I remembered a discussion from a keepers' meeting. "Do you see the sand two feet deep in that yard? That soft surface inside the stalls? That's why their feet are fine, even though Damrey is over forty years old." I couldn't remember exactly how old she was. "How about the full-time veterinarian, the top quality hay and produce, all the effort that goes into environmental enrichment for them? I do not see two sick, miserable animals. I see two busybodies who are wasting time here when they ought to be working for sanctuaries in Thailand and Cambodia and India, that is, if you really do care about elephants and not just about getting your pictures in the paper."

That fired up the young sidekick. Eyes flashing, he half-shouted, "Next I suppose you'll claim that these two are 'ambassadors for their species' and that all their suffering is so that the wild ones will survive. But you said yourself that it isn't working! You drive them crazy in zoos and then you blame them for turning on people!"

I had no idea where to begin with this jumble, but before I could try, the younger one said, "If everyone here is so nice to these elephants, where did Nakri get that gash on her thigh? Could it be that someone took an ankus and ripped her open?"

"No," said a quiet voice. Ian. He must have seen the altercation through the window and come to back me up. "They get browse. Each week. Maple, maple and alder branches. She lay down on one. Poked herself. It abscessed." He turned to me. "Sam called Security."

"Of course he did," said the junior activist. "You can't stand having the truth come out, so you evict us."

"Enough, Dale," said Mr. Bushy. "We've made our point. Let's go look at zebras. See you later, Ian." He turned away, and I stepped back from his sign and backpack as they swung toward me.

"I don't believe that about the branches for one minute," the sidekick called over his shoulder as they retreated.

The security guard rolled up in a little electric cart. I pointed at the retreating signage. "They went thataway." The guard spun the sluggish little vehicle around and did his best to roar off.

I gathered myself back into bird keeper mode. "Thanks, Ian. Stinks to be the target."

He nodded.

"What's *with* those two?" I asked. "They can get into the zoo before it's open, and the big-hair guy knew I wasn't an elephant keeper. How do they know all this?"

"Don't know how they got in. They know you don't work this area because they watch. All day."

"Watch elephants the entire day? Why?"

"Short guy talks to visitors about sanctuaries. Young one hopes we hit one of them. Get it on camera."

"That's disgusting." I was mad all over again.

Ian shrugged and started back toward the barn.

"Ian, he knew your name," I said to his back.

He didn't turn around or slow down. "It's on my shirt."

That was true. I watched him disappear into the barn. But the senior sign-waver sounded as if he really knew Ian, not as if he'd just read his name. I shook it off and got on with my real work.

A little before noon, I dropped by the office to see if Jackie wanted to join me for lunch, hoping for news of Wallace. Mr. Crandall was exiting the Administration building as I approached the door. He brushed a hand over his silver hair and straightened his tie, gave me the briefest of distracted nods, and stepped toward the zoo entrance. I watched him through the gate. He positioned himself in front of the Finley Memorial Zoo entrance sign, facing a cluster of media types who bore an assortment of cameras and microphones. A press conference.

"What's up?" I asked Jackie. "The cubs?"

She shook her head, busy with the phones. I waited while she put three callers on hold and looked up, her face tight with strain.

"Not the cubs. Wallace's sister let the hospital disconnect his life support. He died an hour ago."

I flinched in dismay. Dr. Reynolds was right. Kevin Wallace wasn't going to resolve anything.

Chapter Six

Damrey was not acting in her own best interests. She paced in the front stall, tail stuck out behind her, ears flat to her head, trunk waving around. She rumbled and blew long gusts and generally announced that she was upset, unhappy, and having a really bad day. Nakri wasn't as wound up, but neither was she the picture of pachyderm passivity. The cows milled about the barn, scuffling through straw and wood chips, pacing in and out of the two stalls.

This was a change from their calm cooperation half an hour earlier in the morning. Ian had stood by while I wielded the cup on a stick, tooted the whistle, and pitched out dried fruit. Damrey was no dummy and had searched the floor in front of the hay rack for her raisin reward before realizing that this time I had managed to dunk the wad properly into the hay rack. Nakri was the soul of cooperation. Anything for dried mango seemed to be her operating principle.

But now people were gathering inside the barn, in clusters by the service door and in the aisle along the viewing window. The zoo was not yet open, so no visitors or activists would be observing, or so I hoped.

Damrey was apparently not pleased to have all these strangers nearby. I relaxed my jaw and opened my fists. No one was at risk. It was only an excited elephant safely behind bars. I joined our team—Sam, Ian, Dr. Reynolds, Hap, Kayla, and Mr.

Crandall. Two uniformed police officers, the two who responded to my emergency call when Wallace was first injured, stood with Detective Quintana to make the second team. They all stayed well clear of the elephants.

Mr. Crandall introduced three strangers who had to be the National Association of Zoos committee. Ed Berchtold was a small, handsome man of about fifty, the senior elephant keeper at a major Eastern zoo, wearing jeans, a thick green chambray shirt, and steel-toed boots. Dr. Barry Morgan, a veterinarian specializing in elephants, was casual in boots, shorts, and a Hawaiian shirt. The third, Dr. Lorene Rasmussen, was a research biologist. Mr. Crandall said she had spent twenty-five years studying Asian elephants in zoos and in the wild. She sported khaki safari pants with cargo pockets and a short-sleeved blue shirt with snaps. The three seemed to know each other well.

Mr. Crandall announced the Finley Zoo staff's names and roles. He said, "Having us all here is an opportunity for a complete review of the events that led to Kevin Wallace's death, with all interested parties present."

I heard no gasps. Word had gotten to us all that Wallace had died.

Mr. Crandall continued. "The police are here because every unattended death requires an investigation. I am grateful they agreed to participate with the committee instead of requiring another disruptive session with the zoo staff. Unfortunately the OSHA representative has the flu and can't make this meeting. I'll address their concerns at a later date." He folded his hands in front and stepped back, ceding leadership.

I assumed that the vet in the tropical shirt, Dr. Morgan, was in charge, but it was the tanned, weathered Dr. Rasmussen who led off with a second formal statement. "First, I want to express to those of you who worked with Mr. Wallace that the committee is very sorry for your loss." She let that sit a beat. "Today we are here to determine, if possible, what led to the accident that occurred last Saturday and how to prevent anything similar from happening again. We will walk through background information and then the entire incident. We will follow up as needed tomorrow before we fly out in the afternoon." She turned to Dr. Morgan, who knew his lines.

He said, "I draft the report. Barry and Lorene review it. Fred Crandall should have the preliminary draft in about two weeks. We may or may not have recommendations for managing the elephants here. It may affect the process to get this zoo fully accredited. We'll have to see."

Dr. Rasmussen picked up. "For now, our goal is simply to understand what happened. It is not our job to assign blame. We will begin with background information. Sam, could you describe the history of these two animals."

Damrey stood with her back to us, a hind foot stuck out behind her, and rocked rhythmically. Sam said that both had been circus performers and arrived years ago. "I was working hoofstock when we finished building this elephant exhibit, and Damrey was added to my string. She was pretty thin and had bad digestion when we got her. You could see all her vertebrae. I had to try a lot of different diets to get her settled in. I called five or six zoos for advice. I'd guess the circus sold her because she was such a mess. She was about twenty then, and we think she was originally from Thailand. Nakri came several years later, probably born in Cambodia. She was just a kid, only about six, and this little circus sold her in a bankruptcy before she was confiscated. She was chained most of the time and had a sore on her leg. She healed right up, and Damrey loved having her." Sam's pride in his care of these two animals leaked through his matter-of-fact account. "Damrey's always been dominant, and Nakri's never challenged her. But Nakri takes the lead now more than she used to. Damrey seems happy to follow. She's getting on in years." He added, almost as a plea, "She's always been reliable."

Directed by the researcher's quiet questions, Sam described the daily routine, foot care, training, bathing, cleaning, and so on. Dr. Rasmussen said she was glad to see the soft floor covering in the stalls and the deep sand in the yard. "That's why Damrey walks sound even at her age. We see so many in captivity with arthritis from the hard surfaces. What about exercise?"

Sam glanced at Mr. Crandall. "We need the new exhibit for that. I walked them on the grounds up until a few years ago, even did elephant rides for awhile with Damrey, but the insurance company clamped down on that. Can't even walk them before visitors come in."

Mr. Crandall nodded in confirmation. This was before my time. The idea of two elephants wandering the grounds was startling. I sensed old friction over ceasing the exercise program and wondered where Wallace had figured in that. My bet was he had sided with Sam.

Dr. Rasmussen turned to Ian, who seemed surprised to be asked, and requested that he review the daily and weekly schedule again. Ian looked cornered and kept his answers even more terse than usual. Berchtold, the committee's elephant keeper, asked why they didn't use the door between the back stall and the outside yard. Ian froze up, and Sam explained that the building had settled and it didn't work. "The maintenance staff said it was a huge job. They'll need to tear out and re-pour that whole wall."

Mr. Crandall looked uncomfortable, but all he said was, "That's a problem we plan to address."

I was ready to bet my next paycheck that the zoo would be dinged for the non-functional door in the NAZ report and wondered why the director wasn't more specific about the new exhibit. He might have given a date when he thought it would be done.

Next up were Dr. Reynolds and Kayla, who walked through the research protocol. "Kayla, did Damrey ever swing her trunk at you or act threatening?" Dr. Rasmussen asked.

Kayla was backed up against Dr. Reynolds and Hap. The brash vitality was nowhere to be seen. "Well, I don't know…I mean, I'm not any kind of elephant expert…She—Damrey—didn't seem to like me. She sort of did what I asked, but mostly because Ian or Sam was nearby. I didn't feel comfortable around her…" Her voice trailed off.

"And did she ever act aggressive toward you?"

"Um…it's hard for me to say."

I'd never seen cheerful Kayla look so uncomfortable.

Damrey made herself conspicuous by vibrating her forehead against the closed door to the outside yard. It was hard to hear over the din. We waited while Sam shut both cows outside.

"Did Damrey grab at you or try to hit you?" Dr. Rasmussen asked Kayla

"Once, when Sam and Ian weren't right there next to me. I jumped back."

Sam and Ian both came to attention. Sam looked dubious, and Ian seemed surprised. Sam said, "You should have said something."

"I…I didn't know if it was normal or what. I didn't want you to think…" Kayla looked miserable.

I looked around and saw a sea of poker faces. This did not sound good for Damrey.

I knew what Kayla didn't want others to think. She didn't want them to think she was afraid of elephants. The same concern I had.

I was next and described my two mornings of sample collection. I said that Damrey was initially uncooperative the first day, but was fine after a few minutes and had behaved well today. And, no, she hadn't swiped at me. I didn't add that I'd been careful not to give her an opportunity.

"Sam," Dr. Rasmussen said, "Could you tell us about Kevin Wallace's normal interactions, if any, with these animals? Did he go in with them?"

"He came three-four times a week to help me out. We're shorthanded, what with the elephants and giraffes and so on. The girls did anything he asked. He helped me trim feet, and he kept Nakri quiet when the vet lanced that abscess on her hip two weeks ago, just by talking to her. Wallace was an elephant man before he came here to be foreman, and he never forgot it."

"Did he observe all safety protocols, such as not going in with them when you or Ian weren't standing by?"

Sam said, "Yes, he did." Ian was stiff and silent.

The gloomy detective surprised us by saying, "A word?" He and Dr. Rasmussen stepped out of hearing and conferred. Dr. Rasmussen motioned Berchtold, the elephant keeper, to join them.

They returned to the group, and Dr. Rasmussen resumed questioning Sam. Berchtold tapped Ian on the shoulder and jerked his head toward the work room. They were behind Sam, and he didn't notice when they left.

I didn't get it until I saw Hap nod thoughtfully at the detective, lips pursed. He looked impressed.

The detective had picked up on the tension between the two Finley Zoo elephant keepers and recommended separating them for questioning.

Ian would still be on the spot. If he described what he thought was Wallace's recklessness, Sam would figure it out when he read the report. Ian would hesitate, but the odds of him coming clean in private with Berchtold were vastly better than the odds of honesty in front of Sam and the rest of us.

Dr. Rasmussen was done with background. I was up again and described my morning from hell. Hap, Sam, and the two police officers confirmed my story and added details from their perspective. I didn't learn anything new. Ian and Berchtold returned after a long session. Sam frowned at them.

Dr. Rasmussen looked at the vet in the tropical shirt and some signal passed between them. He picked up the questioning, turning to the police group. "Detective Quintana, you said you would provide information about Mr. Wallace's injury. May we see the medical chart and x-rays?"

"The medical examiner briefed me, and I'll share that with you."

Dr. Morgan looked annoyed. "Very well then. Share away."

Quintana said, "Cause of death was brain trauma. He was hit on the head with the twin to that elephant hook on the wall over there. The old wood one, not those lightweight aluminum ones. Hit twice. The hook penetrated the skull and caused massive bleeding. He lost consciousness quickly and never regained it. Minor contusions on his upper arms, ribs, and back were not medically significant."

"*What?*" Dr. Morgan said. "You knew this from the beginning, and we're learning it *now?*"

Quintana was not a man who flinched. "Medical information is privileged, and the family did not want it shared. We had to respect that, but now it's a death situation. I'm informing you because it's necessary to close out the incident."

The NAZ committee, Sam, and Ian all seemed disconcerted, and I was flat-out astonished. No internal bleeding? No smashed ribs? All that mauling was "not medically significant"?

The big detective continued unflustered. "The question is, which elephant took the hook away from him and hit him. It looks like the older one, but I'd like to be sure."

Sam spoke first, to Mr. Crandall. "I didn't know he was hit with an *ankus*. If Damrey wanted him dead, she would have smeared the floor with him. Why would she fool around with an ankus?"

Dr. Rasmussen said, "Detective, elephants kill people all the time and not by hitting them with little sticks. They use their bodies—step on the head, kick them, or kneel down and crush the victim with their trunk doubled under. Or they smack down with their trunks. All are effective. This news completely changes what we thought happened."

The detective's long face seemed to droop even more. "You're the experts, but you'll need to convince me that this isn't just what it looks like. He goes in with that poker thing and jabs her. She doesn't like it, she takes it away from him and whacks him a couple of times on top of his head. I looked into it. Elephants have the manual dexterity with those trunks. Maybe it's a fit of temper, and she stops there. She seems plenty temperamental. We asked around pretty thoroughly and didn't find any reason for someone to kill him. Let's not make this more complicated than it is, no matter how much you like elephants."

Berchtold turned to me. "Describe what she was doing to his body."

Startled, I described again the fumbling trunk and the big feet shoving him around on the straw and rocking him back and forth.

He turned to Sam. "Did she ever have a calf or was she around a birth?"

Sam shrugged. "She might have seen a birth, before she was captured. Maybe watched her mother's next birth."

Berchtold said, "I think she was trying to get him up. Cows use their trunks to help their newborn calves stand up. And they nudge them with their feet. Without seeing it, I can't be sure, but it sounds like she was trying to help him. She sure wasn't trying to finish the job."

"But she had her *foot* on him," I said. "She was shoving him around."

Berchtold shook his head. "Elephants have almost total control over their bodies. They hardly ever put a foot wrong or misjudge how much pressure to apply." He looked at Ian and back to me. "You're, what, a bird keeper, right? No elephant experience? It must have looked pretty bad. But she didn't actually hurt him."

"Yeah, it looked bad." I was supposed to feel forgiven for getting it wrong, but I was still too stunned.

Mr. Crandall caught Sam's eye and they spoke softly. The NAZ committee conferred among themselves. The detective looked mournful and patient. The two officers behind him muttered to one another.

Another thought came to me, something that had bothered me two mornings running. I hesitated. The pause as each team accommodated the new information and regrouped was long enough for me to find my courage. I was already cast as the village idiot. I didn't have much to lose. "Sam, how well does Damrey see?"

Instead of Sam, the committee turned to Dr. Reynolds. "Her vision is not good. I'm keeping an eye on it." She added a lot of optical technicalities that I did not follow.

Dr. Morgan said, "We should have started with the health exam. Let's take a look at her eyes."

That was complicated. Dr. Reynolds sent Kayla off for equipment. Sam herded us all out into the visitor area and told us to stand well back. He and Ian and Dr. Morgan remained inside with Dr. Reynolds. I stood by myself, trying to wrap my mind around a whole new interpretation of what I'd seen that traumatic morning. I felt lightheaded and vague. Goji berries exhumed from my pocket helped. Mr. Crandall talked quietly with the police. Kayla came back panting, handed Dr. Reynolds a traditional black bag, and joined us in the visitor area.

Sam opened the door to let the cows into the front stall. Damrey walked from one end to the other, trunk waving around. Sam began sweet-talking and handing her apple chunks through the bars. She calmed down and started paying attention, nudging Nakri aside to claim the treats. Ian took Nakri to the other end of the stall for her own quality time.

Damrey was not keen on the vets messing with her, but Sam talked her into it by tugging on her ear, more fruit, and a little help from the ankus. Sam and the vets worked from the people side of the bars, but they were well within trunk range, and Damrey could have eliminated all of them if she'd wanted to. Instead, she stood reasonably still while the docs shone lights into her eyes at great length, and I realized how much intestinal fortitude it sometimes took to be a zoo vet. Not to mention an elephant keeper. When they stood back, Sam slapped Damrey gently on the trunk and let her retreat to the outside yard again.

We reconvened inside. Dr. Reynolds said, "To simplify, the retinal deterioration has progressed rapidly since I examined her a month ago. Damrey is now essentially blind. There is no treatment, but obviously she can function well enough in a familiar setting using touch, smell, and hearing."

Sam turned in triumph to the detective. "She couldn't have scored two direct hits on the top of his head. She couldn't see him."

That explained her groping for her raisins instead of zeroing in as Nakri had. Perhaps it also accounted for her "fussiness." She wanted consistency so she knew what to expect and how to behave. Her control as she fumbled around at Wallace's unconscious body was even more amazing.

The detective said, "What about the other one? Can she see or are they both blind?"

That didn't seem relevant to me, but the committee wanted an answer also. We surplus participants retreated to the work room while Nakri was examined. Her vision passed muster.

Quintana put me on the witness stand again. With both cows shut out, Sam and Ian did a quick bit of housekeeping in the front stall, then Ian played dead, lying on the floor where I'd seen Wallace. Sam set the door the way it was that morning, the committee stood in Nakri's stall, and I described how she'd gone to her knees trying to reach him. The detective refused to rule out the possibility entirely, but none of the zoo staff or committee could take either elephant seriously as the aggressor.

Detective Quintana's sagging face grew even longer. Disappointment resonated in his deep voice. "Okay, folks. What you're telling me is that neither of these elephants killed Kevin Wallace. Some party or parties unknown, presumably human and not an orangutan, came into this elephant barn and attacked him inside the stall. The attacker hit him twice with the ankus thing. One blow brought him to his knees and the other, even stronger, finished him off. Or it could be that he was jumped outside the bars and hauled or shoved in there." He shook his head. "One way or another, I now have a homicide scene that's had two elephants loose in it for five days. Folks, this isn't going to be easy."

Chapter Seven

The committee was done with me. I was shooed back to my job while they conferred and debated and speculated with the police. Calvin had somehow missed hearing about Wallace's death. I broke the news.

"Wallace dead. Well." He spread his short, thick fingers on the table, as though bracing himself. "I worked with him a long time. Can't say I liked him, but still…" He and Wallace had a long and troubled history, but his dismay seemed genuine, and I was struck anew by his decency. He was as amazed as I was that Damrey was exonerated. "Guess I should of trusted Sam. I thought he was letting his heart run away with his head. Teach me to jump to judgment."

It had seemed disrespectful to eat while I told him the bad news. Done, I wolfed down the sandwich I'd brought from home.

He said, "This is a bad situation, not knowing who killed him. It's a shame you're pregnant. You might be a good person to sort this out. You got a sharp eye."

"Calvin, I'm the one who got it wrong in the first place. But I'm with you—I'd like to know who left him to die and set up Damrey to take the blame."

"Yeah, that was a raw deal. In the old days, she probably would of been shot by now. This whole thing put Sam through the wringer. Now we all get to go through it." He stood up. "When you're done, let's see if we can patch that aviary fence. I found a big hole this morning."

I put my trash in the garbage can and pulled open the drawer with leather gloves and pliers. "Calvin? Being pregnant is not like nine months of polio or a broken leg. Really."

He snorted a chuckle. "Wait till you try to bend over and tie your shoe laces in another month. We'll see what you say then."

At the aviary, Calvin squatted, knees cracking, and held out duck food to the nenes—Hawaiian geese—and the little Hottentot teals. The pair of nenes came right up and argued with each other as they gobbled from his hand. They would never eat from my hand, but I chose to believe that they were put off by my face mask and gloves, even after five months, rather than that they simply preferred Calvin. The nenes and I related much as Sam and Ian did, and the little teals were cool to me. My feelings were hurt, but I knew they would like me better on Calvin's day off when I was the only option for special treats.

We'd been struggling with the fencing for half an hour, Calvin muttering about Birds always getting the short end of the budget, when Dr. Reynolds dropped by. She watched for a moment, then said, "Iris, could you drop by my office before you leave for the day? I'd like to discuss the elephant research for a few minutes."

What was so special about the research that she couldn't tell me in front of Calvin? He and I exchanged a glance. Something to do with Wallace.

"Sure thing," I said.

Calvin and I did our best on the aging mesh, then made the afternoon rounds of feeding, watering, and tidying. I filled out the end-of-day reports while Calvin scrubbed the sinks. He would probably clean the Penguinarium with a toothbrush if that meant he didn't have to do the reports. Wallace had promised us computers, no more pencil and paper, but we hadn't seen them yet.

"Gol-darn it," he said. "Forgot my medicine this morning. Too much going on." He rummaged in the people-food refrigerator and found a little glass jar. Thick fingers pulled out little tan lumps.

"Looks like deer droppings."

He was unfazed. "Golden raisins soaked in gin. Supposed to be magic for arthritis. Maybe help my knees."

I'd thought of Calvin as another Mr. Crandall—ageless, permanent. He was a sturdy guy, in physique and in health, but apparently not exempt from getting older, and someday he would retire. I put the thought away. I had enough real changes to worry about.

I left ten minutes before quitting time and walked through departing clots of school groups shepherded by burnt-out teachers trying to survive until summer vacation started. It was Wednesday, my Friday, and I was tired, hungry, apprehensive, and more than ready for a couple of days off. I hoped whatever Dr. Reynolds had on her mind wouldn't take long. Marcie was cooking dinner for me and Denny. I craved a shower, clean clothes, and a break from zoo disasters.

Dr. Reynolds closed the door after me and waved me to a guest chair in front of her desk. She sat behind tidy stacks of books and papers and chewed on her lower lip for a moment. A little centrifuge whirred in the corner. I was impressed once again that this slender woman, a few years older than myself, was managing the health of every animal in the zoo. I suspected she wore a lab coat more to convey her role to skeptics than to protect her clothes.

She flipped stray hair over her shoulder. Her tone was brisk. "Iris, the situation is different now. The police are treating Kevin's death as a homicide, but they are working under difficult circumstances. They have pictures of the original scene, but the stall has been scrubbed several times since then, and of course the elephants trampled everything in their normal activity. They tried a chemical called Luminal to see if they could bring up residual blood smears, but it isn't working properly because elephant stool and the cleaners mask the effect. It's a tough situation."

"I'd hate to see whoever did this get away with it."

She nodded. "No motive has been found, and no one has any idea why Kevin was at the barn so early in the morning. It wasn't typical for him to be there at that hour or to enter the stall without Sam or Ian around."

I didn't disagree out loud, but I wondered. Ian had implied differently.

"Iris, this is another reason I'm glad you're continuing the research project. I'd like you to keep an eye out for anything unusual, anything that might explain the...attack. The keepers will talk to you more than they will to the police or a committee or to me. You know everyone and you know where the bodies are buried—sorry, poor choice of words—and might find out something that no one else will have a chance to discover."

My apprehension was justified. First Calvin, now Dr. Reynolds. Where was this notion coming from? "I wish it were true that people will spill to me, but I really don't think it is."

"You picked up on Damrey's vision problems right away."

That didn't seem particularly relevant.

"Iris, Kevin said he'd seen someone sneaking away from the barn early in the morning. That was a day before the accident. It was only a glimpse. Perhaps you could find out who it was."

This was news. "Did you tell the police?"

"Yes, of course, the same day as the attack. They said they hadn't found anything when I reminded them today." She wound a wisp of hair around her index finger and frowned.

My shoulder twitched. She had this plan in mind when she first asked me to take on Kayla's task. She and Sam had separately manipulated me into the barn, each for their own reason. "I'll keep my eyes open. That's all I can do."

Stress lines around her eyes relaxed a little. "I appreciate your help very much."

"I'm sorry for your loss," I said, awkwardly parroting Dr. Rassmussen.

Dr. Reynolds leaned back. She rotated her office chair to look out the window at leafy branches and a scrap of cloudy sky. Her voice softened. "It wasn't the same, I think, as when you lost your husband. We weren't very far along—a few dinners and a lecture or two—and I don't think it would have gone anywhere, not in the long run. Still, it was nice to be noticed. We agreed it was best to keep it undercover. I liked him, but I suspect he was more optimistic about us than I was. Who knows…"

I said, "He was…cheerful the last few months. He seemed happy. And…it sounds like he didn't suffer. At the end."

"Yes. I think that is true."

We sat in silence for a moment. I said, "I should have visited him in the hospital. I should have thanked him for not firing me when I was screwing up after Rick died. He was cranky and fussy, but he was fair. I think he was good at his job."

She turned back to me and shook her head. "The hospital wouldn't let anyone but family in." She looked out the window again. "I don't know a soul here except Kayla, and I'm coming off a bad divorce. As if there ever was a good one. He was fun to be with." A wry smile.

She'd known a different Wallace than I had. "He had a few failed relationships of his own. Not entirely his fault." Impulsively, I added, "I hope you stay."

She smiled. "I'd like to. The salary here is dismal. I'd buy a house if I could."

I understood that one. Rick's life insurance was all that made my home ownership possible.

"Iris, I hope you and Kayla get along. She doesn't know anyone here either. I seem to feel responsible since I recruited her to come work here. Of course, she's very social."

Another request? "She seems good at her job. And fun. People like her. I wouldn't worry."

The vet nodded and fell into silence, staring out the window again. After a moment, still looking away, "Kevin liked you. You were tough to manage, but a good zoo keeper. That's what he said. He felt that your husband's death was the worst thing that had happened in all his years at the zoo."

I was blind-sided and unable to speak.

Dr. Reynolds turned her chair back to face me. The narrow, serious face was transformed, predatory. "A killer broke into our zoo. We don't know who it is or whether it will happen again. Let's figure this out. Let's get whoever did this to Kevin."

Chapter Eight

Chicken artichoke casserole over rice, green salad, roasted red bell peppers with sweet onions. I had showered and changed before driving over, and I sat in a green sweat suit like a swollen toad with my hair still wet. I ate until common sense finally kicked in, and I could raise my eyes from my plate. "Oh, Marcie. Will you marry me and cook for me forever?"

"I'll give it some thought." Marcie flipped a hand at me, brushing it off, but she had the embarrassed glow she got when anyone said something positive about her, as though it couldn't possibly be true but she couldn't resist being pleased. She had already cleared her plate and Denny's. I relinquished mine in hopes that it would be replaced by dessert. It was—strawberry-rhubarb pie and a cup of coffee.

We sat in her little dining room in her perfectly neat apartment. Marcie was very advanced in home making. That included cooking and baking, so I totally approved. All our plates were from the same set, and they were color coordinated with the place mats, which matched the napkins. The cream and red color scheme did not, however, match Marcie's pale blue pullover and neat navy slacks. That would have been too much. We'd been friends since college, Oregon State U. She got me through sophomore year, my last, and I got her through a breakup that left her man-shy and un-paired, until she hooked up with Denny. He was the last man on earth I would have chosen for her, but she didn't ask.

I had to admit, she looked happy. Sexy, actually. Voluptuous rather than chubby, comfortable with herself in a way I hadn't seen before. For now, being with Denny was working for her. He was more than casual in a faded purple tee shirt and jeans. He looked pretty cheerful himself, but who wouldn't after that meal? The pie was springtime itself.

"You should drink red raspberry leaf tea and not that caffeinated stuff," Denny said.

"It's decaf," Marcie said.

"Buzz off," I said.

"They can hear negativity. Impairs their emotional development. Raspberry tea tones the uterus."

"My uterus is *so* not your business. And not a 'they.' Only one. Don't frighten me like that." I scraped off the last gooey sweetness and decided I really must not lick the plate. Life was, if not good, at least much improved. Clean, fed, no impossible expectations coming at me out of the blue…I relaxed for the first time in a week.

"If you won't tell us whether it's a boy or girl, it's gonna be a 'they.' I am not going with 'it'."

Marcie nodded agreement. I'd kept this secret from her, too, because she couldn't keep it from Denny.

I sagged back in my chair. "Denny, if I tell you, you'll be off and running about genderness and what I should be doing about it."

"I haven't researched that yet. I've seen a lot of warnings about golden seal and dong quai. Pennyroyal is not good either. Stay away from all of those."

"I have never consumed any of those to the best of my knowledge, and I promise not to start now. Meth and cocaine, ditto."

"You think therapeutic herbs are *addictive?*"

Marcie stood up to clear the dessert plates, waving a hand at me to stay seated. "Denny, please. She's pulling your chain. Could we attempt a normal conversation?" She would never adapt to our habitual bickering. A limitation of being compulsively nice.

Denny handed over his plate and filled the empty spot on the table with his forearms. He leaned forward toward Marcie. "What she really needs is something to keep her stress level down. You didn't see her after she found Wallace, and she's been totally reactive about it ever since. It's got to be affecting her pH balance. Not good for Rick, Jr. At this stage of gestation, they—"

"*Drop it*," I snarled. Wallace, Rick, and the baby thrown into a heap ignited an unsuspected pile of emotional gunpowder. They both flinched. After a frozen moment, I said, "I'd better go," and got up from the table. Blinded by tears and unbalanced by new weight, I stumbled. Marcie set down the plates hard enough to risk breakage and grabbed my arm.

"I brought a couple of DVDs," Denny babbled. "We could watch one."

Marcie towed me into her pristine living room and pressed me down onto her white sofa. "Sit for a minute. Pet a cat. Digest." She enforced these commands by plopping The Princess, a rickety old Siamese, in my lap. Princess stood stiff-legged on my thighs, sniffed around to orient herself, and carefully collapsed into a round warm pillow. I stiffened for a moment, thinking about toxoplasmosis, and remembered that cats weren't the threat, only their droppings.

Marcie waved Denny away. "Go do dishes or something." She sat next to me with a hand on my shoulder. "Tell me."

"I'm tired, that's all, and it *is* a boy and, and I'm suddenly starving all the time…Rick and Wallace…The nightmares are back."

Marcie produced a tissue and nodded as though this made sense.

I wiped my nose. "Now it's not just lions and Rick, it's lions and elephants and Rick and Wallace, all gory and scary. Sometimes the baby is there…I'm trapped in slow motion, and I can't help them. My cell phone is stuck in my pocket, I can't remember if it's 911 or 119, my fingers don't work…" I trailed off.

Marcie put on her matter-of-fact therapy voice. "Finding your boss dying brought back Rick's death."

"Yeah, it fried me more than I expected. I was dealing really well, but now…" I shifted on the sofa to help my stomach compete for room with my other internal organs. Princess put her ears back and stopped purring. "Until this, I was okay with Rick gone forever. Not over it, I can't imagine being over it, but moving on, thinking about the kid, not wallowing in stuff I can't change…Lonely, but not whacked out."

"It's been a terrible week."

"I know Rick and Denny were best friends, and he misses Rick, too. This baby is all that either of us have left of Rick, but Denny keeps telling me how to be pregnant. So does Calvin and my mother and everyone else. It's throwing me off. I have to trust *myself.* This single-parenting thing is scary enough without people assuming I can't possibly handle it." I leaned my head back.

Marcie's hand was warm on my shoulder.

"Well, what *do* you want your friends to do to be supportive?" She tilted her head at an "I'm listening" angle.

"Don't ask me that now. Right now I want everyone to back off." I drew a breath. "There's more."

"What?" Denny couldn't stand being out of the loop and sat himself on a wing chair across from me, hunched forward with his elbows on his thighs.

I wanted to wait for a private meltdown with Marcie, but once begun, meltdowns are not easily deflected. "People are *on* me to figure out what happened at the barn. Marcie, remember I told you I'm supposed to collect elephant pee every day? The vet is after me to spy while I'm there. Even Calvin thinks I should root around in this, and I don't want any part of it. Maybe it was a stranger and maybe it wasn't. I hate suspecting coworkers. Those are my *friends.* It's creepy."

We sat in silence for a few minutes. I stroked Princess, who vibrated with forgiveness. The youngster of Marcie's three cats, Impossible, used his claws on Denny's jeans and, after attaining his lap, flopped over on his back bonelessly. Six-Toes slept somewhere out of sight.

"It's not just you," Denny said. "The negative energy is every-where. First we thought Damrey went berserker, and that made us all wonder if our number's up next. Some animal or equipment that you trust comes unhinged or your foot slips, and you're the one on the stretcher. But it was murder. The press is all over the zoo. Crandall is getting creamed, even with the new cubs."

"I can't fix it," I wailed.

"No," Marcie said. "Of course you can't."

"But if we never find out who killed Wallace, it's my fault."

"That's silly," Marcie said.

Denny thought a minute and nodded.

Marcie said, "Don't *agree* with her! How could it be her fault?"

"I can see it," Denny said. "You called it wrong at the beginning, thinking Damrey was smashing him. So the cops treated it like an animal attack and didn't totally work the scene. Now the evidence is trashed. No CSI instant answer."

I nodded.

Marcie frowned. "Don't be so quick to give up on the police. They're the experts."

Denny swung a foot back and forth, jostling the cat on his lap. "Everything that happens changes what goes forward. Sometimes you have to follow the trail back to understand it and realign it."

"Not you, too," I said.

Denny shrugged. "You need to restore your harmony so the kid's not marinating in stress hormones. Sounds like you've got Dr. Reynolds talking to you and access to the barn. That gives you the advantage."

"Not so much."

"Iris, no one has any right to put you in this position," Marcie said, her hands folded tightly in her lap. "Denny, please do stop encouraging her. This is a really bad idea. Iris has other priorities right now. This is a police problem."

I considered that. "My priorities are staying healthy, doing my job, and getting ready to deal with a baby." A baby. What was wrong with the world that a basket case like me would end up responsible for a baby? My friends were right to worry. "Having my work scene, the zoo, in a mess isn't good. It's going to stay in a mess until we know what happened and why. I *want* to know."

"Iris, this is not your problem." Marcie's voice had a flavor of calm that would be shouting from anyone else. "You are talking yourself into interfering, and that is unnecessary and maybe dangerous."

"Not interfering. Trying harder to notice. I've got the inside perspective and the lead detective's phone number. If I'm proactive—is that the word?—maybe the nightmares and flashbacks will slack off. I won't do anything dangerous, and I'll call that Quintana guy if I learn anything he might not know."

"We can work together," Denny said, energized. "I think we should start with the activists. And Ian. There's something not right between him and Sam. Another thing—"

"Denny. Please." Marcie said. "You and I need to talk, but not now. We're going to stop discussing this and watch one of those DVDs you brought."

"Okay, fine. You want *Raising Arizona* or *Rosemary's Baby?*"

Chapter Nine

One of the better reasons for living with dogs is that they are oblivious to shame, especially when their brains are flooded with hope for a run in the park. Winnie and Range did not care in the slightest that I awoke feeling like a cretin. At Marcie's the night before, I'd been unstable, unpleasant, and incapable. The dogs hadn't been there to observe gluttony, hair-trigger rage, and sniveling, and wouldn't have cared anyway. With a leash in each hand, I radiated the glory of a goddess.

It was my day off and doggie entitlement got me moving. Mt. Tabor Park wasn't far, but I was in no mood to walk. The dogs hopped into the pickup, I tied the leashes to eyebolts in the middle of the truck bed for safety and hauled my unwieldy self into the cab.

The legality of doggy freedom comes and goes in Portland parks, as does enforcement. On this early Thursday morning, neither got in our way. Parents walked their preschoolers, birders with binoculars wandered around making "pish pish" noises at little birds in the trees, crows investigated whether eatables had grown from the ground during the night. A woman flung a tennis ball for her golden retriever. Winnie hijacked the golden for a romp while Range stole his ball and brought it to me. I tossed it to the owner, a hefty woman in shorts, and hurled my own tennis ball for him.

It was a beautiful spring morning full of birds and blossoms. I scooped poop with a better heart, although Kevin Wallace kept intruding. I thought I'd made a decision to find out what happened to him, but in the light of day, I couldn't see where to start. My musings circled back to what Calvin and Dr. Reynolds had suggested in the first place: keep my eyes open, especially at the elephant barn. There must be something more, but nothing came to me. The dogs exercised themselves happily for most of an hour, and we all went home.

In the driveway of the teal bungalow with cream trim, 3 bds, 1 bath, new rf. and elec., I wondered if I'd ever quit thinking I should park on the street like a visitor. Everyone said my new house was cute and perfect, and I liked it myself. It was only that I felt I was house-sitting for the real owners, probably an older couple or maybe a family with a dad and mom and twin eighth-graders. I invented occupants whom this house would wrap around and shelter. None of them were single mothers still mourning their husbands or zoo keepers with vague ambitions to find out why their boss was dead.

The dogs flopped on the living room rug, licked themselves tidy, and fell asleep. Energized by sunshine, I started on the home version of what I did at work—cleaning. The household version required a lot less brain power. I focused my unused cognition and started loading the dishwasher, stopping occasionally to make a note on scrap paper.

After the pans were washed, the counters wiped and the kitchen floor swept, I reviewed the water-spotted piece of paper. Under the heading "Scenarios" I'd listed the following:

1. W argued with X, X lost temper and killed W

2. W found X doing something wrong, X killed him to hide it

3. X found W doing something wrong, W attacked X and lost the fight. X afraid to admit it.

4. X plotted to kill W and blame it on the elephant, lured him to barn.

5. W plotted to kill X, lured him/her to barn. W lost the fight. X afraid to admit it.

6. Mistaken identity, W killed in error. Who was it supposed to be?

7. X, Y, and Z ganged up on W. Who are *they?*

8. Killed elsewhere and dragged to barn, stuffed through bars into stall

9. One of elephants really did kill W with ankus

I fixed a cheese sandwich and stuck it in the toaster oven. While that was heating, I crossed out everything after number five as unlikely. That left way too many possibilities. It was also distasteful. I'd been optimistic that Wallace's killer was someone from outside the zoo, but that was wishful thinking. I had no idea.

I switched from chewing on the pencil to chewing on the sandwich, pulled another piece of paper out of the recycling bin, and wrote: "Who is X?"

Male or female?

Known to Wallace—zoo staff or from somewhere else?

Stranger—how in barn? Why in barn?

Stalled out, I mopped the kitchen and vacuumed.

Time for a cookie break. I shared cookies with the dogs. Re-read my notes. Zero inspiration. What to do next?

Giving up sounded good. My left brain was tired and so was the rest of me. Time for the subconscious to pick up the slack. I gave it every chance by crashing on the sofa. I slept like the dead, catching up from a week of troubled dreams and clouded leopard watches.

Barking dogs woke me up hours later. I blundered to the front door and my mother bustled in, bright in a yellow sweatshirt. She set a bushel of pink peonies on the dining room table. "Hello, dear. Color isn't right for this room, but aren't they lovely? The lilacs are already gone and the dahlias aren't open yet."

"Mom? Was I expecting you? Did I forget?" I'd have to plead mental disability due to pregnancy if I'd forgotten they were coming to dinner, a humiliating prospect. I buried the papers with my notes under a stack of mail. A neat stack.

"No, no, sorry. Your dad said we should call, but I forgot. I took off work an hour early so we could shop for a new washing machine, and we decided to drop by."

My mother developed supplemental math units for elementary schools, floating from school to school, sprinkling pre-algebra everywhere she went. I had not inherited her short stature, double-dose of energy, or math gene. In fact, my school performance had caused her many years of self-doubt about her parenting skills and profession.

My father wandered in like the calm after the storm, carrying a big shopping bag in each hand. I blamed his genes for my dark hair, height, and lack of academic ambition. A self-employed sign painter, he lived for gold leaf and up-scale designer jobs.

The dogs greeted both visitors politely, and the parents settled in the dining room. Ducking into the kitchen gave me a few minutes to collect myself and to put water on for tea. Splashing water on my face dispelled some of the grogginess. I checked in with my subconscious and found it had declined to do any heavy lifting. No inspiration about Wallace. On the plus side, I'd slept without nightmares.

I joined my parents in the dining room and, after fielding inquiries about my health and that of my unfinished offspring, undertook the now-customary opening of packages. This batch included another crib sheet, diaper covers, a musical mobile, and maternity pajamas. The jammies consisted of a pink top and pink plaid bottoms, totaling enough fabric to outfit a clipper ship. "This is great. Thanks so much," I ritually responded. Baby gear was piling up in the second bedroom while I still had no idea what I needed. It was daunting and premature. The baby wasn't due until August, after all, and it was only June.

"Tell her, Jim," my mother nudged.

"I maybe found a car for you," he said. "A Honda CRV, lot of miles, but runs good. Friend of a friend is getting divorced and needs to sell it fast."

What was the rush? I had *months* yet. I tossed out the first objection I could think of. "So I wouldn't get a trade-in on the pickup. I'd have to sell it myself."

"Got that covered. Aaron, the guy from Fresno who's been helping me in the shop, wants the truck. He'll pay the low end of Blue Book, which is pretty fair for that thing."

"Dad, it runs great. That truck has never failed me."

"This is a good deal, Iris. I don't think you're going to get any more for that truck."

"Maybe." My obstetrician and any number of free baby magazines assured me that riding in the front of a vehicle is lethal for an infant. Only back seats are suitable and only if equipped with an infant carrier incorporating space-age technology. My parents had provided the car seat within hours of learning I was pregnant, but I still lacked a back seat. My truck had to go, and I was struggling with an inappropriate attachment to a mechanical object, or so my mother told me.

My dad seemed mildly puzzled by my lack of enthusiasm. "Tomorrow you can come by the shop and show Aaron the truck. Then I'll go with you to look over the Honda. If you like it, you'll be ready."

"Ready," as in for a baby not safely housed out of sight, a baby requiring a skill set other than eating for two and wearing a face mask at work? No way would I be "ready." "We'll see. We can talk about it tomorrow."

My mother looked pleased, confident that I'd been nudged another step toward responsible parenthood. "Have you gotten a crib yet?"

"I checked prices on Craigslist," I lied.

Apparently that was sufficient because she moved on. "The circus is coming to town."

"How about that," I said cautiously, thinking this might be a metaphor.

"Next week, I'm taking a classroom of fifth graders. I want you to come, too. You can tell them about the animals. The kids will love it. It's a week from today. Two o'clock. I'll get you a free ticket."

Not a metaphor. "Um, I might have other plans?" Plans that didn't involve rowdy ten year olds. "Tigers jumping through hoops makes me queasy. It's undignified. People shouldn't get their kicks watching tigers being bossed around."

"I thought you'd love the idea. They have elephants and horses, too. Not enough parents signed up to help, and I'll have to cancel."

She wasn't the sort to overact with a sad face, but I could tell she didn't want to cancel. She didn't often ask my help. Usually she was helping me. Had I always been so vulnerable to arm-twisting? "Okay, fine. Sure. You do remember that the clowns terrified me the last time you took me to the circus?"

"You were six years old. You ate popcorn and licorice until you threw up."

"No way. I've always hated licorice."

"Loved it until then, but don't blame the circus. We'll have a good time. You'll see. Oh, that reminds me. I've been saving this clipping for you for months." She dug in her purse and pulled out a newspaper clipping. It showed a picture of Damrey with the little girl who'd won the art contest.

I glanced at it, thanked her, and set it on top of the stack of bills.

She said, "I read in the paper that the foreman died. What was his name?"

On to the next item on her agenda. I was barely keeping up. "Kevin Wallace."

"What a horrible thing. I wonder if they'll be able to figure out what happened."

"The police? Sure they will. They do it in an hour on TV," I said, unsure where she was going but hoping to deflect her. I didn't want to share the details of finding Wallace yet again or, worse, explore the fact that a killer might be loose in my workplace.

"I should think you would want a desk job at this point. You have two to think about, and your job is risky in your condition."

I should have seen that coming. This campaign had started long ago. "Mom, I'm a bird keeper now. I might get pecked. On the finger."

"You always make light of it, even when you were working with lions. Is there an office job maybe available? You should think about it. You shouldn't be doing heavy work."

"Nope. No office jobs. How's *your* work going? How did you get roped into this circus thing?"

"I love circuses. Who's your boss now?"

"Mr. Crandall is acting foreman."

"That dinosaur. I can't imagine why he doesn't retire. If he's your boss now, you could ask him about another sort of job, couldn't you? I mean, it wouldn't hurt to ask."

I wasn't *that* much of a wimp. "Mom, it would hurt. I'm an animal keeper. It's what I do. You shouldn't worry. It's perfectly safe. The doctor told me to exercise."

"Gloria, it's getting close to dinner time," my dad said.

My mother jumped up. "Right. Come to dinner with us. We're going to that new café on Division."

I wasn't hard to convince since sleep had won out over shopping for groceries. Maybe the café would be noisy enough to minimize conversation. Six months hadn't been near enough time for my mother to adjust to the idea of a pregnant daughter. I was exhausted by her worries and suggestions, and the real action hadn't started yet.

As we got into the car, she said, "Honey, I just want everything to go well. You've had such a hard time of it. Tell me to back off if I'm too, too…"

"Bossy?"

"Involved."

An opportunity to lower my stress level that I should not pass up, but this was the tricky interpersonal stuff I was terrible at. What would Dear Abby or Amy or Carolyn advise me to say? I silently rehearsed the phrasing. Stilted, but the best I could do. "Mom, I know you feel that I'm not able to handle this, and I appreciate everything…"

She snatched up the bait before it landed. "No, no, that's not it at all! I—we—have complete confidence in you. You are extremely capable. We only want to help!"

Feeling wildly successful and a little guilty, I said, "It's good to hear you think I can handle being pregnant and getting ready for the baby. So, Mom, there's no need to try to think of everything and push me to do it."

"I know, I know. I'm over-doing it. It's just that I'm, we're, excited about our first grandchild. It's so brave of you to tackle this alone."

"Bravery hasn't anything to do with it. I really do appreciate the support, but—"

"I promise to lighten up. I won't press you anymore."

"That would be great." I sat in the back of the car, totally pleased with myself, and silently counted seconds. "*One Mississippi, two Mississippi…*"

At "*fifteen Mississippi*," "You will get a crib tomorrow, won't you? Make sure the bars are close together. You don't want the baby to get his head stuck."

Chapter Ten

My Monday, that is, Saturday, came around all too soon. My father had succeeded in pulling off the Great Vehicle Swap and I drove to work in a "new" green Honda CRV, fully equipped with tires, roof rack, and, crucially, a back seat. The cargo area was tight for two biggish dogs, and the car had been detailed with odiferous petrochemicals, but it drove fine, and I could breathe perfectly well if I kept the windows rolled down. I'd handed off my truck to Aaron and hoped he would love it. My Country Chick persona was evicted, Suburban Mommy had the wheel. At least it wasn't a minivan with a "Baby on Board" sign dangling from a window. Dad promised a custom painting on the cover of the spare tire bolted to the rear. A clouded leopard portrait would de-bland the Honda and—maybe—make it mine.

The Honda had a certain zip to it, I couldn't deny, or perhaps commuting in daylight put the zip into me. Mornings and evenings of the longest days of the year are often wasted under clouds in the Northwest, but today was clear. Approaching the old Interstate 5 bridge, I glimpsed the blunt, snow-streaked top of Mount St. Helens. Pictures taken before I was born showed a perfect cone. That peak was now scattered over a lot of acreage, and the mountain was a thousand feet shorter. Geology isn't theoretical in these parts, it's to be taken seriously.

Mount Hood loomed severe and snowcapped to my right as I crossed the bridge against the rush hour traffic migrating into Portland. The Columbia River gleamed below. My father had taught me the old names of the mountains, from the people who were here before our kind. Lewit for St. Helens, Wy'East for Mount Hood. It's a gracious thing to see a mountain or two on the way to work.

I pulled into the zoo in a better mood than I'd left it two days before. Walking toward Elephants, I wondered if I'd be able to locate my new wheels after work, given the two other green Honda CRVs in the employee lot. My license plate started with W. Or maybe Y. It had a 9. Possibly.

This was my third shot at collecting elephant samples. Knowing that Damrey hadn't killed anybody took most of the anxiety out. I rounded up the broom stick and cups. Ian was working alone in back, hauling bales to the hay racks with an ease I envied. I watched by the front stall's hay rack, musing that human strength means nothing against an elephant—hay bales are where the muscles count. "Sam's day off?" I asked when he brought a bale over. "You and I must be on the same schedule."

He nodded as he clipped twine, broke up the bale, and shoved flakes into the rack. Mr. Sociable.

Nakri and Damrey were slouching around the front stall. Damrey swiped at bits of hay on the floor. Some she put in her mouth, some she tossed onto her shoulders. What made one bit "food" and the other "adornment"? Nakri slurped from the giant trough, blowing gallons of water into her mouth and dribbling gallons more onto the floor. The stall was littered with droppings the size of tea kettles. I'd have to claim a few for my mother. A dedicated gardener, she regarded herbivore manure as a natural resource equivalent to silver or timber.

Ian joined me and reminded Damrey what the deal was. She sniffed at the raisins, but was slow to offer up her liquid treasure. I could tell Ian was about to call a time out and usher me back to the work area when she wheeled around and presented her butt. I collected a half-cup of what she produced and tossed the clod of raisins into the hay rack. Nakri backed up to the bars, eager for her turn. I turned away to signal that I wasn't ready, left to put Damrey's sample in the work room fridge, and came back armed with a fresh cup. Ian stood silent and still by the bars. Nakri saw me returning, and I had to trot to catch the last of her premature contribution. She was really into dried mango and not into waiting around for sluggish research assistants.

I put the lid on the cup. Ian and I stood for a moment watching the big animals go on about their business, idling around the stall, brushing against each other, blowing softly through their trunks. I pulled the newspaper article my mother had given me out of my pocket. "Ian, why are their tails so bare? Nakri had that long tuft on the end two months ago when this picture was taken."

Ian took the picture and studied it for a few seconds. He shrugged. "Reported it. Vet took skin scrapings. Didn't find anything. Growing back."

I stuffed the picture back into my pocket. "Weird. The male cougar lost hair on his back a couple years ago. We added fish oil to his diet. Cougars don't eat fish in the wild, far as I've ever heard, but it seemed to work."

"Giving amino acid supplements. Might grow back anyway, no matter what we do." Never relaxed, he did seem a little less tense than usual.

"True enough. Sometimes you never know. Do you think we'll ever know what happened to Wallace?" I asked not because legions of co-workers were lined up demanding that I pump him, but because I honestly wanted to know what he thought.

"Hope so." He looked at me sideways like a frightened horse.

"Who could get into the barn?"

He edged toward the work room. "Lots of people can get in."

I trailed behind him. "I guess the blindness explains why Damrey is so particular."

He stopped and turned toward me. "Also not well trained. Not aggressive, but doesn't know the commands she should."

The door from the visitor area opened as he spoke, nearly bumping him.

"Hey, Sam, thought it was your day off. What brings you in?" I said.

"Had to. Wallace used to come in on the weekends and check on things. He'd call me if he found any problems. Everybody thinks this area's out of control. I never know what's going to happen when I'm gone."

Was he referring to shadowy skulkers or the attack on Wallace or Ian?

It was clear how Ian took it. A flush rose from his neck up his face. The rims of his protruding ears slowly reddened. I tore my eyes away from him and took a step back. The two men faced each other with tight shoulders, tight focus.

Sam stepped to the open door to the workroom and looked inside, both ways, then stepped back toward us and examined the barn like a health inspector at a suspect restaurant.

Ian said, "Never called you because he never found anything wrong. Wallace used to come play, *play* with them."

Sam snorted. "Wallace understood elephants better than you ever will. Must be nice for you to know all there is to know, so early in the game. Who needs experience?"

Shocked, I took another step back. I'd known Sam for years and never seen him *mean*.

Ian looked like a man who had finally been pushed too far. His voice rose in volume and pitch, words tumbling out in jerky bursts. "Right. I *don't* have thirty years with the same, same two cows. I worked with, with a dozen elephants in four facilities. Including bulls and calves. So, so don't preach to me about *experience.*"

Sam reared his head back. "What did you learn from it, besides teaching tricks? Have you thought about running away and joining the circus? Might be a good fit." He glanced at me. Was I the real target of this argument? I'd learned that Sam was happy to use me. Ian didn't seem to think that way.

"I can get a job, a job anywhere in the country. I'm here to make it better for these animals. Could train standard commands. Help with accrediting. If it weren't for you. Anything new is a challenge to the herd bull. Has to be beat down."

"Damrey behaves fine with *me*," Sam said in that same cold voice, "and she did with Wallace. Now everyone knows that." He spoke to me, ignoring Ian. "Crandall is nuts to go for accreditation. Why do we need curators and directors from other zoos telling us what's good for our animals? Did you know the animals have to be trained to tolerate us sticking probes in their rears?"

I'd heard Dr. Reynolds on that subject. "Sam, what's the big deal? The vets want ultrasound because they can see what's going on inside the animal. You know it's a good tool, and the cows don't mind as long as the treats keep coming."

"It's disrespectful. There's more to elephant-keeping than this kind of training."

"Yeah, a *lot* more." Ian was still hot. "Especially in a dump. Like this. Only reason to keep these animals here is that new exhibit. That I don't see happening. Those picketers are doing more than you or me to get them decent housing. More space."

The elephants started pacing and ear-flapping.

Sam forgot me again. "Oh, is that it? You think those sign-wavers know what's best? That's rich. Every week I sit in some brain-snuffing meeting busting my ass trying to get the new exhibit moving, and you're ready to pitch it all out for some fantasy of a perfect sanctuary."

"So why, why isn't it happening? You and Wallace were such buddies."

"Because I don't run this place, and I couldn't get him off his rump any faster."

"And why was that?" Ian pressed.

Sam shrugged, losing energy, losing the offensive. "He was staging the construction. It was coming up."

Ian's eyes gleamed. "Don't think so. Think he took another look at the plans and realized, realized that you'd invest millions in a new exhibit. And it would still be too small. Finley Zoo doesn't have the acreage. You'll never get an exhibit big enough, not for more than two cows. No way to breed them. No way to keep a calf. Much less a bull. Reason small zoos aren't keeping elephants much anymore. That's what I think Wallace figured out."

"If he did, it was because you told him so, and he was dumb enough to believe you."

Ian said, "The next foreman or a new curator will take another look—"

Sam interrupted. "Yeah, and that might be me. We'll know soon. Won't that be interesting?"

Ian shut up, and I stopped cowering and came to attention. Mr. Crandall had decided to split the old foreman position in half and put the animal part into a new curator position. The foreman would hire and manage the keepers. Sam must have applied for curator. He was a senior keeper with years of experience. Why wouldn't he? Because, I realized, he'd have to leave Elephants. But a promotion might position him to get the exhibit he wanted.

"I got work to do." Ian walked stiff-shouldered to the work room. After a minute, the door to the outside grated open. The two elephants stepped out briskly, putting hostilities behind them.

"I'll see you around, Sam." I put my second cup of pee in the fridge and got out of there.

Cool wet air was a welcome relief. Clouds and drizzle had moved in, the weather as changeable as the people I worked with. The old giraffe was out in his yard near Elephants. He swung his head down toward me, hoping for a treat or just being sociable. Lord love a duck, what an emotional cesspool the elephant barn had become. Ian and Sam were a match made in hell. Ian said "you" and not "we" when he talked about the new exhibit. I wondered whether he planned to stick around. He must have some guess or theory about what had happened to Wallace, but he wasn't sharing it with me.

The elephants were messing with a big pile of browse Ian had set out for their amusement. I couldn't resist stopping for a moment. Nakri selected a long branch from the pile and tugged it free. She stood on one end of it, wrapped her trunk around the other, and yanked up. The limb snapped in two with a strip of bark still connecting the pieces. She stood on one and pulled on the other to separate them and began stuffing the leafy end into her mouth. I could hear wood being crushed to pulp. Damrey didn't bother with the preparation. She stuffed a leafy end into her mouth and chewed. The branch worked its way slowly up into her maw until she'd had enough and bit it off, the thick end falling away. Wood chippers were far noisier and less effective than those two.

As I walked to the Penguinarium and my nerves settled, I considered what Sam had said. Wallace's death opened up a career opportunity that no one had expected for decades. Sam might have two options for advancement: curator and, soon, foreman. Clearly he was interested. If Ian was right and Wallace no longer supported the new exhibit, his death also removed an obstacle to the better housing Sam wanted so badly.

Surely these were not sufficient motives for murder. No, not for a planned killing, but the depth of Sam's anger frightened me. Arguing with Wallace? A sudden, violent release of frustration…Where in my list of scenarios had that been? Number Two?

No, Sam was not a violent person. One shouting match didn't mean anything. I was over-reacting. Pregnancy hormones, maybe.

On Saturdays, the zoo was jammed with kids of all sizes and their adult shepherds. Jackie worked Saturdays, like Mr. Crandall. She and I leaned against the wall in our usual spot, hidden from staff and visitors alike. I shifted sides as soon as she lit up and I could figure out the wind direction.

I listened impatiently to her gripes about Mr. Crandall and the press and how black cohosh pills weren't helping her hot flashes. When I'd completed my quota of sympathetic murmurs, I broke into her critique of the contractors for Asian Experience and their expectations of the office staff. "Jackie, what's going on with replacing Wallace? Has Mr. Crandall posted the position yet?"

"Nope, and he's not going to. Not for a while."

"How's that going to work? He can't be foreman for months. He doesn't know what he's doing. We're coasting on what Wallace set up."

She took her time, blowing smoke out of the side of her mouth away from me, her idea of etiquette. "Don't get your knickers in a bunch. I think he's got another plan. He's going to recombine foreman and curator for now, hire somebody right away from the curator candidates, and deal with the foreman job later. Splitting them was stupid anyway. So maybe next week."

"Huh. That fast. I guess that's a good thing."

She quirked her eyebrows at me. "Sort of depends on who he hires, right?"

"Any internal candidates?"

"Yeah. Sam. The rest are from outside."

I thought that over while Jackie puffed. "So who's it going to be?"

She shrugged. "Can't say."

I was pretty sure that meant she didn't know.

"So," she said, "you know about the senior keeper position that's posted? It's for Bears and Felines. You could apply."

The keepers had wondered if this position, funded by the bond measure, would ever be created. "I'll think about it." Trying for senior keeper was full of pros and cons. I changed the subject. "Have the police said anything about who killed Wallace?"

She shook her head. "Nothing. Could be anyone with keys to the elephant barn or Wallace could have let someone in. I don't see how they can ever find out." She waved the smoke away from her face, frowning. "Icky." She ground out her butt. "That big old cop looked in Wallace's file cabinet and took his computer."

Wallace's files immediately seemed like a source of crucial information, now that they were out of reach. Damn. "Just unplugged it and took it? Is he going to bring it back?"

"How would I know? We've got another one for the new guy, whoever it is. A better one. Wallace didn't want to upgrade and have to learn a new interface."

"Won't New Guy need Wallace's files?"

Jackie gave me a pitying look. "We do have backups, you know. We aren't living in the bronze age."

Of course. "What about Wallace's email? Is that backed up, too?"

"It's all on a server. We've got everything except what Wallace kept on his hard drive and didn't save to the server. He wasn't good with computers. Mr. Crandall is even worse. I spend half my life straightening out his files. He does this Save As thing and has all these versions of the same file and then he—"

"Jackie, I want to take a look at that computer."

"Why? What do you care about it?" Her brow furrowed in alarm. "You want to see Wallace's files. Why?"

"Why do you think?"

"To find out if anyone had a reason to want him dead? Not your problem."

"You don't think the cops are going to figure this out, do you?" I asked.

"Might."

"Is Mr. Crandall in or not?"

"He's got a telephone conference in his office for..." She looked at her watch. "Another forty minutes. What could you find that the cops couldn't? You're wasting your time."

I waited out her struggle between common sense and professionalism on one side and a little excitement on the other.

Her eyes narrowed. "He might come out to go to the bathroom or something. It's a risk. It's set up with Wallace's logon. He's still getting email, and I have to deal with it. You'd never guess that the password is 'neofelis.' If I'm out of the office, I'd never know who went in there, would I?"

"No, you come, too. You're *supposed* to read his email. I'll look over your shoulder."

Jackie thought this over. The pheasant stepped up to the poacher's snare and hesitated. I couldn't come up with any corn to sprinkle on the ground. Jackie shook her head. "Nah. You're on your own. Mr. Crandall's already crabby."

"Have a nice lunch," I said, and she tossed her stub into the mulch and headed for the café.

Inside the office, I found the summer intern, a chirpy high school girl in a skimpy tank top and big hoop earrings, there to handle the phones and run errands in the busy season. She beamed a welcoming smile.

"Um, I'll be doing some data entry using the computer in here," I said, walked into Wallace's office, and closed the door. It didn't feel right to be there, anymore than it ever had. The room was small, with two ordinary wooden arm chairs for guests, gray carpet, a wooden desk with a monitor. Cheap wood paneling. An army green file cabinet. Swivel chair behind the desk with a cushion dented in the shape of Wallace's butt.

Nothing good had ever happened to me in that room. That was where keepers were chastised for their sins, where I'd learned Rick was dead, where I was busted from Felines to Birds. The photo of a younger Wallace with an elephant was still on his desk. Not Damrey, an elephant from a different zoo. The room smelled stuffy, with a hint of elephant. I wandered to a small closet and opened the door. A warm-up jacket, rubber boots, a white shirt neatly hung on the rod, a blue tie draped over it. I checked the jacket pockets and found a package of dried mango slices, a piece of monkey chow, and a grocery receipt.

I put my butt on the chair behind the desk and looked in the drawers. One was locked, probably full of personnel files. A chance to inspect my own file? And Denny's, which probably shared some of the same disciplinary forms. But I couldn't find the key in any of the other drawers. Wallace hoarded paper clips and pads of yellow sticky notes. I stood up and checked the file cabinet, which wasn't locked. Every drawer held folders labeled by species or year or topic. It was stuffed with paper. No way did I have time to examine all that.

This seemed hopeless. I didn't even know what I was looking for. No, I did. I was trying to find out who he met or found at the barn.

I turned on the computer. It came to life much faster than my own. Did Wallace have a personal calendar? If he did, the police probably took it. Maybe he used an online calendar. I logged on and opened his email. It was the same software I used at home. I clicked on the Calendar button and was excited to see that

Wallace actually used it. Every day had entries. I hit the back arrow until I got to the day of the incident. Nothing for seven in the morning. The first entry was a meeting with the senior keepers at ten. I rummaged around, looking at the week before and the week after, and found nothing interesting.

Disappointed, I clicked on Mail. He'd received a gazillion emails since he'd died. Many of them were newsletters from wildlife and zoo organizations. Most hadn't been read. Jackie wasn't keeping up.

Feeling criminal and not in a competent way, I took a closer look, trying to sort out the personal emails. Those were few, judging by the subject lines. I paged back, sampling anything not quickly identifiable. I tried sorting by "From." Reading emails from Dr. Reynolds seemed intrusive, but I did it anyway and learned that she had requested that the zoo pay her way to a zoo vet conference in Georgia. Also that she was over budget for lab tests she sent out. Nothing juicy.

I skipped all the emails from Mr. Crandall once I figured out that they were forwarded memos to and from the city council. I skipped the zoo newsletters.

I opened three emails from names I didn't recognize. One was a link to a YouTube video of a woman old enough to know better hugging an adult male lion she'd raised. Another notified him of his high school reunion coming up and reminded him to come dressed as his favorite movie character. The notion boggled. The third was from his dentist reminding him to come have his teeth cleaned.

This was not working. It would take many hours to paw through all of the emails. I checked my watch. I had twenty minutes before Mr. Crandall's meeting was scheduled to end.

As though I'd summoned him, the door opened and Mr. Crandall put his head in. "Iris? What are you doing here?"

Flustered, I clicked the mouse and missed the spot to close out the email. "Oh, hi. You startled me!" I prayed he couldn't see the screen from where he stood.

"Are you on light duty today?"

"Yeah, I mean, yes. My ankles are swelling, and Calvin said I could find something to do sitting down. Jackie set me up to enter animal records."

"Well, good. You take care of yourself now. No heavy lifting. No ladders." He pulled his head out and shut the door.

Rattled, I gave up on emails. I scrolled up to the top and moved the mouse to reset the sort back to Date instead of From, covering my tracks. Before I clicked, I saw that at the top was one from Ateam_mom@email.com, with the spam-like subject "Your letter," sent two weeks ago. I opened it. The message was short and to the point: "Too little, too late. I hope you rot in hell, like I am." No signature. I jerked back as though I'd put my hand on a hot stove.

Mr. Crandall was chatting with the intern when I walked out. "Done?" he asked.

"No. I'm not comfortable in there. Too much Wallace. I'll find something else to do."

He nodded. "Yes, I miss him, too. It's a hard adjustment."

My nerves shredded, I found Jackie and told her how close I'd come to being busted.

"Good save," she said. "You'll be doing identity theft before you know it. Big money in that. You're a natural criminal."

When I glowered at her, she said, "I'll cover for you, but you owe me. Did you find anything good?"

"Not sure. Who's 'A Team Mom'? She's really pissed at Wallace."

"A visitor, some soccer mom? Maybe one of the petting goats bit her kid. Let me know if you find out."

"Deal."

"Do you think we'll ever know what happened?" Jackie was almost plaintive.

"We'd better."

How do you track an email address back to a name and street address? I had no clue, but I was going to find out.

Chapter Eleven

I had an armful of outraged spectacled owl when my radio crackled. The owl was clamped between my right elbow and my hip, with my right hand clutching his legs tight together so those powerful talons couldn't get at me. I fumbled around with my left hand and got the message: "Iris, call Felines." Dr. Reynolds' voice. I was immediately certain that Losa had killed her cubs. No, I was surely overreacting. Surely. With an effort, I continued checking out the bird.

What inspired my meddling was that the owl had skipped breakfast and was fluffed up and dull eyed. As Calvin would say, he looked "crumpy". A minute ago, I'd casually poked around in his exhibit like I always did, then made a fast back-handed swipe at his ankles with a leather-gloved hand, wiping him off the perch and into my clutches. This would not work twice. If I didn't examine him now, we were facing an ugly scene of chasing and flapping. If I used a net, he'd still end up exhausted and possibly with broken feathers.

In my five months under his supervision, Calvin had done his best to teach me how to examine a bird. A check of the owl's breast muscles confirmed that he was too thin. Mouth looked okay, feet were fine…Maybe the cubs were all right, but Losa had died of some post-partum infection. I re-focused, parting feathers on his back and peering at the bases, nudging my little white face mask with a thumb so that I could see. Ah-ha.

Feather lice. He was old and tired and not keeping up with his grooming. I carried him to the little shed outside the aviary where Calvin kept cardboard boxes and stuffed him inside one. Powerful as the feet and wings were, the owl couldn't break out of a cardboard box and wouldn't even try. He would be safe and quiet. Later I'd take him to the hospital for treatment. Maybe Linda had saved one of the cubs.

I called Felines and got Dr. Reynolds.

"Iris, I thought you'd want to be here." Steely professional voice, emotionless, calm.

I panicked again.

"Rajah can't get up this morning, and it's time to put him down."

Shit. I wasn't prepared for that, either. "You're doing it now? I'll suit up and be right over." I couldn't do that steady voice, not even close.

"I'll wait for you."

"Losa's okay? The cubs?"

"No problems there."

One more loss. I stood still outside the aviary shed and forced myself to think like a professional. Leave the owl and the leather gloves in the shed. Remember to disinfect the gloves later to get rid of any lice contamination. Uniform was contaminated also. I stripped off the coveralls, down to maternity jeans and a tee shirt, wadded them up, and dumped them in the shed. Locked it. After sloshing through the footbath at the Penguinarium and washing my hands, I rounded up vinyl gloves and a fresh face mask. I found Calvin's spare clean overalls and pulled them on.

Oh, Raj, I'm so sorry…

I walked to Felines remembering, barely noticing the drizzle seeping from a gray sky. My first days as a Feline keeper, three years ago, with Harold training me in the two weeks before he retired. Wallace hanging out with me on my first solo day, suspecting correctly that Harold hadn't done much more than show me how to put meat into feeding chutes. I was more afraid of the foreman than of lions or leopards. My terror led to clumsy mistakes, and Wallace had elaborated on each one and how it might have led to my death. Looking back, his extra training had helped keep me alive.

Raj, old even then, was the bright note those first weeks as I struggled to get the job done and survive. Soon he permitted a little face scratching from the beginner, two fingers through the mesh of his night den—prohibited, unsafe, irresistible. After a month, he greeted me with the growly poof that is tiger for "hello" and I still loved rumbling back.

I remembered when a naïve visitor dumped a pair of white domestic ducks on the zoo grounds, probably envisioning a happy life for them forever. One flew well enough to land in the tiger exhibit and had made Rajah's day. I picked up white feathers in the exhibit for weeks.

I'd salted his log and rocks with different scents—perfume, zebra manure, cloves—and watched him explore and react— intent, fierce, and gorgeous.

I pushed aside a memory that still sent iced lightning through me: the day we ended up in the outdoor exhibit together, and he chose not to kill me. He snarled and stalked, but he let me back out and slam the door on him.

Raj was my best animal pal. We were cross-species buddies, imperfectly, awkwardly, giving what we had. Tears had me pretty well blinded by the time I turned my key in the door to Felines. I had to be there, and, with precautions, my flutter would be safe. Half the pregnant women in America live with cats.

The tiger was lying flat on his straw bed, Linda and Dr. Reynolds waiting in the hallway outside his night den, Kayla hovering behind them. Old and underweight, dying, he was still so beautiful he made my eyes sting and my throat ache. His food sat in an untouched pile a yard away from his nose, of no interest. I said, "Good morning, Raj" and he raised his head a little, then lay back down, relaxing, ribs rising and falling slow and shallow.

In the last year, he'd survived dental work, an infected claw, and arthritis. Dr. Reynolds and Linda had bought him an extra six months, a comfortable six months, with diet, medications, and careful husbandry while his systems failed. Despite a special diet and medication for his failing kidneys, he was too damn old and sick to go on. Unquestionably time to say good-bye, but it was hard, hard.

Near death, he still commanded respect. Dr. Reynolds waved us out of her way, took her time, and darted him with her pistol through the mesh. He barely flinched. His eyes closed. Dr. Reynolds loaded a pole syringe. She couldn't reach him through the bars. Linda opened the door, the vet stepped in, jabbed Rajah in the rump, and stepped back out.

After a long, long time—a minute or two—his ribs grew still. At Dr. Reynolds' gesture, Linda opened the door to the den again and the vet walked in alone. She injected a syringe-full into his foreleg. He didn't move. After a bit, she crouched to put her stethoscope to his ribs. "It's over," she said, standing up. We filed in to pay our last respects.

"Poor old thing," Kayla said softly. "Are you sure he's dead?"

Dr. Reynolds nodded.

He seemed both bigger and smaller than before. I rubbed his cheek for old time's sake and ran a hand down his shoulder and leg, my first and last chance to feel the coarse fur and now-slack muscles. His feet were enormous. I tried to smooth an eyelid down with a white plastic finger. Linda's face was wet with tears as was my face mask. We touched him respectfully and bid his spirit a silent farewell. I wished him a verdant jungle with fat stupid deer, lovely lady tigers, and no people.

Dr. Reynolds murmured something and I looked up. "What?"

She was talking to Linda. "I left the zoo van outside with a litter. We'll need some help lifting him."

Kayla asked, "What do you want to do with him?"

Dr. Reynolds said, "I'll take a look, a standard necropsy. Maybe I'll find something that might help with the next tiger or other cats. Then we'll donate the body to one of the universities. You can make the calls to see which one wants him."

Kayla nodded.

"I'll call Hap for help," I said and walked to the kitchen to use the phone.

He showed up with Denny and Ian. At my raised eyebrow, Denny said, "Takes manpower to lug tigers, Ire. You shouldn't be lifting. By the way, you look ready to decontaminate Chernobyl."

"Price of admission." I adjusted the face mask, which managed to let air leak around it while still impairing my breathing.

Ian didn't say anything.

Denny and Hap brought in the empty litter and stood for a moment in the den, looking at the old tiger. Linda and I stood with them. Denny put an arm around my shoulder, a brief half-hug, and let it slide off. Hap shook his head and said, "Sorry, Linda. Comes to every one of us." We'd worked together, in our different roles, for enough years, enough triumphs and disasters, to share an understanding of what Rajah's passing meant. I wouldn't cry over a deceased snake myself, but I knew why Denny might want to and that I would attempt a word of comfort. Hap didn't work with the zoo animals as directly, but he raised parrots at home, and he knew.

Ian and Dr. Reynolds and Kayla waited quietly. A tickling wiggle in my belly made an obvious but helpful point about the cycle of life. The moment passed. We lifted Rajah's legs to roll him onto the litter, an ignominious procedure. Linda draped a stiff blue tarp over his body to hide him from visitor eyes. The zoo wasn't open yet, but someone might be on a special tour. Hap and Denny were clear that I was not to help. I stood around as Denny and Hap took one end. Linda and Kayla arranged themselves together, Ian took the fourth corner. Hap said, "On three," and counted. The litter sagged and they adjusted their grips and posture, then carried him out into bright sunshine. In his prime, Rajah had weighed almost four hundred pounds. He'd lost weight steadily this last year, but he was still a lot of cat. Dr. Reynolds opened up the rear of the van, and they shoved the litter inside.

"Put him on the necropsy table," Dr. Reynolds said. "One of the sun bears has a bite wound, and I have to get over there. I'll notify Mr. Crandall later. He'll put out the press release."

Five of us climbed into the van, a big white box, anonymous since Maintenance hadn't gotten around to sending it out for zebra stripes and the zoo logo. I was of no use, but neither was I ready to let go of Rajah. Ian chose to walk rather than crowd in with us.

We sat with our tiger on his semi-final journey, Hap driving, Denny in the passenger seat, Linda crouched alongside Rajah's tarp-covered back. I was near his head, Kayla sat by his hind legs. Linda and I each laid a hand on the tarp, as though to steady or comfort the body beneath. The van smelled of cat, a hunter's scent. We were all silent, even Denny. Hap slowly steered this funeral cortege toward the fence that separated the visitor area of the zoo from the restricted Commissary, maintenance barn, and hospital side. He activated the key pad to open the gate, drove through, and turned left to drive along the alley toward the hospital, between the visitor fence and the outer perimeter fence. The gate swung shut behind us.

Rajah was hand raised as a cub and lived his entire life in a zoo, never missing a meal but never killing for himself. Well, except for that luckless duck. He'd had the best life we could give him, but a limited one. It was easy to picture a different life in the wild—hunting and mating, cooling off in jungle pools with tropical orchids overhead. The picture included local villagers stalking him with guns to protect their livestock and for the princely sum his hide would bring into their impoverished lives. Wild tigers weren't living in any paradise these days. Populations were on the skids, and the extinction alarms were sounding. Raj wouldn't have lived this long if…

Kayla erupted with something along the lines of "Aggh!" and, jarred back into the real world, I looked toward her and saw Rajah's hind legs twitch under the tarp. Then, next to me, his front paws moved, reaching out from under the tarp with claws extended.

I also said something a lot like "Aggh!" and yelled, "Hap, he's not dead! Let us out!"

Hap glanced once over his shoulder, gunned the motor, spun the van into the space between the Commissary and hospital, and killed the engine. We emptied that van in milliseconds, piling out through the front doors. Somehow Kayla scrambled out before either Linda or I did. Hap slammed one door, Denny slammed the other, and Hap clicked the "lock" button on the key ring.

We stood in a huddle like alarmed primates. "What the hell?" Hap said. "I thought he was supposed to be stone dead."

"Holy crap," Denny said.

"Twitching after death is normal," Kayla said with a complete lack of conviction.

"You bailed out like your hair was on fire," I said.

Linda spoke into her radio. "Dr. Reynolds, mission was not totally accomplished. There is still activity," she said, calm enough to use words that would not alarm anyone overhearing. Stress overtones were thick in her voice, but the lousy sound quality might mask that.

After several seconds of silence, Dr. Reynolds' voice crackled back. "Negative. Mission definitely accomplished. Normal activity. Don't worry."

Don't worry. "No way are we opening up that van." Denny spoke for us all.

"We'll wait for you before we move him," Linda said into the radio.

"And another dart," I squeaked.

"Holy crap," Denny said again.

We stood around in the rain for several minutes, peering into the van now and then. Ian joined us. The blue tarp twitched once for sure and maybe a second time. Kayla and Hap explored the concept of undead tigers in a zombie zoo, Kayla giggling. Linda and I couldn't switch moods that fast. Ian stood back and said nothing.

"She's not coming any time soon," Hap said. "Call me when you need me." He ambled off toward the Commissary, and, after a moment's hesitation, Ian followed.

Linda said. "We might as well wait inside."

We took a final look at the blue tarp through the van windows, agreed the tiger was definitely probably dead, and walked in. The hospital had a small sitting area next to the entrance.

Linda and Denny and I settled at the table and chairs. My face mask was sliding around, and I pulled it off.

"I might as well get some work done," Kayla said. "I'll be in the quarantine rooms if you need me."

Denny waited with us, reading a *Natural History* magazine that was on the coffee table. Linda and I told Rajah stories and debated how long we should wait before returning to our areas. I asked about her ceramics and she told me about a class she was taking. "It's more sculpture than throwing pots."

"Did you ever get your own kiln?" I asked.

"No. The landlord won't permit it. He thinks I'll set the building on fire. I can't afford anyplace else." She looked frustrated. Ceramics were serious with her, and Birds had beautiful leaf-like water bowls as a result.

Sam came in to drop off giraffe and llama fecal samples, annoyed because Ian wasn't on the job. "I sent him to the Commissary for a salt block, and he never came back." We explained that he'd been hijacked. Sam picked up an ointment for a split starting in one of Nakri's toenails and left.

"I should go," I said. "You don't need me here." I opened the door to leave at the same time Dr. Reynolds opened it to enter.

"So what's the problem?" she asked, a little curtly.

"He moved," I said. "A lot. So we left him in the van. We wanted back-up."

"Well, back-up is here. You saw normal agonal twitches, which is post-mortem muscle activity. That animal is dead. Let's get him into the necropsy room. Where's the van?"

"Right outside," I said, and walked out onto the little porch. No van.

"Maybe Hap moved it," I said. Why would he do that? He was as scared as the rest of us. I called him at the Commissary.

"You ready to move him?" he asked. "I want the vet or a shotgun."

"Hap, where'd you put the van?"

Hap hadn't put the van anywhere. The van had vanished, tiger and all.

Chapter Twelve

It was a good half hour before we were all convinced the van was really gone. Hap used the hospital phone to check that no one from Maintenance or Grounds Keeping had moved it. I checked that neither Administration nor Education had taken a notion to use it. We put the word out over the radio asking if anyone could see it. Nada, zip, goose egg.

Back outside, standing in the road, Hap waved toward the gate and diagnosed the situation as a carjacking. "Somebody on Finley Road drove by, saw the van, grabbed the opportunity. Didn't even know the tiger was in there. That douche bag is going to get a big surprise. Be sweet if the tiger really is alive."

We contemplated that for a moment as the sun broke out from cloud cover and dimmed again.

"He is not alive, and I'm not convinced the van was stolen," Dr. Reynolds said. "Someone took it for zoo use. When we find out who it is, I'm going to have a word or two with them. You can't take off with a zoo vehicle any time you find one idle. Let me know when you find it." She went back inside, the door closing firmly behind her.

Hap held out his open palm, showing us the key ring. "Didn't use these."

"It's a joke," Denny said. "Somebody's idea of a prank. Maybe Arnie or one of the maintenance guys."

"It's only a prank if they know the tiger's in there. Otherwise, it's just irresponsible," Linda pointed out. "They wouldn't know about the tiger unless they watched us load him. I think one of those Education volunteers took it for a program in a park somewhere."

"Some crook got through the perimeter fence and jacked the van open," Hap said. "Hotwired it. Quick on his feet."

"Or someone grabbed another key off the key board at the maintenance barn," I said. "I've got to get back to Birds. I'll stop by Maintenance and ask where they keep the keys."

"Good luck," Hap said. "Those boys are loose with keys."

He was right. I talked to Ralph and José, who pointed me to the key board. They picked through the jumble and found another key they thought was for the van we'd used, but couldn't come up with a definite answer as to how many keys to that van actually existed. "They get lost, we get new ones made," Ralph said. "Don't worry, that van is around here somewhere."

I'd heard that before. It was more convincing the first time. "Did you see anyone take a key in the last half hour?"

They hadn't, but both had been working in back and wouldn't have noticed.

It seemed that the zoo's borders were surprisingly permeable. Picketers, thieves, and maybe a killer were coming and going freely without anyone seeing them. It was unsettling. I went back to Birds and the longer I worked, the madder I got. Some idiot had stolen Rajah. Once the creep figured it out, the old tiger's body would be dumped in a ditch on some lonely road, covered with brush, and forgotten. The van would be chopped and sold. We'd never find out what happened. Raj would rot like road kill.

I forgot the elderly owl in the cardboard box until late afternoon, and, stricken with guilt, carried him to the hospital. Dr. Reynolds was in her office at the computer. "Here's the owl. Where do you want me to put him?"

She organized her hair behind her neck. "You can leave him here. I'll have Kayla set him up in a cage. I've been looking for a chance to talk with you. It's been chaotic today—the van missing, sun bears fighting, reporters calling." She put her arms on the desk, hands clasped together. "I want to apologize for asking you to investigate what happened to Kevin. Please don't make any inquiries or call attention to yourself. You shouldn't put yourself in danger in any way."

This was a switch. Only a few days before, she wanted in the worst way for me to be her eyes and ears in the elephant barn. The exemption from spy duty was a relief, but puzzling. Why was she suddenly worried about me? "Any special reason?"

"Only that it could be risky, considering the situation as it is today. In fact, it's fine if you stop collecting the urine samples and stay out of the barn entirely. I'll find another way."

She wasn't going to tell me the full story. I was sure she really wanted those samples. Mr. Crandall did, too. What was the problem, now that Damrey was declared innocent? Neither Sam nor Ian would go nuts and whack me for no reason. I was going to be on leave a lot in the near future, and I could use the brownie points. "I think pee collecting is safe, like you said. I don't mind doing it."

"I'll look for an alternative anyway. It may take a few days."

She was frowning when I escaped, a concerned frown.

I was halfway back to the aviary when I remembered the nasty-gram I'd found in Wallace's email. Go back and tell her? Keep it to myself for now? I didn't have any reason to keep it secret, but I didn't feel like walking back either. Next time I saw her, I'd mention it.

By day's end, I was exhausted physically and emotionally. I wanted to go home, eat dinner, grieve for Rajah, and get some sleep. At the time clock, Hap was stacking cans of marmoset food and turtle diet on the tall metal shelves that filled much of the Commissary. He was still working the missing van. "People steal cars to commit crimes," he told me. "This carjacker will hit a bank or convenience store or whatever, drive the van to some meeting point, get picked up by his buddy, and leave the van behind. He might never even look under that tarp. Cops are watching for the license plate. We'll get it back."

Denny was still hanging around and overheard. "I told Jackie to be sure the taxidermists are notified. He might find Raj and want a tiger skin rug."

"Ugh!" I said. "That is too gross."

"Well, yeah," Denny agreed. "I'm just saying it's a possibility. Here's another one—"

"Bye," I said and scooted out the door.

"Ire, wait!" Denny came barreling out after me. "We need to plan. Synergy. Find out what happened to Wallace like we agreed."

"Like we agreed?" This must be debris from my meltdown at Marcie's.

"Don't you want to walk through strategies? I figure I should look into alibis while you focus on motivations. Take advantage of male and female energies."

Where did he get *his* energy? He was forever fidgeting, pacing, and waving his hands. Watching him wore me out. Maybe I needed more goji berries. "Let's talk later. I'm beat. It's been a bad day."

"Yeah, that it's been. I want to check out the construction crew. Also, Crandall might tell me if Wallace was working on something secret. I'll give it a try."

I was moving toward the employee lot, but this stopped me. "Denny, these are terrible ideas. You'll get the crews upset, and Mr. Crandall will nail your hide to the wall."

"Okay, okay, I'll work the taxidermists. And alibis."

"Great idea. Let me know what you find out."

"Oh, try to sleep on your left side, okay? More oxygen to the baby."

He was relentless, and I was not in a good mood. "Denny, do you spend all your spare time on the internet finding this pregnancy stuff? Aren't you supposed to be playing video games and trading comics? Take Marcie to a concert or something. Obsess elsewhere, like at your girlfriend."

He opened the door to his van looking embarrassed. I didn't expect it to last.

I parked the Honda in the same spot every day by the back fence of the employee lot so that I could find it even when tired and hungry. When I opened the door, Sam popped out of his old Volvo two rows over. Waiting for me, it turned out.

"Iris. Got a minute?"

"What's up?" I hoped my voice didn't reveal the wariness I felt. I backed into the driver's seat and sat, leaving the door open.

"Something I should have said this morning." Sam put a hand on my car roof and leaned toward me.

"What's that?"

"Don't be alone with Ian, especially not in back of the barn where no one can see. I think he's nuts. You be careful. That's all." He straightened up and started back toward his car.

"Sam! You can't lay that on me and walk away. Come back and tell me what Ian ever did to make you think that."

Whether he heard me or not wasn't evident. He shut the door of his car and drove out of the parking lot. A beige sedan pulled out from where it was parked on Finley Road. I couldn't see the driver clearly, but it looked like a man. Black hair. He followed Sam's Volvo.

Chapter Thirteen

I woke up before the alarm the next morning, thanks to aching hips and a fragmentary dream of a Komodo dragon loose in the house with the dogs. While an improvement on dreams of dead people, it was not a pleasant introduction to the day. Why couldn't I have a sweet dream of baby pintail ducks or a visitation from Rajah's spirit to tell me he was happy in the afterlife? Or I'd settle for sleeping until the alarm went off.

I sat alone, not counting the dogs, at the dining room table and ate my granola, blueberries, and giant pregnancy vitamin pill. I had time to fire up the computer and check the news online, hoping that someone had found Rajah. Monday's *OregonLive.com* and Vancouver's *Columbian.com* carried stories about his death and theft, featuring current photos of Mr. Crandall and old ones of Rajah in his prime. Police were investigating. Anyone with information was encouraged to come forward. Both articles closed with a sober mention of the fatal incident at the elephant barn.

Talk radio, on the other hand, on the way to work, considered tiger-napping a hilarious antidote to stock market declines and a plane crash. What a bunch of clowns those zoo keepers were! I snapped the radio off and drove the rest of the way rehearsing a vehement phone call to the station.

I walked to Elephants, but not to the viewing area or the outside exhibit. Instead I unlocked the nearest gate to the visitor perimeter fence and strolled behind the barn and then across a twenty-foot-wide swath of mowed grass to the zoo's outer perimeter fence. Dr. Reynolds couldn't switch off another person's curiosity, at least not mine. I had my own reasons to figure out what had happened here. Eight feet of stout mesh with three strands of barbed wire at the top kept intruders at bay. Small trees grew in clumps in the space between fences, maybe the source of some of the browse fed to the elephants.

A big shed sat behind the barn, close to the outer perimeter fence. Inside was a huge pile of manure and bedding, sitting there to compost for use on the zoo grounds and Vancouver parks. The open front of the shed was designed for easy access by the small front-loader parked nearby. The shed's metal roof sloped toward the back. I checked out the space between the outer perimeter fence and the shed roof, perhaps eight feet of clear space. I couldn't see any way to get out of the zoo by that route or into it, either. The fence looked good both directions from the elephant barn, no holes or washouts. I shrugged and gave up and walked back through the gate.

I watched the elephants for a moment from the visitor area, stalling. I wasn't eager to face the anger and tension inside the barn. Now that I knew for sure she was blind, I noticed the way Damrey moved, touching walls and the floor lightly with her trunk and sniffing around constantly. Still, she walked with confidence and didn't bump into anything. The whole facility, inside and out, did seem awfully small for two big animals.

Sam appointed himself my guardian for the day's sample collection, but his role was undemanding. Damrey and Nakri delivered the goods, and I paid them off. We stood at the front stall while Ian hosed out the back stall, out of ear shot.

I couldn't help asking, "Sam, why don't you do this yourself? You don't really need me."

Sam shrugged, annoyed. "Didn't seem like a good idea to be locked into a new responsibility when we're short-handed. Like today, we've got TB tests scheduled for the girls. That takes time. I thought the pee samples would take longer than they do. Anyway, it's not my job to carry out other people's projects."

Even if it benefits elephants? I let it go. "Last night you told me Ian was nuts and dangerous and to stay away from him. What makes you so sure? What's he done?"

"I'm not sure of anything. I just don't want anyone else getting hurt."

Was it that simple, or did he want me to be suspicious of Ian?

Sam gave me a look I couldn't interpret. "I've got to get going."

"That's pretty strong stuff if you've got nothing to back it up."

"Nothing you'd take seriously."

"Try me."

Sam shook his head.

I asked, "What do you think happened to Wallace?"

"I wish I knew."

He turned toward the person door, curving an arm to shoo me out.

I ignored the body language. "Why was he here alone so early?"

"Beats me."

This was going at least as well as my chat with Ian. "He saw someone sneaking around a few days before the attack."

"Yeah. Dr. Reynolds mentioned it. I haven't seen anyone. Sometimes people come over the fence down by the duck pond, but they've never gotten into the barn or caused any trouble."

Any trouble at Elephants. Vandals caused plenty of trouble elsewhere in the zoo.

Sam looked at me, considering. He said, "You know that Dr. Reynolds and Wallace were seeing each other?"

Where did that come from? "Yeah, I finally caught on."

"Wallace wasn't the only one who liked her. Ian can't take his eyes off her or string two words together when she's around."

Ian couldn't string two words together at the best of times. But I took his point. "And?"

"Something to keep in mind. We'd all like to know what happened here."

"Are you saying that Ian clocked Wallace to have a clear shot at Dr. Reynolds?" This was chilling on multiple levels—that Sam would think so, that he would share it with me, that it might even be true.

"No, no. But you have to wonder if it fits in somehow, Ian obsessing about her. Did you notice that Ian didn't say a word to stick up for Damrey when everyone thought she'd killed Wallace? Kept his mouth shut and let it roll."

"At lunch one day, Arnie called her a rogue and Ian said she wasn't."

"Not exactly a stirring defense. He's worked with her long enough. He should know she wouldn't kill someone. That was a damned dirty trick, to kill a man and set it up for Damrey to take the blame."

These were deep currents, and I was adrift. "Disagreeing with you about elephant management doesn't make him a murderer."

"Of course not. He's probably just an ordinary jerk." Again that considering look. "There's a lot Ian doesn't ever admit, a lot we don't know about him, but for some reason Wallace trusted him. He's supposedly got all this experience in other facilities. He and Wallace ganged up on me about one procedure after another."

I had to be led by the hand to see the obvious. "They were talking to each other and not to you." No wonder the man was pissed.

Sam watched Ian across the barn. "Wallace took to him like his long-lost little brother and quit being straight with me. I couldn't tell if he'd changed his mind about the new exhibit or the money ran out or what. He tap-danced around it and told me what wonderful ideas Ian had. I thought he respected me, but if he ever did, it evaporated. He completely undermined my authority with Ian."

"You'll be in charge if you get the curator job." I wouldn't want to be in Ian's boots.

"I shouldn't have said anything about that. I was mad, and I talked too much. I've got to get some work done. Don't go telling tales, all right?" He edged me toward the door.

I sent out a tendril toward a waning friendship. "Sam? You saved me and Damrey, when she was messing around with Wallace's body. Hap would have had to shoot her. You were amazing over the phone. I hope someday I can be that cool in a crisis."

Sam shrugged. "It's my job. You're surprised I'm good at it?" He looked at me through lowered brows, a second's hesitation, and opened the door for me.

Nothing I had to offer would soothe that lacerated pride.

Outside, with every step toward the Penguinarium, I grew more certain that Sam was again manipulating me and that, at least for now, our friendship was on the shelf. Was he trashing Ian's reputation as preparation for firing him, if Sam got the promotion? Would he lie about Ian's infatuation with the veterinarian to implicate Ian in Wallace's murder? I felt queasy and depressed.

By three-thirty Calvin and I were looking forward to ending the day in good shape, as least as far as caring for birds went. Calvin was sneezing and snuffling from a head cold and chewing on zinc tablets. He fretted several times about transmitting it to me. I assured him that both my unborn child and I could survive the sniffles. Arnie stopped by to shoot the breeze. Calvin always had time for him and never seemed to notice that Arnie was not the most industrious keeper. I kept my head down, wrote up the reports, and succeeded in evading Arnie's interest. I wondered if I had what it took to be a senior keeper. Would Arnie do what I told him to? Doubtful.

"About time to head for the barn," Calvin said, as he did at the end of every day. But the phone rang and he picked up. It was Jackie, reporting that one of the Children's Zoo parrots had bitten a kid. It must have been a tall, illiterate, and unsupervised kid, given the cage design and the warning sign on it. Calvin trudged off to deal with the parent and the snappish psittacine, Arnie trailing behind.

I finished the reports and clocked out a little late. The security guard chugged past, delivering Dr. Reynolds to her car. My back ached. I wanted a long, hot shower, the companionship of two fine dogs, and a whole lot of dinner. As I drove by the front of the zoo, I saw a familiar young man with black hair walking the picket circle alone. His sign read, "Tiger's body destroyed to hide fatal abuse?"

Chapter Fourteen

At Elephants the next morning, the girls delivered the goods without fuss. Ian was tense and distant. Too bad. There for a bit, it seemed he might relax and become less of an outsider.

Calvin had the penguin feeding mostly done by the time I got there. He said the spectacled owl was ready to be picked up at the hospital and I might as well go get it. I ran into Denny on the way.

"Ire, come see this and view me with new respect. This is big, big, big." Denny was almost skipping, not easy while carrying a sizeable plastic storage box.

I took a guess. "You've got space-age micronutrients and powerful antioxidants in a revolutionary new formulation. Something the pharmaceutical industry and the medical establishment have concealed for decades to maintain their profits at the expense of our health."

"What? Don't be ridiculous. I've got four—count them—four *Manouria emys* juveniles. Can you believe it?"

I couldn't pronounce it, but I could believe it. "Let's see."

He put the box down on the asphalt and opened it with a flourish.

I peered in and recklessly flaunted my herpetological expertise. "Turtles. Four brown turtles."

"Asian tortoises, from this guy in Longview. Remember I told you weeks ago? He's a turtle nut, and he bred them himself.

Incredible. You should have seen the habitat he made for them. I took pictures. I'm going to change one of the reptile exhibits for Asian Experience the same way. Aren't they great?"

I didn't remember the conversation. "And this herp-head gave them to the zoo?"

"He's moving to California and can't keep them all. I traded some excellent comics for these. He's a collector."

Uh oh. This I would have remembered. "Denny, the zoo didn't buy these? You arranged the sale? I don't think you ever mentioned that part."

"No worries. I said it was a donation. And it is. From me."

"Denny, I do not want to know anything more about how the zoo got these…things. Please, please, never mention my name in this context."

He looked puzzled and hurt. "Anyone can buy them on line. Expensive, though." His enthusiasm swept back. "Aren't they cool? They'll get bigger, a lot bigger. Forty pounds and up. One of the most primitive tortoises. I have to find out how old they are before they breed. The female doesn't dig a hole for eggs. She actually builds a nest and guards it for a few days after she lays the eggs. Very unusual for a chelonian. Oh, and they grunt and moan during sex. Extremely vocal."

I edged away. "Dr. Reynolds knows about them?"

"Of course. That's where I'm coming from. They're just out of quarantine. They're perfect for the new Asian exhibit."

"I'm happy for you, and I hope you don't get fired for illegal acquisitioning."

He bounced off, still jubilant.

I gazed at his back, hoping he hadn't figured out yet another way to get into trouble with zoo management. What was left of zoo management. Please let this turtle not be on the endangered species list.

At the hospital, I looked around the reception area and the hallway without finding the owl set out in a box for me to pick up. Nor was Dr. Reynolds in her office. I stuck my head in the the necropsy room. She wasn't there either.

Farther along were three little quarantine rooms and the sound of hosing came from one of them. I opened the door, not to go in, which was forbidden since it was, after all, a quarantine room, but to ask Kayla where the owl was.

Kayla was hosing the floor near the door with her back to me. I glimpsed three rabbits in a cage, no doubt intended for the Children's Zoo, and a fennec fox that I remembered hearing about. The beautiful little canine was an ill-advised pet of somebody Mr. Crandall had to please and therefore Dr. Reynolds had to treat. "Kayla!" I hollered over hose noise. She jumped a foot, and in an instant I was soaked from head to toe. She shut the hose off at the nozzle, and we faced each other, equally amazed. "And a fine morning to you, too," I sputtered, wiping my face on a wet sleeve.

"Hi, Iris. Sorry. You startled me."

No kidding.

"I'll be done in a minute." She went back to hosing.

Just "sorry?" I dripped outside, trying to decide how mad I was. I decided and started rummaging in the supply closets lined up along the hallway across from the quarantine rooms. I found clean towels in one. Another was a utility closet for mops and brooms with a big sink on the floor.

The sound of hosing stopped. I waited in the hallway by the door drying my face and hair with a little white towel while Kayla presumably put the hose away and wiped down the floor with a squeegee. The door opened, and she stepped out.

My pitch was good. Two and a half gallons of water arced out of the bucket and landed on her chest. It wasn't precision work, of course, and a fair amount hit her head. Face, actually.

Kayla reacted with the same paralysis I had, but it was brief. I flung the towel away and was galloping down the hall when she reacted, but she was close on my heels when I reached the bathroom. That woman was quick, and I was racing under weights. I yanked open the door and slammed it behind me. I had to lean my full self on the door to get it closed and shoot the bolt. Panting, I shouted, "Serves you right! You got me first."

"It was an *accident*, and I am going to *kill* you!" She slammed her shoulder against the door, which didn't split. Better construction than I expected. "Yellow-livered chicken! Coward! Scaredy-cat! Yellow belly! Come out and fight like a woman."

Then silence. A standoff. I'd run out of strategy, and I couldn't spend the rest of my life barricaded in the hospital bathroom dripping on the tiles. For one thing, someone might want to pee. For another, I had work to do. Time was against me. "Now we're even. Truce?" I yelled through the door. Weak. She would never go for it, and she would figure something out pretty fast, something evil.

Silence. I waited, wondering what she was up to, and decided it was safer not to give her much time. I opened the door a crack, my foot positioned to block any assault. No Kayla. I threw caution to the winds and stepped out.

Screaming like a banshee, Kayla leaped at me, all ten fingernails arching toward my face. I fell back against the wall and threw up my arms. She doubled over, choking with glee. "You look like...like..." Words failed her.

"A drowned gerbil," I suggested and slid laughing to the floor with my back against the wall. I climbed right back up. "Uh-oh!"

Kayla started to say something, but I pointed down the hall behind her.

Detective Quintana stood a safe distance back. "Whatever happened to you two better not happen to me. I've got a gun."

"Yessir," I said. "How may we help you?"

Kayla stifled a giggle.

He said, "I thought I might have a chat with Dr. Reynolds, but I suppose I could arrest you both for assault with a liquid weapon."

A joke? From Detective Quintana? A giggle escaped me. No, more dignified than that. Sort of a chortle.

Kayla said, "She's not in her office?" At his sober nod, "She'll be done with her rounds and back any minute. Why don't you take a seat in the reception area by the front door? Can I get you a cup of..." She made a snorting noise. "...water?"

"Thanks for the offer, but no." He retreated back the way he'd come.

"About that owl…" I said. Best to keep her distracted.

Kayla sobered up. "He's in Room 3. Could you catch him up? He's the only thing in there, so it should be okay as far as quarantine goes." She shed her soggy lab coat, which had done little to protect the low-necked, short-sleeve top underneath. It was pale green and now almost translucent, revealing a lacy little bra. Her necklace was jade leaves. Kayla found another of the white towels, swiped at her hair and chest, and gave it up.

The owl anticipated the worst from me, but he was stuck in a small cage and his talons were ineffective against the leather gloves Kayla provided. He put up a fight when I grabbed his legs with more vigor than he'd shown the day before. Dr. Reynolds' lice treatment, rehydration, and a couple of shots had perked him up considerably. I corralled the wings and stuffed him into a fresh cardboard box for the journey home. Kayla pointed out the bottle of anti-lice cleanser Dr. Reynolds had set out for me to use on all the raptor exhibits. I stuck it into a damp pocket.

Kayla walked me to the front door. Quintana wasn't there, so Dr. Reynolds had come back or else he'd given up. She said, "Even though you're a total puke, I can't tell you how glad I am that you're doing the elephant thing. Is it working out okay?"

Once upon a time I wore jeans like hers, jeans with a waist. "No problems. I take it you don't want the job back, even though Damrey's cleared."

"Nope. It's all yours. She tried to smack me, and I think those elephant people are all kidding themselves. And being in that barn makes my clothes and hair smell like elephants for the rest of the day."

"Kayla, just wondering—did you ever see anyone leaving the elephant barn early, before the keepers got there?"

"Dr. Reynolds and the police and that committee asked me. No, I never did." She slumped into one of the chairs.

The box with the owl wasn't heavy, but it was awkward. I set it down on the little coffee table. "If you remember anything else, let me know."

"Why? I mean, why are you so interested?"

Good question. I punted. "We all want to know what happened, right? Everyone's trying to figure it out."

"Yeah, I suppose so. I guess Damrey really didn't do it. But I don't want to be around them anymore." She made a face.

"Elephant phobic? Can't afford to be if you're going to work here." Like I had the right to lecture.

"It's a one-year job. Jean—Dr. Reynolds—said she'll try to get funding to keep me for another year. But even my old clinic job paid better than this."

"So working here is just to pay the bills?" I thought of all the people eager to work with exotic animals, the flood of applications for every zoo position posted to the public.

Kayla shrugged. "I'll stay if Dr. Reynolds wants me to. She saved my bacon. I left the clinic when I got a job as office manager at a business that imports bamboo flooring, but the son of the owner and I...well, he pissed me off, and I quit." She touched her jade necklace. "This was the best thing I got out of *that* relationship."

"Beautiful."

"Anyway, then I couldn't find a thing and was totally depressed. I've got the vet tech degree *and* a bookkeeping certification and couldn't find anything. I was a mess, and Jean pulled me out by the scruff of my neck. She was the dorm mentor in my freshman year in college, and we stayed friends. She's the one who's always there for me. I wish there was a career path for me here."

"I barely made it through two years of college." Marcie had gotten me through those two years and thought I should finish up. She apparently didn't have the same clout as Dr. Jean Reynolds, or I was a tougher case than Kayla. "Maybe you'll get addicted to the zoo. I did. I started here as a volunteer with the education animals at school programs. A keeper position opened up, and here I am. Senior keeper is as far as *my* ambition goes."

Kayla stood up and plucked at the front of her blouse to unstick it from her skin. "I like being around the animals, and I like the people, especially Mr. Crandall. He's such a sweetie. Mr. Wallace was always nice, too."

Zoo management had never eaten out of *my* hand.

She combed through her wet hair with her fingers and shook her head to settle it back down. "I've got meds to do."

I nodded. "Nice hosing with you."

"Back at you."

Outside, I remembered I was supposed to find Dr. Reynolds and tell her about the ugly note from A Team Mom. Some other time. I stopped for a moment to study the area by the hospital where the van with Rajah had been parked. A black sedan was there now, presumably Quintana's. Whoever stole the van would have driven it back the way we'd come and gone left through the perimeter gate to Finley Road.

Getting the van through the perimeter gate would be no problem—it was on a motion detector to let delivery and service vehicles out. Getting in required punching a code on a key pad, a code Hap shared with delivery companies. Maintenance staff knew the code also, but since I never used that gate, I didn't. I knew the one for the employee parking lot farther down.

Around the corner of the hospital from where I stood was Dr. Reynolds' office. The day had turned warm, which I appreciated in my sodden condition, and the window was open. It was not my fault that I could hear her voice.

"…hardly relevant and due to circumstances that won't occur again. I can't see how it will help your investigation to damage my reputation at this zoo, and it certainly won't help the zoo. My professional competence was never in question."

I couldn't make out the words from Quintana's deep voice and stepped closer.

"Yes, of course. I'm not going anywhere." She sounded angry and maybe a little sad.

More from Quintana.

She said, "I'll let you know if anything else occurs. You know your way out."

I took my owl and stepped away from the building, Rajah forgotten for the moment. Dr. Reynolds was the last person I would ever think was hiding something. Something that Quintana had found out and come to talk to her about. Something Kevin Wallace had found out?

I heard the car behind me and stepped to the side of the road to let Quintana drive by. He gave me a little wave. I watched the gate open as he pulled up in front of it. He waited and drove through, turning onto Finley Road.

Across the road, near the employee parking lot gate, stretched a grassy hill with a few trees on top. A bird watcher sat halfway up the hill with binoculars obscuring his face, a backpack at his feet. The man was facing the zoo, not the best habitat for wild birds. No pileated woodpecker or western tanager around that I could see. An Anna's hummingbird tweeze-tweezed on a phone line above me, bushtits zipped around in a maple on the zoo side of the visitor fence. I took one more look around at the van's probable path and gave it up.

Her professional competence was never in question…what the hell did that mean? What *was* in question?

Chapter Fifteen

The deadline loomed, my future was at stake, and I had no idea what to do. I took a poll.

Marcie said over the phone, "I don't think you should. You have enough on your plate with a new baby. A new job is too much."

Linda looked up from her crossword puzzle and said, "Bring it on! Mr. Crandall can tie a four-foot rope to our left wrists like they did in old California. He hands us each a hoof knife, and we fight to the death. The winner is Queen of Bears and Felines."

Dr. Reynolds paused in her weekly inspection of the aviary. "I don't see why not. Felines has not had a senior keeper to represent it at meetings with Kevin...with the foreman. Neither has Bears. You have feline experience, and you'll be able to work that area as soon as the baby's born."

Hap put down a crate of broccoli. "Whoa! Are you *serious*? *You* in management meetings? Not that you wouldn't be good at the job, I mean, you'd be great..."

Denny waited at the time clock to tell me this: "I figured out why you're falling apart. It's your Saturn return. Saturn is back in the same position it was when you were born. You're getting reborn, including the painful part. Everything changes, everything falls apart. So you'll be a new person. Or maybe you already are, I'm not sure where you are in the process. You have to decide your new relationship with power: totally corrupting or leveraging your positive energy."

I didn't ask Calvin. What if he said it wasn't a good idea? That I wasn't ready to be a senior keeper? That would sting.

I didn't ask Jackie, because she would spin it into some deep psychological disaster I was courting, either way, and then tell everyone.

I had no idea how strong a candidate I was, but the odds of success were at least a little better if I actually applied. Soon. If Mr. Crandall didn't choose an applicant from the current staff, the position would be advertised nationally and hundreds of people would apply.

I could always turn the job down if it was offered. I couldn't decide whether that would be smart or hopelessly lame. Maybe it would get me black-listed, forever rejected as a senior keeper. Better to decide up front whether I wanted the job or not.

Easy to say.

When I left work on Wednesday, I did not drive straight home to feed my dogs. I took a different freeway exit and cruised across the Columbia River to Oregon using the broad, wide-open Sam Jackson Bridge instead of the old Interstate Bridge with its thicket of green struts overhead. After winding around through a light industrial area—you-pull-it junk yard, a body shop, Foster Feed & Seed—I parked in front of Oakley Signs and Banners and hauled myself out of the Honda.

The black Dodge Ram parked in the next space spoke truth: my father was inside. He stood at a thick plank propped up on a workbench. Five numbers were carved into the surface, and he was carefully filling them in with gold leaf. The contrast between the gold and the rough wood looked sharp. "Hey," he said, "come to see how honest people earn their living?"

"No, that's two doors down. I came to see sign painters slacking."

The shop was barn-like with a high ceiling, concrete floor, and a row of windows along the back. While he finished laying the leaf, I examined a round cracked mirror on a chair. "Wolcutt's Barber Shop Shaves Haircuts Beard Trims" ran in blocky old letters along the top and bottom. Dad said, "Aaron found that at a flea market. We're trying to date it, maybe 1920."

I drifted around the shop, ran a finger along the rim of the big sink stained with years of washing out brushes and rollers, admired the tidy tool rack, the screwdrivers and hammers lined up neatly. A huge Christmas cactus hanging under the skylight looked even more limp than usual, so I poured a mug of water into it. The water ran out immediately, so I took it down and set it in a bucket to soak properly.

I sat in a tall swivel chair and twirled while he dabbed another scrap of leaf into the top curl of a six. The shop was soothing.

"You coming for dinner?"

I sighed. "No. I have to feed the dogs. Need some input."

"Input. Is that the same as advice?" He put the little booklet of leftover gold leaf into a drawer in the workbench.

"Could be. There's a senior keeper position over Felines and Bears that's come up. Take a step up the food chain or stay a grazer? More money, more meetings, supervising other keepers."

"You want to supervise other people?"

I thought about that. "Not much. It's mostly the money that appeals."

"I thought you were doing okay financially." He cleaned a brush at the sink.

"Surviving."

"We could help."

"You could save for retirement."

"It's a three-bedroom house. Could rent a room." He spun the brush dry and stroked it smooth. Hung it up on a nail with similar brushes.

True. A paying housemate. Would that be the same amount of stress as a bigger job? I hopped down and wandered to the back windows and looked out at cabin cruisers and drift boats on trailers waiting for the boat repair shop next door. "I'm going to need flexibility with the kid. Might be harder to get if I'm a senior keeper. I hear babies get sick a lot."

"Yup." My father took a rag, dampened it under the faucet, and wiped the top of the workbench.

"I'd like to show Mom that I'm on a career path." The Christmas cactus had soaked enough. I set it in the sink to drain.

He took a push broom and swept the floor where he'd been working. Bits of gold leaf took flight and floated at knee height, glinting in late afternoon sunlight from the windows.

I held the dust pan. "No, taking care of the baby is what matters. I'm not going to torque my life to impress anyone. But I'd love to get back to Felines, and it might be fun to help design new exhibits."

He put the brush away.

I emptied the dust pan into the garbage can and hung it up.

He re-hung the plant and put little paint cans away, organizing them by a system that wasn't clear to me on the metal shelves that ran along one wall.

"Linda's going to apply. I've got more experience. I think I'd ace her out, and this opportunity won't come around again for a long time."

He stepped out of his white coveralls, splotched and dribbled with many colors, and hung them up on their hook.

"But I'd be happy to see her get the job, and I like Birds better than I thought I would."

He washed his hands using paint-removing goo, with special attention to his fingernails.

"Thanks, Dad. I appreciate the help." I leaned close to give him a peck on the cheek. Fresh paint will always smell like security to me.

"So which is it?"

I smiled. "Give Mom a hug for me. Bye now."

Chapter Sixteen

The Vulture's Roost featured four dozen different beers, twelve of them on draft; three kinds of bad wine; and raspberry lemonade. I stirred ice cubes with a straw and wondered whether berries or chemicals contributed the intense pinkness. The vivid cheese on the nachos didn't look any safer, but I was too hungry to pass them up while I waited for a burger.

Hap had whooped at me as I clocked out after a blessedly uneventful day. "Cowboy up, Oakley! We're going to the Buzzard for team building. We've been bummed out too long. Time for *Brew Therapy*." He had rounded up Arnie, Kayla, Linda, and Denny. Ian, looking confused and reluctant, failed to escape. It was Wednesday and tomorrow was my day off. Why not attempt a little fun?

Vulture's Roost, AKA The Buzzard, wasn't far, and we swept into their little parking lot like The Invasion of The Smelly People. We sat in a half circle at a corner booth, a scarred plank table in front of us, pressing gently against my belly. I was between Linda and Ian. The tavern wasn't crowded and the music was an inoffensive mix of Hank Williams and Jimmie Dale Gilmore. Some of us were still in the pants-and-shirt style of uniform. Those who wore coveralls were in the clothes we'd had on underneath. Kayla wore a low cut top in a crinkly silver fabric, silver disks dangling from her ears. The woman had more style in her little finger than I had in my entire bulging body.

I was giving it an hour, then home. The dogs had excellent internal clocks and well-defined expectations, expectations I had not been meeting lately.

Hap launched into stories from his biker days. Kayla leaned forward to listen, and I watched Hap enjoy the cleavage and Kayla enjoy his interest. Arnie pitched in with rodeo anecdotes he believed were humorous. Denny argued with the blond bartender about not having a vegan selection on the menu, which was foolish not only because he wasn't a vegan, but also because she was a big-boned gal who could probably bench-press twice his weight. Ian, of course, was silent. He sipped a Coors in this shrine to microbrews and looked trapped. He also kept his eyes on Kayla, who was laughing and jabbing Hap in the ribs.

Denny gave up trying to convert the bartender and swung his attention back to the table. "We're on the cusp of a new era. Who's going to be the silverback?" he asked.

Arnie stumbled to a halt in the middle of a story about a rodeo goat who balanced on a medicine ball. "Huh?" he said.

Hap and Ian looked baffled. Kayla cocked her head.

I made the catch. "Jackie says the interviewing's done. The foreman position is combined with curator again. She's waiting for Mr. Crandall to pull a name out of the hat. We should know soon."

Heads nodded in comprehension.

"Did any of the senior keepers apply?" Linda asked.

I shrugged. Sam had asked me to keep quiet. "We've got more changes coming up, with that new senior keeper position. Anybody know when the winner will be announced?"

Nobody did. My burger arrived and I dug in.

"The third transformation might not happen until the new boss is in place," Denny said darkly.

Kayla bit. "Denny The Mysterioso. Auf Englisch, bitte."

"Transformations. Usually you get three. As far as I can tell, we've had two." He held up his index finger. "Wallace dies under mysterious circumstances. The consequences are still being revealed." His middle finger. "Rajah, an iconic animal, dies and disappears. We won't know the implications until his body is found, maybe years from now." Ring finger. "Next? Whatever it is, I think it's going to affect one of the buildings. Or maybe a visitor."

"And why is that?" Hap asked.

"The first affected a staff person, the second an animal. So it makes sense that the third would be a building or a visitor. Or maybe it'll be meteorological. An earthquake." He brightened. "Yeah, an earthquake. That would do it."

Hap wearied of humoring Denny. "I hope he's good. We want someone to fix what's broke and leave the rest alone."

"He?" Linda asked, with teeth.

"Or she. I got no problem with that," Hap said, unflustered.

"Finley Zoo is on the upswing," Arnie chirped. "Fine time to join up."

"Yeah," Denny said, "a dead foreman is always auspicious." He added, "That was sarcasm."

"Worst part is not knowing who did it," Linda said. "Could be anybody."

"I don't think it was one of us," I said.

"Good. Why?" Linda asked.

"Gut feel." More like wishful thinking.

"Doesn't help. Still ugly, still somebody roaming loose." Linda looked around the table. "Sorry to pop the bubbles."

"Hey, we are here now to stop thinking about just that thing," Hap said. "Moving on."

"Can't until we know who did it," I said. "Let's see if more nachos cheer us up." The burger was history.

"C'mon," Kayla said to Hap with a tough-girl grin. "I need to make some money." She led him to the foosball table and grabbed the poles. "Quarters? Seven goals."

She and Hap fished for pocket change and started in. It didn't take long. "Next?" Kayla sang out.

She beat Hap again and persuaded Arnie and then Linda to take a run at it. They saw the writing on the wall and were good-natured about losing. I claimed my belly wouldn't let me close enough to the table and stayed put. Ian did, too, and Denny was busy scarfing nachos. I said to Ian, "Seems like Hap and Kayla are in living color and the rest of us are in black and white." He looked at me in alarm and got out of the booth. He stood in the background and watched the others commence a pool game.

That left Denny and me alone. "Here's what I got on alibis," he said. I'd forgotten his self-imposed assignment. He slid closer to me and spoke fast and quiet. "Arnie and Kayla and Jackie were home alone, no alibi. Hap's wife is all he's got. I'm trying to be friends with Ian and then ask him, but he's so remote, a tough vibe to engage. I haven't figured out how to ask Mr. Crandall yet. Dr. Reynolds sort of got mad at me for asking her."

Imagine that. "Denny, how deep are you going with this? The fry cooks? City council? Mr. Crandall's already annoyed with you."

He considered the possibility. "Didn't think about them. Good point."

"Denny, I'm kidding."

He forgot the muttering and spoke at normal volume. "I'm working the construction crew next. Oh, I called Brent and asked what gym he and Sam used, said I wanted to join one. He confirmed that he was with Sam when you called to get help shifting Damrey. I timed the drive from the zoo to the gym. Sam could have clipped Wallace and made it to the gym in time to take your call. Assuming he really was at the gym. I talked to one of the trainers, but she couldn't tell me whether he'd been there that morning. They don't save the sign-in sheets."

"So nobody's eliminated."

"Well, we know more than we did."

"We do? Now everyone at the zoo knows you're asking about alibis. That is not going to help." I considered mentioning the fragments I'd overheard from Dr. Reynolds and came to my senses. Denny would run amok.

He leaned back in the booth, looking disgusted. "So what have *you* come up with? You were supposed to find motives."

"I'm working on it. I'm trying to find out who was hanging around the barn in the early morning." I evaded revealing how little I'd accomplished in that direction by getting out to watch the pool game. Three people were up for it, so the game was Cutthroat. Hap moved like a semi-pro, Arnie was casual but competent. Kayla pushed up the bangles on her arms and shot hard and fast. Hap took the first game, Kayla the second. She winked at Arnie and nudged him with an elbow before she demolished him. He seemed to like it.

Hap said to Kayla, "I tagged you as drinking mango martinis with the cool dudes, but you're just another a brew-swilling pool shark."

Kayla tossed her hair back and wiggled her shoulders, all sexy lady. "Ah kin ride a horse, catch a steelhead, and dress out mah own deer." She straightened up and bobbed her head. "Really I can. Daddy was a hunting guide for awhile. But…" She squinted at Hap, "I can also cut you up good with my Nordstrom's card, so don' you ever cross me."

Hap cracked up.

"Darts for dollars?" she suggested, but a new pitcher had arrived, and we regrouped at the booth.

Kayla had lightened the mood, and while we couldn't stay that frisky, we could talk about the new Asian Experience complex instead of grimmer topics. All agreed it was coming along nicely, with something for everyone—big orangutan quarters, a tall clouded leopard exhibit, spaces for birds and reptiles, all drawn from the diversity that falls under the label "Asian". Some of the exhibits were turning out smaller than we expected and the drains might be inadequate, but it was all better than anything existing at Finley. Seeing the clouded leopards in a big exhibit where they could leap around in a high tree canopy…worth the price right there.

Linda turned to Ian, who was immune to both hijinks and amiable work chat. "What about elephants? Any word on starting construction?"

He shrank back a little and shook his head. "No news."

Linda cocked an eyebrow at him. "I'm surprised. Those sign-wavers out front should be keeping it on the table."

"Too bad Sam's not here," Arnie said. "He'd know what was going on."

If Ian took offense, it didn't show.

Hap said, "I'm thinking it's not going to happen. The construction foreman told me they're over budget. They had bad luck with the late rains, slowed everything down, and the soil analysis wasn't right. They had to go deeper for the foundations than they estimated."

"Have you heard anything about replacing the aviary?" I asked.

No one had.

"Still," I mused, "the place is improving. We're not going to get everything we want, but at least it's not static like it has been for the whole time I've been here. If visitors like Asian Experience, maybe we'll get another bond measure passed before we all retire."

"That's what we want to hear," Hap said. "Sunshine, it's been a long time…Hey!" he called toward the bartender, "How's about another pitcher?"

The conversation veered into music and movies. Hap was right, it was good to get together and talk about something other than murder, death, and disruption. Denny lectured Arnie about cross-species genetic engineering. Hap went back to telling stories, and Kayla kept flirting with him. Actually, that was worrisome. I'd have to tell her about his wife soon, the one with the pet rattlesnake. Benita would open Kayla up like a sardine can and throw away the key. Other than a little worry about that, hanging out was fun.

A glance at my watch made me nudge Linda. "Pumpkin time. Need to get out and hit the road."

She scooted over and I started to slide out when a man pulled a chair up to our booth and sat himself down, glass in one hand, pitcher in the other. A well-fed, bushy-haired guy in overalls, a backpack slumped at his feet. "Hi, Ian," he said, and went around the table greeting us each by name. "I'm Thor to my friends, Bill Thorson to the press, William G. Thorson to the law. Never been here before. Regular hangout for you guys?"

"Howdy," Arnie said with a big smile.

"Where's your picket sign?" I asked. "Are you wired? Is your sidekick in a van outside recording the conversation?"

Kayla's smile faded, and Linda's eyes narrowed.

"It's a private party," Hap said. "Table's full."

Thor filled his glass and passed Linda the pitcher he'd brought. "Relax. I'm sharing."

"Not the issue," Hap said, and started to climb out of the booth.

"Well, Ian, are you going to own up that I'm a friend, or are you going to let this gorilla toss me into the street?" Thor looked at Ian over the rim of his glass, draining half of it.

Hap stood up and the bartender drifted our way. I'd never seen Hap in action. He was muscle where Thor was only broad, and he was a lot taller as well. This would be interesting.

"Say, honey," the bartender cooed, "maybe this isn't the right spot for you. Let me set you up somewhere warmer."

Thor smiled up at her. "No problem, m'am, but thanks for your concern."

Hap stepped up to Thor and put out a big hand to bunch up his shirt at the collar.

"We worked together," Ian said, barely audible, and Hap paused.

"See?" Thor said and rested his wrists on the table, relaxed and cheerful. "I thought it might be nice to chat. Have Ian introduce me to his new playmates, that sort of thing." Hap stood at the ready.

"Why?" I asked. "You know we think you're a jerk and a blister on the heel of progress." What did he hope to gain? Surely not friendship.

"Colorful! No, I figured you guys haven't ever seen an elephant sanctuary, except for Ian of course, and I could tell you about the one I know, in Kentucky. Where Ian and I used to work."

The bartender drifted away from our table and leaned against a support post, keeping an eye on us. Hap eased back a step. All eyes were on Thor. I admired the stagecraft. So he'd come to pitch us. Annoying, but gutsy. "You want us to ship a blind elephant to a new facility. Somehow that doesn't sound all that humane. Or, of course, we could ship off her companion of almost twenty years and leave her alone. That would be so much nicer."

Thor sipped his beer. "They could go together. Damrey could adapt. Ian knows how to do a careful introduction to a new space, right?"

Ian didn't say anything, but the flush started up from his throat.

Thor turned his chair sideways and crossed his legs. "Let me tell you about this place. A hundred acres, trees and rolling hills, two ponds. They've got five elephants now, three of them Africans, and they have room for four more. They're all loose on the grounds, with a barn in case one of them gets sick."

"And an on-site vet with elephant experience?" I asked.

"A vet's available when needed."

"Lame." I still needed to get home, but this was interesting.

"Who inspects the facility?" Linda asked. "I haven't heard of a sanctuary accreditation program that's up and running yet."

"It will be soon. Let's not forget that Finley Memorial Zoo is not accredited, either."

"On the path to it," Hap said. "It's conditional until we get the new projects done." He sat down on the end of the bench that ran around the booth.

"Was a biological survey done on the hundred acres of natural land before they turned five elephants loose on it?" I asked. "It's not like they're a part of that ecosystem."

"North America was full of elephant relatives at one time." Thor was ready for that one.

"Yeah, and it was full of dinosaurs at one time, too. So what? The elephants will trash the place. It's what they do. Africa has had millennia to adapt to it. Kentucky hasn't."

Thor tilted his chair back. "You should try opening your minds a tiny bit. It won't hurt as much as you think. Really, the thought of elephants roaming free has no meaning to you at all?"

"Not free," Denny said. "A bigger pen. That's all elephants are ever going to get in the whole world. Africa is getting chopped up and fenced in, like the American West and the bison. Same with Asia only worse. Elephants live like outlaws with a bounty on their head, the poachers on their trail."

"Freedom's a strange concept now," I said. "Problem elephants wear electronic collars that send a text message to a ranger's cell phone if they come too close to crops. The rangers show up to chase them away so they don't have to be shot."

Denny started to get wound up. "Like ankle bracelets. Elephants are too much for us, too much *like* us. We have to evolve into a new species ourselves to survive for the long term. Soon we can tailor our own DNA so that enlightenment is within reach of everyone and not only those who study for years. Then there's hope that—"

"I have to take a leak," Arnie said. "Pardon my French, ladies." He wandered off in the wrong direction. The bartender turned him around, waved a thick arm toward the Men sign, and went back behind the bar.

Ah, Denny…He was making a valid point about the future of wild elephants before his synapses went rogue. Thor briefly displayed the disoriented look people got when Denny did that. He set his chair back on the ground. "Have the police figured out yet who took a bull hook to your foreman?"

The papers had described it as "a heavy object." Zoo staff knew it was an ankus. Who had told Thor—Ian? Or was it a lucky guess?

Thor didn't get an answer, only shrugs and silence. I scanned the table. Thor wasn't going anywhere. Linda, Hap, Kayla, and Denny were rooted and sullen. Arnie would be back soon. If anything interesting came up in conversation, Linda would tell me.

Ian slid out of the booth and so did I. "It's been real, Thor," I said. I dropped bills on the table. "See you," I waved at the others.

Ian muttered, "Bye."

I followed him outside to his scruffy Jeep. He opened the driver door and looked up, surprised to see me watching him across the hood.

"Ian, tell me about working with Thor." I kept my voice soft.

Ian shrugged, the flush rising up his throat again. "Nothing to tell. A few months, months at that sanctuary. Didn't work out." He stood at the open car door poised to bolt, one hand on the door, one on the roof.

"Tell me what you think happened to Wallace. Was that Thor guy involved?" I tried not to sound challenging, but Ian acted as if we were in a little room with a single light bulb dangling by its cord, and I was slapping a baton into my palm.

"No clue. Truly." The cloudy brown eyes were frustrated.

So much for that. I gave up. "Sam used to be a decent guy. I wish it weren't so ugly between you two. It must be awful to work together." I meant only casual sympathy. Wariness wouldn't have surprised me, but the scarlet racing up to his brow did.

"I made, made a, a mistake. At the beginning. Stepped in it."

Ah. "You didn't catch on quick enough that his life partner is not female."

Ian's mouth opened, but nothing came out.

"You made some stupid comment that got you started on the wrong foot, then you kept telling him how to work the elephants, pressing him to train up to national standards. Right?"

Ian tried again. "Misunderstood what I meant. Just bullshitting with, with him. Don't care one way or the…Never gave me a second chance. I tried, tried to back off, but that didn't work. Either. Won't trust me with, with anything. Now it's like he blames me for Wallace." He looked desperate.

"Where were you when it happened?" Hard to make that sound innocuous.

"Alone." More words seemed to be trying to escape, but they failed.

I waited, but he slipped into his car, closed the door, and started the engine without looking at me. I stepped back to let him flee.

He rolled down the window. "You need to, to stay away. From me."

A plea? I watched him drive off, bewildered. Stay away for his sake or for mine? I opened my car door and sat, wondering once again about Ian. I'd seen him pushed to anger. I couldn't guess what would trigger violence. He was so strange…Would he attack Wallace, his supporter and buffer against Sam? To eliminate a competitor for Dr. Reynolds, a woman he was terrified to speak to and had no chance with? Was sympathy for the outcast blinding me to reality?

One all-too-obvious reality was that Ian's social incompetence was a perfect mismatch for Sam's pride and sensitivities and that Wallace had made the situation a thousand times worse. What a train wreck. I could not imagine how this could ever be set back on the rails.

I turned the key in the ignition and glanced around before backing up. And nearly jumped out of my skin. Dale, Thor's sidekick, leaned his face inches away from mine, only the driver's window between us. I almost wet myself. He straightened up and stepped back, mission accomplished, his sullen, triumphant face framed by messy black hair. Mowing him down was almost irresistible. Back up, shift to Forward, crush him against another car…I flipped the locks down and pulled out of the lot. Murder had never seemed so reasonable.

Chapter Seventeen

My father sat in the Honda's passenger seat, unclear about what I was up to, but willing to cover my back. I told him, "She's Calvin's daughter, and I need to talk to her about zoo business. She's likely to get mad."

"What are you up to?"

"I can't say without causing trouble. I should keep it confidential." The last thing I needed was my parents panicking again about Wallace's death. He started in with the silence and the look that compels the whole truth. I scrambled out of the car.

The house was a shabby white bungalow in Lents, not the most prosperous neighborhood in Portland. I walked up an uneven path through an unkempt yard and studied the front door. An all but illegible note on a white card instructed me to knock, which I did. The doorbell had apparently perished long ago. That happened at my house and I fixed it with a twelve-dollar, no-wire, battery-operated doorbell in about ten minutes. Janet hadn't bothered.

Finding the address of A Team Mom had turned out to be simple. I sent an email saying I had information about Kevin Wallace that I needed to discuss. Period. She had taken the bait. A short phone call led to this meeting.

The surprise came when I put her first name and connection with Wallace together. She was Calvin's daughter and had worked at the zoo administration office before my time. Jackie told me all about her. Janet and Wallace dated until one day the gate receipts were found in her purse, and she was fired for theft. Several months ago I accidentally discovered that she was set up in an act of malice by another zoo employee, one who hated Wallace and wanted to ruin his romance. I'd told Wallace and Calvin, expecting that one or both would tell Janet that her name was cleared.

It was Thursday, my day off, and the first opportunity for this visit. While the dogs romped in the park, I'd thought about my appointment with a possible murderer. At the last minute, I'd abandoned the logic that Janet had to be smaller than my current size and therefore was no threat. I called my dad for backup.

The door opened and a woman said, "Yes?" The hair was still blond, with assistance, but the cute figure in Calvin's photos of the young Janet had become a series of overlapping spheres—breasts, belly, hips all rounded and flowing into one another. She was still short, but the confident grin was long gone. She wore a loose chartreuse blouse over stretchy black pants, black flats, a little makeup. Her hair was curly and neatly brushed.

I waved toward my car as I said, "I'm Iris Oakley. My dad wants to wait in the car." She glanced at the Honda, not interested, and let me in.

She sent me to a sofa covered in gray vinyl. It skidded a little on the worn oak floor when I sat down. No rugs anywhere. A teenage boy sat at the dining room table hunched over a drawing with a pencil clenched in his fist. He didn't look up, and she didn't introduce him. All she said was, "My other son is out."

She seated herself in a matching gray chair. "You're from the zoo. A friend of Kevin's?" Her voice wasn't friendly.

"Not a friend so much. I'm a keeper, so he's—was—my boss. I'm a bird keeper, so I work with your dad."

The house smelled of air freshener underlaid with cooking grease. No sign of a cat or dog. She nodded and waited.

"The zoo has to conduct an investigation into his death. I have a few questions." The first sentence wasn't a lie, exactly.

Janet sat back and crossed her legs. "A cop was here already. He asked a bunch of questions and swabbed all my shoes. So why you?"

I nodded as though that were old news. Points to Detective Quintana. "The zoo has to file its own reports on the death."

Janet looked at me thoughtfully. "And they sent a keeper?"

She was no fool. I shrugged. "Like the job description says, 'Other duties as assigned.'"

"Because you're pregnant and can't do the heavy work."

"Right." The all-purpose explanation. "I know that you worked at the zoo years ago and left under a cloud. Your dad must have told you that new evidence cleared you of the theft charge. I hope that Wallace—Kevin—apologized for the zoo and corrected your personnel file."

Each hand gripped a corner of the chair seat, the fingers chubby and tight. "Apologize? Correct the personnel file?" It was my turn for silence. "That's rich. You're still young. You don't know what it's like to have God flick his finger and knock your world apart. You still think that things can be fixed."

She had that wrong. I knew how fast life can change and that some things stayed broken forever.

Her upper lip curled with irony. "I thought I was strong. I should have been. I was pretty and smart back then, and my parents loved me. That should have been enough, right? Take a hit and bounce back, right? You don't know shit."

I recoiled a little, and she smiled from some dark well of cynicism.

"I lost my job, my reputation, and my fiancé all in one hour. I was a thief—a criminal—and I was supposed to be grateful to get fired and not arrested. Kevin kicked me out, *bam*. No chance to figure out how that money got into my purse. I was set up, and I knew it, and I couldn't do a thing about it. Kevin adored me one minute and despised me the next. He never doubted for an instant. The only one who believed me was my dad."

"Calvin was pretty bitter about it. He lost a lot of respect for Wallace."

"Lot of good that did. He wanted to quit his job and Mom wouldn't let him, so I was to blame for them fighting and for him stuck in a job he hated. He thought she got cancer from the stress, and he blamed Kevin for that, too."

Calvin liked his job, that I was sure of. I let it pass. "The truth came out. I hope that helps."

"Yeah, my dad told me months ago, but Kevin couldn't be bothered, not then. After my entire life is down the toilet, I finally get a letter from him, and that's supposed to make it all better. It came the same week my second husband walked out on me. Nice timing, huh?"

"When did you get the letter?"

"A few weeks ago."

Wallace had known Janet was innocent for six months. I wondered why he hadn't acted sooner. Then I wondered what *did* trigger him to write. Maybe starting a relationship with Dr. Reynolds. "So you got in touch with him?"

"Yeah. I'm in recovery—AA—and my group thought it might be a good idea. So I met him at a Starbucks. I'm fat now, but he knew who I was. We talked. It didn't change my life."

"Why did you send him the email? The one about rotting in hell."

"We talked, and I remembered that I once actually cared for him. My group said hating him only hurt me. But I came home, came back to *this*." She waved a hand. "He never gave me the tiniest benefit of the doubt. He'd known me for six, seven months, worked with me, dated me, knew my father, said he loved me. We were engaged, for God's sake. I was twenty-one. You know I've never held a job for over a year? Not since then. Every time things would get tough at work, I'd quit so they couldn't catch me by surprise and fire me. I married the first guy who asked me, and he wanted me to work, wanted the income. I couldn't do it, not for more than a couple months at a time. So I drank, and he left."

"You got home and the hate came back, so you sent the email."

"Hate him? That's way too simple. What can you say about the guy who wrecked your entire life? He didn't mean it? It was all a mistake? My mother used to say, 'Sometimes *sorry* isn't good enough.' What an understatement. Yeah, I wasn't going to let him think he'd fixed everything up nice. He hadn't done shit except stir it all up again."

I looked and I couldn't see Calvin in her, nothing of that square, silent, kind man, except the ability to hold that same bitterness for years. "Um, Janet, do you think he deserved to die?"

She looked at me sharply. "That's for God to decide. And I guess he did, all right."

"You wouldn't have wanted to help that along?"

Janet's mouth twisted, something between a smirk and a wry smile. "There was a time I would have, but it wouldn't do me any good, would it? It's not like me forgiving him or him dying makes any difference, does it? I'm stuck here on the A team." She nodded toward the boy, who hadn't moved a muscle except for tiny finger movements on his sketch pad. "Aaron and Adam, autism and asthma. And me: alcoholic and abandoned." The summation sounded rehearsed. It seemed to please her. "You're pregnant. Good luck with that."

She sat still for a moment. Her face softened and aged. "I can't figure out whether I failed God's test, or I got caught in his struggle with the devil, and he forgot to come back and pick up the pieces. Either way, I'm on my own, no matter what AA makes me say." She came back to the present and stood up. "I got stuff to do, if that's all you're here for."

The questions I still needed to ask weren't enough to keep me in that house.

My hand shook turning the car key in the ignition.

"Go okay?" my father asked.

"Remember the Robert Frost poem about the world ending in hate and ice? That's the woman to do the job." I drove to his shop in silence, checking carefully at all the intersections, and dropped him off. At my house, my house that smelled of bacon from breakfast and the peonies my mother had cut for me, I sat on the floor with Winnie and Range and let the dogs lick the bitterness off me.

Chapter Eighteen

My mother had scored excellent seats, six rows back from one of the two rings. Each ring was defined by foot-high barriers and covered in wood chips. Above stretched a tangle of wires, lights, ropes, nets, platforms, and mystifying contraptions understood only by circus roustabouts. The visibility was great, the noise was a thunderous combination of over-amped pop music and screaming children. Instead of a Big Top tent, we clustered in the cavernous Portland Rose Garden, the stadium where the Trail Blazers play basketball and big-name music acts perform. Confetti drifted in the breeze from giant fans above. Popcorn scent was thick, with a hint of horses. I shared my row with four fifth-graders to my right and five to my left. Most of the kids wore the little red clown noses the ticket-takers handed out. My mother sat a row forward to my left and a parent sat to the far right in my row, a military-like deployment over "our" two rows to maximize adult presence.

I'd tried to get Marcie to join me, but no luck. She and Denny were off to a concert. A small girl behind me kept kicking my seat. I turned around and glared at her with zero success.

On the way in, an earnest young woman in a long dress had handed me a brochure about circuses mistreating animals. I'd tucked it into a pocket to study later.

My job was to be a responsible adult. My skills did not yet lie in that direction, but no problem. The kids were safely entranced by clowns goofing around in the ring, except for one red-headed boy on my left who focused on catching the floating confetti. This scene was all about entertainment, with a capital E. It totally obliterated the morning's soul-stain from Janet née Lorenz.

The clowns invited a few kids from the audience to practice tight-rope walking and circus-style bowing in the ring in front of us. Our bunch nearly stampeded that direction, but my mother employed The Voice, and they sank back in excited defeat.

The audience was a standard Portland crowd dressed in drab tee shirts and jeans with sensible shoes. The high-wire couple above us shimmered and glittered in purple and silver, the clowns vibrated in fluorescent green, red, and yellow. Dark-clad roustabouts—men in a range of ages—hauled gear around and set up wires and platforms. The men were swift, efficient, and nearly invisible. I suspected that few in the audience noticed them at all.

The first acts, or maybe pre-acts, were low-key despite the relentless music. Clowns zipped around in tiny cars, young men jumped sturdy bicycles through hoops, a little white dog ran around and got into trouble with the clowns. The kids shrieked and parents smiled. It seemed hokey and unspectacular, until I realized that this non-scary action acclimated the little kids so they wouldn't freak out at the more high-powered acts. I'd been one of the freak-outees in my early years, and I appreciated the thought.

The real Big Show kicked off with a parade around the outside of the two rings. Pretty horses, some white, some black, with silver spangles. Two elephants with huge red and gold spangles on the harnesses adorning their heads. More clowns. Family groups of performers, each family in a different bright, tight costume, waving at the crowd. More horses. Zebras, of all things. A pack of fluffy dogs. Two more elephants.

I tried to notice more than spectacle. The animals in the parade looked well fed and surprisingly relaxed. They bustled along as though they knew exactly what to do. The zebras, who seemed to be young fillies—hard to tell for sure—looked pretty bratty, but they mostly did what they were supposed to. I suspected that an adult zebra would hold circus discipline in contempt, no matter how long the buggy whip.

Two elephants trotted into the ring nearest us, trunk of the second locked onto tail of the first, a red and gold costumed woman on each neck. Damrey and Nakri used to live this life of constant travel, new situations, noise and confusion. They, too, had spent long hours chained or confined in a boxcar stall. Neither of these elephants showed a pink scar around an ankle like Damrey's. One looked like Nakri with the addition of little tusks—"tushes"—at the corners of her mouth. She sat on a stool while her leggy rider did a headstand on her forehead. Then both elephants stood teetering with all four legs on the little stools, curling their trunks up. I felt embarrassed for them, but unclear about what all this was like from their perspective. Perhaps the performance was a welcome respite from boredom and inactivity. Even if it was, did that justify a life so different from what they were built for? Perhaps their winter quarters were warm pastures where they roamed free for months in payment for entertaining our young. Perhaps not.

The elephants exited and were replaced by clowns, then a trapeze act. The high-wire performances made me anxious, despite the net. I rubbed my belly to reassure my child that we were safe on the ground and no one would fall to their death. The kids in our bunch were riveted, leaning forward with open mouths. So was my mother, except she kept her mouth closed.

When I looked back from scanning my charges, the lighting had changed, and somehow a netted ring full of tigers had materialized in front of us. I'd been expecting this, yet all the setup slipped right by me, and I flinched to see the cats so close.

Some of the tigers were normal gold and black, like Rajah, others were white with black stripes, and one was all white. They did not look as accepting of their jobs as the elephants. The trainer earned snarls and threatening paws as the cats leaped from stool to stool, jumped through hoops, and rolled over on the ground. He carried a lightweight pole and the cats were trained to respond to its position. Several times the trainer's hand passed swiftly by tiger mouths, handing out little meat rewards. The kids would never notice. The unhappy body language was troubling despite the sleek coats and healthy weights. I couldn't pretend the tigers enjoyed the performance. When the trainer was focused on a complicated stunt with the white tiger, one of the normal-colored animals slipped off his stool, ears flat, body crouched, moving behind the man. The trainer caught it in his peripheral vision, turned, and flicked the whip, shouting. Busted, the tiger climbed back onto his stool. The episode could pass for part of the act, but all my instincts insisted that sooner or later, that trainer was doomed. Like Rick. I was glad when the act ended.

I relaxed at the liberty horses. Black ones and white ones, bridles and belly-bands glittering in silver and gold, they pranced in formation, guided by flourishes and taps from a light whip, whirling and rearing with long manes and tails billowing. Amazing grace. The sensual display of power under control. A willing partner-dance with their trainer. I hoped.

After acrobatic performances, more trapeze daredevils, and a dog act, we arrived at the raucous final crescendo—another parade of human performers, elephants, horses, and dogs with the loudspeakers straining to achieve new decibels. Then we edged out through the crowd, trying to keep our kids together in the crush. I saw them all onto the school bus, with my mother boarding last. I hadn't contributed more than a warm body, but that seemed sufficient for her.

Still half-deafened, I drove home thinking of the many peculiar ways humans interact with animals. Thor was right that Nakri and Damrey deserved better quarters, but it looked to me as if they might prefer what they had now to returning to the circus. They had freedom of movement and as much entertainment as the elephant keepers could devise. In the zoo's case, it was the elephants who were being entertained.

I greeted my dogs and, scratching under a collar with each hand, considered the contract we'd made with wolves. Humans ensured, more or less, that dogs ate regularly without the risks of chasing down and biting hoofed mammals, and also that their offspring had a good chance of survival. In exchange, dogs more or less did what we told them to, and humans got to tinker with their DNA. Winnie and Range seemed content with the deal.

The deal with elephants or any wild animal didn't feel the same. I stroked my dogs and tried to work it out. Wolves became dogs by domesticating themselves around campfires and villages, and house cats may have done the same. Elephants hadn't volunteered. Originally people wanted their muscle power for logging and their terrifying appearance as war machines. Now we wanted mostly to be around them, to see these huge, strange creatures up close, and, being the primates that we are, to touch them with our hands if we could. Elephants who weren't party to the captivity deal were losing ground. We change all the land and seas for our own uses, and wild animals get the scraps. Wild elephants who raid crops—what else to eat when the forest is cut down?—end up dead. And, of course, the ivory trade devastates elephants on two continents. It was all so sad and hard, it made my head ache.

I gave it up and took a shower, feeling briefly guilty for adding another person to the planet. Someday, if all went well, I would be the parent of a fifth grader. Unimaginable, but easier to face than a tiny newborn.

In bed, struggling with multiple pillows to find comfort, the image of elephants sitting on stools in the midst of noise and confusion returned. Damrey and Nakri had lived the circus life for years, had once had the same nerves of steel. That tolerance must have worn off, considering how upset they were when the NAZ committee met in their barn. They hadn't liked the crowd of strangers at all. Odd.

What would the new curator do about better housing for them? Maybe he or she would get the new exhibit moving forward. I should ask to see the master plan. Where, exactly, would this new exhibit go? Asian Experience was occupying the logical space.

Janet's poisonous depression seeped back now that I was quiet and unoccupied. I thanked my lucky stars that I didn't live in that mind. She seemed fully capable of braining the man she blamed for her troubled life.

Janet could get a key to the elephant barn from her father, with or without his knowledge.

Detective Quintana was on her trail. Would the shoe swabs Janet had mentioned prove she'd been in the barn? Why hadn't I inquired about her alibi for that morning? My skin crawled at the thought of returning to ask where she'd been and who could back up her story. Maybe I could wait and see what the police came up with. After all, Dr. Reynolds had told me to back off.

At last I slept. The only dream fragment I remembered featured myself as a four-year-old in my beloved lavender tutu with silver glitter.

The next day, Marcie took me crib-shopping at Target so I could pacify my mother, but the concept of paying a lot of money for a wooden cage for my child unnerved me. Marcie made me eat lunch, then we tried again. We discovered something called a co-sleeper, a three-sided bassinet thing, that would park the baby next to me in his own little space at the same level as the mattress. The clerk assured me that the baby would be close for nursing, but I wouldn't be able to roll over on him. That sounded good. Marcie told me to suck it up and pay the money rather than shop for a used one.

She cooked dinner for me and Denny—spaghetti with home-made pasta and homemade sauce and homemade everything but the parmesan. Denny waited until she was busy in the kitchen to share that Ian had no alibi for the night Wallace was attacked. I gathered from his caution that Marcie objected to him messing with police matters as much as she objected to me doing so.

Ian's lack of cover was not news, but it gave me a reason to summarize my visit to Janet. "Why don't you ask her neighbors where she was that night?" I suggested. "Don't talk to her because that will get Calvin mad. Just ask the neighbors. Be discreet, for once in your life." He spun off onto finding aerial photographs of her neighborhood with timestamps. He was sure the military or one of the mapping services had such records and that they would show whether her car was parked at her house when Wallace was attacked. He dropped the subject when Marcie returned to the table with an experimental pudding-thing with lychee nuts. It was strange but delicious.

I drove home feeling pleased with myself for the baby-corral solution and for enlisting Denny to do what I didn't want to. He might actually go ask Janet's neighbors. I considered whether using him as my cat's paw was irresponsible and decided it wasn't. People had been manipulating me for weeks. I was entitled to try my own hand at it.

Chapter Nineteen

Saturday morning at the employee parking lot and there was Thor Thorson, bad hair, coveralls, and backpack. I lacked the time but had the inclination to investigate. "How did you get in? What are you doing here?"

He seemed delighted to see me. "Good morning, Iris! I'm leafleting cars. Here's one for you."

I stuffed the paper into the pocket of my coveralls. "How'd you get in?"

"I enjoy a challenge. Let's say that the gate to this lot isn't much of one." He put down his backpack to pull out another handful of brochures.

The gate was eight feet of mesh fence with barbed wire at the top. Not a challenge? I followed him from car to car as he lifted windshield wipers and slipped little brochures underneath. "What, you slip-streamed through on someone else?"As cars pulled in and parked, Thor smiled and leafleted them. The drivers climbed out and retrieved the piece of paper, looking puzzled or annoyed.

The shaggy little troll shook his head at me as if I were dim.

I got it. "That was you sitting on the hillside with binoculars. You watched people coming in and scammed the combination for the keypad."

"Bingo! We'll make an activist out of you yet. Now I want you to read that handout and really think about it."

"I think what I'll do is call Security."

"Suit yourself. But I'm done here. Have a nice day!" Most vehicles had brochures, including Hap's motorcycle, where it was rolled into a tube and jammed under a cable on the handlebars. Thor ambled toward the gate.

"Hey, wait a minute."

Thor turned around. "Want to talk about natural environments for elephants?"

"No. I want to talk about Ian Sullivan. You showed up at the tavern to discredit him with us."

Thor shook his head. "Not at all. I wanted a chance to talk with you guys in some place relaxed, and he happened to be there. You have a suspicious mind, you know that?"

"Now Ian looks like a mole feeding you information. Which, of course, he could be. How did you know Wallace was hit with an ankus?"

"Easy enough to guess. I have to do my own guessing and digging. Ian doesn't want to talk with his old friends. He turned on us, turned on our whole mission, and came here."

"Why is that? I'm thinking it's more than Ian feeling guilty. What happened at that sanctuary? Ian didn't like maintaining elephants on a shoestring budget?"

Thor hesitated, then shook his head. "Nah, he's embarrassed about bailing. Did you enjoy the circus? The cow with the tushes—did you see the scar behind her ear? Not recent, I'll admit. From a different outfit."

Two could play at this. "You were at the barn, early in the morning. The day before Wallace was killed. And the next day, when he died."

Thor cocked his head. "You are *so* fishing. I had nothing to do with his death." He hitched his backpack over a shoulder. "Tell me, do you ever date guys shorter than you? Let me know if the idea appeals. I'll be around. But now I have other places to go, other people to charm."

I said to his back, "Keep Dale away from me, and tell him to quit following Sam."

Thor stopped and turned around. "I'll look into that. But I don't own Dale."

At the gate, he waved his hand over the motion sensor. It creaked open, obedient to anyone or anything exiting. He passed through, turned and walked backward a few steps to wave at me, and walked away on Finley Drive.

I shook my head to clear it. As my dad might say, the guy had some bark on him. Six months pregnant, "Calvin" on my bulging brown coveralls...He'd hit on me. Nobody had hit on me for a very long time. Was it a trick? Should I be pissed off? My brain got back to business. How did Thor know I'd been to the circus? Because he or his sidekick had seen me there. Had to be.

One thing I knew for sure—Thor starred at getting in and out of zoo areas. I thought about that on my way to clock in. I recalled running into him at Elephants before the zoo opened. Maybe his story then about the main gate being left unlocked was fresh, steaming organic fertilizer. Maybe he'd lied about reconnecting with Ian, maybe they'd been hanging out discussing old times. Simple enough to steal his keys and have them copied. As Janet might have stolen Calvin's. Thor might break into the barn to take pictures of Nakri's wound as evidence of abuse. Thor bumping into Wallace. Wallace yelling at him... Thor reacting out of fear or anger...

I was finding way too many people with reason and opportunity to do away with Kevin Wallace.

George, the security guard, steered the electric cart around me, heading toward the gate to the employee parking lot. He waved hello. Too late, Thor was long gone.

At the time clock, I found a notice for an unscheduled keeper meeting that was half over. Mr. Crandall hadn't included an agenda. Probably an update on the NAZ committee report or on hiring the new curator.

Ian wasn't at Elephants and neither was Sam. It was Sam's day off, although he kept showing up anyway, and Ian must still be in the meeting. Ian arrived before I got too restless and anxious about my other work. I asked him about the meeting.

"Hired a new curator," he said.

Good news, I hoped. Mr. Crandall was looking haggard, our work schedules were goofed up, and we needed a leader who could make informed decisions about animal management, if that wasn't too much to ask. "Any details?" I realized what I was hoping for was something along the line of "just like Wallace, only nice."

Ian shrugged and turned away without answering. Skittish or hostile? I couldn't tell. So much for a relaxed relationship. I would ask Jackie about the new hire, such as the start date and whether this person knew a kiwi from a kudu.

Damrey and Nakri had gone ahead with their big morning pee, judging by the puddles. Ian stood by in stony silence as they did their best to deliver, but the process took longer than usual and left me even more behind schedule.

I hastened to the Penguinarium, where hungry, irritated penguins brayed at me. It was Saturday, Calvin was off, and I was almost an hour behind. This was not going to be my best day as a zoo keeper. I set my brain to Efficient and worked hard and fast, but circumstances continued to conspire against me. Mrs. Brown ate less than usual and stood with her head pulled in. I suspected a broken heart since she'd had to watch her ex making whoopee with that immoral hussy, Mrs. Green. Or it could be aspergillosis, a fungal disease deadly to captive penguins. Or avian malaria, or any number of other ailments. After consideration, I decided she didn't look bad enough to call Dr. Reynolds. I would mention the poor appetite in my daily report.

I was still at the counter fixing food pans for the aviary when the door banged open. "Who the hell are you?" I asked the guy who barged in. I'd been focused on cutting fruit as fast as possible, and I'd nearly lopped a finger off.

"Your new boss. You missed the meeting this morning."

He was a little taller than I, maybe five-foot ten, about thirty-five or forty years old, a round head with close-cropped light brown hair above a broad, tense set of shoulders. Vivid blue eyes in a tanned face. Short-sleeved white shirt, jeans, dark leather boots.

Wrong day to be late. "Um, yeah. An unauthorized person was leafleting cars in the employee lot. I got rid of him. I was due at Elephants." Why hadn't Ian said anything about the new guy actually starting? Because Ian did not communicate.

"Next time call Security and come to the meeting. That's what "all hands" means. It means you. What were you doing at Elephants?"

I strained to keep my voice even. "Collecting urine samples for a research project."

"And why are *you* doing that and not one of the elephant guys?"

"Ask them. Or Dr. Reynolds. Not my idea."

"I'll do that." He looked around the kitchen like a realtor calculating the market value.

"I'm Iris Oakley." Good. No hostility leaking out.

"I know that. I saw your file. I want you all on the same page about my management style. I went over this at the meeting. I've got the same expectations for everyone—the same policies and the same consequences. Making up your own rules as you go along is a non-starter. Plan to clock in on time. Meetings are not optional."

So I was one of the bad kids, and the teacher was starting off tough. A bit of insight thanks to being my mother's daughter. "I was hoping to learn your name."

"Oh. Neal Humboldt."

"Okay. Do you want a tour of Birds? Calvin's off until Monday."

"I took a look at the aviary and the duck pond. It looks like a stamp collection. One or two of everything. Is there any theme or organizing principle?"

"You could ask Calvin about that. He keeps hoping for a great collection, but we never get any money for decent exhibits." Wow. Talk about hitting the ground running. I needed to warn Calvin before he walked into this buzz saw.

"I'll look at the priorities. We should close that aviary down. Tear it down. And those ratty cages by the pond with the owl and the hawk. We could keep the duck pond until we need the space."

Maybe he was just musing out loud, but I felt like I had hoof prints all over me. This guy made Denny seem sluggish. "Sounds like you've already made up your mind about a lot of things." I couldn't keep the resentment out. I turned and leaned my back against the counter, as much to brace myself against this onslaught as to ease my spine.

"First cut only. I'll need a full review of the master plan." He looked me up and down and gave a little groan. "Oh, no. I suppose you're going to resign and leave me another keeper down. Play out your family leave and decide you'd rather be a mommy than shovel shit."

"Not likely. I like to eat, and nobody else is going to pay the bills." Slipping a little, voice-wise. Breathe. Breathe.

"What, no husband? Did you skip that step?" A tight little smile.

"No. I. Did. Not. The lions killed him, you stupid bastard."

"Oh." A pause.

I wasn't going to cry. I wasn't going to care if he fired me. I wasn't.

His stance changed, a subtle crouch, a readiness. For what? Ah.

The forgotten chef's knife was still in my hand. I gently set it on the counter.

He said, "I should have read that file a little more carefully. Let's start over."

"I have work to do. Come back later." I was definitely going to cry.

He met my eyes for a moment and backed away and out the door. It closed softly behind him. I crashed into a chair at the little table and buried my face in folded arms, rage, grief, and anxiety ebbing and flowing in rip tides.

I bumbled through the rest of the morning, dropping a full food pan on the kitchen floor, banging my head hard on a branch at the aviary, and jabbing my palm on a protruding bit of fencing at the spectacled owl. I stared at the blood welling through the vinyl glove, perversely relieved that something so real could happen despite the emotional chaos. The survival-oriented part of my brain examined the blood and said, "Chill out, or you're really going to get hurt." The rest of the cortex stepped back and chilled. A little. I took a breath, found a Band-Aid, and continued my work with a stinging hand and a steadier heart.

I didn't have time to get the scoop from Jackie, but I had to anyway. I ducked into our spot under the eaves of the Administration building and called the zoo on my cell phone. The intern answered with a long, perky greeting. "Let me talk to Jackie," I said, more curt than I intended.

"HowcanIhelpyou?"

"Jackie, it's Iris. Can you come out? I don't want to run into that Neal guy."

"He's off the grounds."

"He might come back. Come on outside."

"Can't. Had my lunch already. Come on in."

I stepped into the office, ready to stampede for the high grass.

"I've got to copy this stack," she said. "Come down to the basement with me."

We climbed down the steps and stood in the windowless little basement with the copy machine gasping and thunking. It was cool and the air was stale and tainted with strange copy machine odors. Claustrophobia nibbled around the edges of my awareness.

"Tell me about Neal whatshisface."

"Humboldt. He's a piece of work. Ex-military. Ran some kind of little zoo in Peru or Ecuador, I can't keep those countries straight. Then he was a training consultant for big corporations on some software, nothing to do with zoos. Then he took a bunch of zoo management courses. Kind of zigzagged around. He doesn't seem like Mr. Crandall's type, but here he is. He's already thrown out most of the stuff in Wallace's office."

That made this all too real. "He stopped by Birds. I think I'm in trouble already."

"That was fast. Let me guess. He made you mad, and you mouthed off."

"Could be. Is he going to fire me?"

"On his first day? I think he'll wait until tomorrow. Go kiss up if you're worried."

"I'll pass, thanks all the same. But call me if he says anything." Like asking whether Iris Oakley often stuck a knife into her superiors.

The copy machine stopped cold. Jackie filled the paper tray with unthinking proficiency and pushed a button to reanimate it. "He may be way better looking than Wallace, but he's trouble. Now I have to take minutes at all the manager meetings. He assumed we take minutes. That's going to be a ton more work if he keeps it up."

"Oh. I almost forgot. Thor, that bushy-haired guy with the pickets. He has the code to the gate at the employee parking lot. Better get it changed and tell Hap."

Jackie leered. "'Thor' is it? You're on a first name basis with him now?"

"Yeah, we're dating. He wants to take me to Hawaii. The sex is fantastic."

"Don't be sarcastic. Ruins the complexion." She took the stack of copies and tapped the edges even on the top of the copy machine.

We climbed the steps back to the planet's surface, where the air was better.

And there was Neal, stepping out of his office. One look at me and his face clenched into a scowl. I turned to flee and bumped into Dr. Reynolds as she entered the building. "Oops. Sorry. I was just leaving."

She stepped out of my way. I fumbled with the door and heard Neal's surprised voice. "Jeannie Franklin? Is that you?"

I hesitated with the door half open, wondering who that could be.

"I'm Dr. Jean Reynolds, the zoo's veterinarian." They stepped into his office.

Interesting.

The picketers were walking their circuit in front of the zoo like Shetlands at a pony ride. I hustled back to Birds in the futile hope of catching up on work. And froze on the path. Locked in place because the notion struck me that carjacking might be included in Thor's felonious skill set. He seemed to circumvent locks with ease. Why would Thor want a zoo van? What would Thor do with a zoo van containing a recently deceased tiger?

I unfroze. This would require some thought.

Chapter Twenty

Sunday was uneventful. No sick animals, no Neal, no implosions. No Linda to talk to, she'd taken the day off.

Monday, I stepped out of the Commissary to walk to Elephants. The security guard's electric cart, coming from the employee parking lot, stopped, and Dr. Reynolds stepped out of the passenger seat.

"Iris."

The cart moved on, and I waited for her. She spoke in her sober way. "I have a little information for you. I ran into a police lieutenant at a veterinary mixer last night, a cocktail party the Vancouver veterinary association put on. His wife's a small-animal vet. The husband said he'd heard they would close the case on Kevin's murder soon."

"Any hint of who did it?"

"No, sorry. I'll be so glad when this is over. It won't bring him back, but it will clear the air, and the NAZ committee can finish their report. I still regret that I tried to embroil you in this."

We agreed that this was good news and went our separate directions. I hoped that the police had the right person. But why wouldn't they? It was their job, and that dour detective seemed capable enough. I could quit feeling responsible for screwing up the investigation. I expected to feel relief, but mostly I felt anxious about who would be arrested.

At the elephant barn, Sam stood by while I collected the samples. That done, I was dumb enough to tell him I was sorry he didn't get the curator job. Ian was in the rear of the barn, out of earshot.

Sam's mouth went hard. "I wasn't surprised. Management's looking for outsiders. Nobody here stands a chance of promotion, not for a good long while. Not until they figure out that knowing something about this place actually matters." He gave me a look I could not decipher. "What did you tell Mr. Crandall and that police officer about Wallace and Damrey? About what I had to do with it?"

My head jerked back. "What are you talking about? You were there. You know exactly what I told them."

He crossed his arms over his chest. "No, you had other conversations, with them and with other people. Did you tell anyone you thought I'd killed him?"

I almost dropped the cups of pee. After a second's paralysis, I said, "*What?* Of course not." Which was true. I'd kept my vague speculations to myself.

He didn't relax. "I know there's a lot of suspicion and distrust around here lately. I'm wondering if you're stirring it up. Denny is, and I figure you're working together."

I didn't know what to say. Tears prickled the backs of my eyes. "I'm not making up any stories, especially not about you, and if Denny is, I don't know anything about it." Denny asking about alibis was a different matter. "Weren't we friends once upon a time, or am I wrong about that?"

The air seemed to fall out of him, and he put his arms down. He looked older and tired. "I used to love this job. Now it's turned rotten. No matter what I do, nothing's going to change. And I can't get out of it." He turned toward the workroom.

I drew in a deep breath and walked with him. "Sam, it's not all bad." I couldn't come up with anything better.

"I can't trust anyone, no one at all. Wallace backed off on the elephant exhibit because Asian Experience is over budget. Wallace! The guy who should have been leading the charge. Look out there." He turned back and his wave took in the elephant door to the outside and the viewing window. "Did you know that kid picketer is videotaping us every day now? No one should have to put up with that on the job. I'm accused of hurting animals I've done my level best to take good care of. Who knows what Ian's up to, or what he's already done? I sure don't. He's the one nuts enough to murder someone, and I have to work with him every day. It's not that hard to get somebody else killed in this line of work."

"Sam, before you start looking for a rope to lynch Ian, there's a rumor that the police will make an arrest soon. I didn't hear anything on the news this morning, so maybe tomorrow."

I followed him into the keeper work area, labeled the cups, and put them in the fridge. I could hear Ian hosing the back stall.

He said, "I doubt that. The cops have nothing. I've tried and tried to figure it out. Ian's all I can come up with. He won't say where he was that night, tap dances all around it. But there's no proof. Nothing. If he did it, he's going to get away with it." He hefted a box of carrots onto the counter and started sorting through them, pulling out the really wilted ones and tossing them in the garbage.

Ian drifted through the work area and out toward the front stall without a word to either of us.

Sam said, "I'd be really happy not to work with that guy anymore. And I wish my damn back didn't hurt all the time. This is not a good job to get old in. And I'm stuck. Nothing else will open up for years."

I had no remedies to propose and left with a troubled heart. I'd thought Sam was my friend because he'd been helpful and thorough with my training, because we'd been in hundreds of lunch conversations, because he showed up at Hap's parties and we drank beer together. Sensible, competent, secretive about his private life. But he'd manipulated me into the elephant barn before the committee visited to show me how docile Damrey was and filled me with his suspicions and convictions about Ian. Now he was looking for reasons to blame me for not getting a promotion.

I wished for the old Sam back, the one I thought I knew, who brought grace and steadiness to his work and, I'd thought, to his relationships with coworkers.

I gave Calvin a version of my encounter with our new boss as we prepared vitamin-enhanced fish. I omitted my personal melodrama and most of Neal's comments about demolishing the bird exhibits. "He, ah, seems to have a lot of changes in mind."

Calvin said only, "We'll see how that works out." A few minutes later, he added, "A new broom sweeps clean, but the old broom gets the corners."

I told him the Wallace's-murder-solved rumor. He looked thoughtful, no doubt wondering, as I was, who would be tagged, and didn't say much after that.

The good news of the day was bite-sized. Calvin thought that Mrs. Brown looked fine. No need to catch her up for tests. The spectacled owl was eating well. The duck pond had at least fifteen baby mallards in three or four broods, cute but unwelcome given that mallards were wild free-loaders. The male Brazilian cardinal in the aviary was carrying bits of leaves around, planning a nest. Soon he would be diving at us aggressively as part of his parental duties.

Dr. Reynolds came up to me at the duck pond under a sky regressing from sun to gray. I told her that Mrs. Brown was eating and that Calvin thought she looked all right. "Good," she said. "Let me know if that changes. She's a geriatric bird." We talked about the water quality in the pond, always a problem when the weather warmed up. Calvin and I would need to drain and refill it soon, a mammoth task.

She seemed relaxed, and I took a chance. Sam claimed that Ian was infatuated with her, and this was one of his hints and allegations that I could verify. "Um, I've been meaning to ask you...Has Ian been acting strange toward you?"

Dr. Reynolds looked at me in alarm. Her voice was sharp. "Why do you ask? Is there a special reason?"

"He's been a little odd toward me."

A silence hung between us, full of unspoken concerns. A mallard drake quacked.

Looking at my belly, she said, "If Ian does anything inappropriate, anything at all, please let me know immediately."

So I wasn't going to get an answer without serious digging. My courage failed.

Dr. Reynolds watched ducklings for a moment, then said, "How is your pregnancy going? You seem to be managing well, but it must be a challenge."

An attempt at friendliness, if not outright friendship? After my talk with Sam, I could use a little friendship. "Everything's normal. I feel pretty good, and the job is fine. The mask is a nuisance, but it's tolerable. I wish I could hang out more in Felines and see the cubs, but I'm staying out until the baby is born."

"Wise of you. I know your husband is deceased. Did he have family? If I'm not prying…" Dr. Reynolds sounded a bit lonely.

"No, no, it's fine to ask. His parents are dead, and his sister vanished long ago. Rick thought she'd probably died from drugs or alcohol, or he would have heard from her. I never had an aunt or uncle in my life, and I guess my kid won't either. Just me and my folks."

She nodded and gazed beyond me at the swans swimming side by side. "Life can be even more difficult with a partner."

Ah, the bad divorce. "So I've heard."

She turned to leave. "Let me know if I can help with anything. Anything at all."

"Thanks. I really appreciate it." I couldn't think of anything warmer to say, any other way to connect. She was, after all, the veterinarian, and I was only a keeper.

Weary and still behind, I staggered to lunch through a June shower. Linda and Denny sat at an inside table defending two empty chairs. The café was crowded, and I wouldn't have had a seat otherwise. "Don't say a word," I said to Denny, "until I get this down." A chicken burger and carton of milk later, I came up for air.

Linda said, "Hyenas after they pull down a zebra."

Denny shook his head. "More like piranhas and a wounded tapir."

"Hilarious," I said.

Kayla showed up to claim the last seat. She was her usual stylish self, this time an apricot blouse with gold earrings that had sparkly bits embedded in them.

"Hey," I said, and scooted over for her. "Nice ears. That ex-boyfriend?"

"Nope. Vintage. Inherited from my aunt. They were clips and I got them changed to studs for pierced ears. It's tough to find anything to wear at work. Rings get beat up fast."

"Watch out for monkeys grabbing at those," Linda said.

"Has anybody seen Neal around today?" I planned to be scarce for a few more days.

"What happened?" Linda asked.

Was I that transparent? "I met him—the new curator—on Saturday. I missed the all-staff meeting, he caught me by surprise. It did not go well."

Linda said, "Denny came in late, and you didn't show up at all. Neal was not happy. We're a bunch of slackers, and he *vill haf deescipline* from now on."

"My tire was slashed," Denny said. "Could happen to anyone. Happened today, too. Neal left me a note about being late. His letters slant left. Not a good sign."

"Two tires cut? What's up with that?" Linda asked.

"I think it's a neighbor. I'm going to have to deal. It's very negative."

So I wasn't the only one off to a bad start. "I have news from Dr. Reynolds. There's a rumor that the police will close the case on Wallace's murder soon."

"Close as in 'giving up'?" Linda asked.

"No, I don't think they do that. You read about all those cold cases they keep working on."

"Jean didn't say anything to me." Kayla seemed bothered. Not much bothered Kayla, and she shook it off. "She's been distracted. There's this vet inspection team reviewing every medication, all the stock and the records. It's routine, but she's in a really bad mood."

"I think it's that Thor guy," Denny said. "He whacked Wallace off-site and stuffed him through the bars as a message."

"Denny, that's nuts. He wouldn't let Damrey take the blame." Why was I defending the guy? I considered him a prime suspect myself.

"He knew we'd figure it out, and Damrey wouldn't be affected. Yeah, that sounds right. A warning to us. What about weight gain? You're looking really big."

"Play nice!" Kayla said.

"We sexed the cubs," Linda said before I could retaliate. "I lured Losa into the shift cage and Dr. Reynolds and I pulled them out of the den. They look great. They are *loud* when they're pissed off."

"I got to hold one," Kayla said.

Jealousy stabbed me hard. I hoped my face didn't show it. "Losa didn't get too upset? What are they?"

Linda said, "She calmed down as soon as we put them back. Two males, one female. One of the males is smaller than the other two, so we'll need to check them again in a week to make sure he's not being out-competed at the milk bar."

"Are their eyes open yet?"

Kayla and Linda shook their heads.

Lunch took a different turn as Arnie joined us with a chair he dragged across the room. He wore his usual big smile, big hat, and big belt buckle. "Howdy, ladies!" he said. "And gent," with a nod to Denny, "but it's Linda I've got news for." He beamed at us.

We waited, chewing, all of us declining to ask.

"Neal said I got the new senior keeper job for Felines and Bears. Found out this morning. We'll be even more of a team."

Linda and I did not choke on our food.

After an awkward pause, Kayla said, "Congratulations!"

Denny asked, "Who else applied?"

"I did." Linda folded her potato chip bag into a tiny triangle.

"You'll get your turn after a few more years," Arnie said generously.

"Gotta go," I said. "I'll talk to you guys later." My head was ready to explode. I put one foot ahead of the other without seeing a thing until I was standing in front of Wallace's office door. It was open. Neal was sitting at the desk signing papers. I knocked politely, he said "Come in," and I closed the door behind me.

"Iris. What's up?"

"You made Arnie Linda's boss," I said. My voice squeaked just a little.

"That's right. He was promoted to the senior keeper job."

"You took the least reliable employee at this entire zoo and made him a senior keeper. Can you tell me why, so that I can understand your management style? And then maybe you can cancel it?"

"Sit down and calm down."

"I'm *not* yelling." I sat down.

He turned the swivel chair back and forth, restless. "I don't owe you any explanations. I'll tell you anyway because I do owe you an apology for my comment when we met."

"Yes. Explain. Please."

"He applied and Linda applied. He's got eight years more experience than she does, a perfect attendance record, and a great reputation. There was no real—"

"A great reputation. With who?"

Neal leaned forward for the kill. "The director of this place and Calvin Lorenz."

I closed my eyes and opened them again. "Mr. Crandall is clueless about the real work. Calvin has carried Arnie for years. He thinks Arnie is a damaged soul who deserves every break. Arnie was wounded in Vietnam, probably by shooting himself, and then he got busted up riding rodeo broncs. Wallace would never fire him because that would mean crossing Calvin, and their relationship is, was…complex. We all help keep him out of trouble by fixing whatever he forgets when he's our relief keeper. We *conspire* to keep him employed. He's not a bad person, just… This is *pathetic.*"

Neal leaned back, looking annoyed. "You didn't apply, I notice. I don't see that you have much grounds for complaint. Arnie's got a new set of expectations to meet, and I'll see that he does his job. It's a done deal. I suggest you adjust your mindset and get back to *your* job. Excellent performance is what is going to work out best for you, I guarantee it."

"That has *not* worked out. Linda does work that is freakin' great. That's why we have clouded leopard cubs, and now she's got to take orders from a guy who's, who's…Those cats are at his *mercy.*"

"You don't have to work here under these unacceptable conditions, you know." The blue eyes were icy.

I closed my own eyes again. Brain parts throbbed. I opened my eyes. Before I could speak, he started in.

"Let me tell you something else. I can already see that no one wants one single thing to change at this zoo. Everyone wants best practices as long as they don't have to do anything different. Well, I was hired to get this place accredited, and I'm going to do it. Arnie is not afraid of change. I suggest you try that on yourself." A pause for effect. "Now beat it. And keep this in mind: you get one shot at barging into my office and yelling at me. Do not do that again."

"I did not barge, and I did not yell. This is going to bite us all."

I retreated, defeat bitter on my tongue. Seemed that whatever Sam had, it was going around.

The day's disasters weren't over. At the Commissary, ready to clock out and crawl home, I found Denny sitting on the counter swinging his legs and waving one hand. His audience included Arnie, Hap, Linda, Ian, and Calvin and they all looked fascinated by whatever he was saying. I braced myself for yet another torrent of almost-facts and half-baked theories.

No theories. He was describing real life, this afternoon in fact.

He saw me and said, "Wait. Let me back up 'cause Ire just got here." A pause for me to join the group. "You won't see Sam clock out today because he's done doing that. He went and talked with Neal about the new elephant exhibit this afternoon—I asked Jackie—and it ended up with yelling. Jackie said it was about to get physical, so she got Mr. Crandall. He went in, and Sam stomped out."

Hap said, "Neal came down and changed the schedule on the board. Really had his warrior on. Looked like he was ready to pulverize the next guy who said 'hey' to him. He took Sam off Elephants and put him on Children's Zoo for the rest of the week. Sam blew in half an hour later and erased his name from the schedule. I asked him what was up, and he said he was outta here for good. Ian?"

Ian was not ready to pick up the ball. He took a step back.

"What happened at the barn?" Denny asked with what was, for him, considerable patience.

Ian stood his ground, for the moment. "Sam took a call. Said he quit. He left."

"What else?" I asked, my stomach churning.

"Said Elephants was all mine." His faced tightened. "How's that going, going to work? I can't do it alone. Just, just walked out."

Hap raised both hands, palms out, commanding our attention. "This fumblebum Neal hacked Sam off to the max. He's high up the tree of righteous rage, spitting sparks and razor blades. You all know he's a good man, and we need him. Who's going to man-up and talk him down?" He looked around, waiting for one of us to accept the challenge.

Why did he look at me like I was the lead candidate? Denny started to say something. "I'll try," I said. Chewing my hand off at the wrist was a more appealing prospect.

At home, I found good reasons to put this off. For starters, the dogs had a vet appointment. I loaded them into the Honda, and they experimented with hopping from the back to the rear seat and then to the front passenger seat. I explained once again that the rules had changed, and they were required to stay in the back. All the way back. This made no sense to either Winnie or Range, but I pointed out that, unlike in the truck bed, they weren't tied up. That could change if they didn't cooperate. Range, ever the peacemaker, flopped down in the rear, and Winnie sat beside him with an injured air.

I had picked my veterinary clinic partly because they were open late two nights a week. After exams, shots, and treats, and a fascinating discussion about heart worms, we made a pass through Burgerville for my dinner and drove home for theirs.

I took an early shower and decked myself out in the pink jammies from my mother. I called Marcie. Denny wasn't there so we talked for half an hour about nothing much. Denny was taking her to a comic book convention. "I'm trying to care," she said, "but I'm taking a paperback. Give me a mystery any day over a graphic novel. They're all so dark." The TV news had nothing about an arrest. My inhabitant wiggled and jiggled inside of me like the spider in the kid's song.

Being adult is all about making yourself do what you ought to but don't want to. I never asked to grow up. A mental search for additional reasons to wait came up empty. The stomach twitches weren't at all like baby calisthenics. I sucked it up and called Sam's house. Brent answered and muffled the phone while he checked whether Sam would talk to me. The wait seemed long, and I prayed Brent would come back so I could leave a message to have Sam call me when he felt like it. But Sam came on the line.

"Iris."

"Yeah. I heard you quit. I got elected to talk you out of it. Hap and Denny and Linda and so on. We want you back."

Silence. I braced for the blast.

What I got wasn't bitter or angry. More like resignation. "No, it's my time to go. Brent's wanted me to quit for months now. He thinks we can get by on his income, and I guess we'll have to try. He wants to travel, and we can't with my job. It's done, Iris. I'll miss the people, most of them, and I'll surely miss the girls, but it's over. I can't fix anything there, I can't do anything but the regular routine. It's making me crazy, it's going to get worse, and I need to let it go."

There wasn't much to say to that. I asked him to keep open the possibility of coming back.

"No, I don't think so. I apologize for the way you saw me behave. And the way I turned on you. There was no excuse for that."

"Sam, it's forgotten. Really."

"Iris, do not trust Ian."

"Is that why you wanted to carry a gun?" That had worried me for weeks.

"I don't even own a gun. I didn't want him or anybody else to think I was a sitting duck like Wallace was."

I promised to be careful and signed off, relieved that the Sam I knew was back, sorrowful that I would not be working with him. Or seeing him at all, for that matter.

But a few minutes later, wandering the house to tidy up while my nerves finished settling, it came to me that Sam would likely be out of the country soon...out of reach of any investigation. I shut down the thought. Sam was never *that* angry, never that crazy...

The phone rang as I was brushing my teeth. It was Linda.

"I just watched the late news," she said. "Calvin's confessed to murdering Wallace."

Chapter Twenty-one

Detective Quintana did not answer his phone at seven in the morning. The papers had nothing, but television had a still of Wallace and one of an elephant hook, followed by a few seconds of video showing Calvin from the rear, head bowed and hands cuffed behind him, as he was escorted from the police station to the county jail. It almost broke my heart.

I drove to work and called Detective Quintana at seven thirty from the phone by the time clock. No answer. I stared at Linda's handwriting on the whiteboard: "*Neofelis nebulosa* 2.1" Two males, one female. Even that didn't cheer me up.

I needed to interrogate Jackie, but elephants came first. Sam was gone and Ian had to do all the work alone. But Ian said I was out of the pee business. "Neal says I do it now."

"He could have mentioned that to me."

Ian twitched a "not my fault" twitch.

"I talked to Sam. He's not coming back. I hope he's eligible for retirement."

Ian nodded. I left.

Jackie was pale and almost as uncommunicative. She said that all she knew was what was on TV. Mr. Crandall's office was empty. Neal was seated in his office with the door open. I ignored him, walked back to the Penguinarium, and called Quintana again. Again, the voice message.

After the penguins were fed and the food for the aviary prepared, I made a cup of coffee—the one a day I was allowed—and took a short break, scarfing a health-food muffin and a banana.

My IQ rose with my blood sugar. I'd been thinking like a friend. Time to try thinking like a parent. Calling Quintana might not be the brightest way to support Calvin. This situation put me in a quandary.

Linda knocked as she opened the door and sloshed through the foot bath, looking as upset as I was. She grabbed the second chair. "Why didn't you come find me for break? We have to talk. First Sam, now Calvin. This is *insane*." Penguins studied us through the baby gate.

"I needed to think. Sit."

She sat and fiddled with a tea bag in one of the beautiful cups she'd made for me. "You work with him. How could he have done this?" She glared at me. "Talk."

"Linda, this has to be just you and me. No discussing any of this with Denny or Jackie or anyone else."

"No promises. Tell me now, or I'll steal all your food."

"What kind of a deal is that?" Feeling bullied, even by a weak joke, I said, "First off, there's no budging Sam. Brent has the bit in his teeth. I predict he will whisk Sam out of town within the week, off to some romantic vacation. Brent wanted him to quit because this place was making Sam crazy. Which it really was."

"It's making *me* crazy."

"Yeah, it's going around."

"And it started with *Calvin* killing Wallace?" Linda shuddered. "Is there LSD in the hot dogs or something?"

"Calvin didn't kill Wallace any more than you or I did. He thinks his daughter Janet did, and he's protecting her."

Linda sat back. "Oh."

"That's what I want you to shut up about. Here's what's going on." I reminded her about the old story of Janet's entrapment and firing, and told her about my visit to her house. "Wallace wrote Janet a month or so ago and apologized. I think he meant to clear the slate for a new relationship with another woman.

He must have known how ineffective that was, but he probably couldn't see anything better to do for Janet. They met and talked. She went along with the reconciliation at the time, but once she got home and remembered how the accusation led to her crappy life, she sent him a hateful email. The police read it, I'm sure. They tracked her down and talked to her before I did. Anyhow, something convinced Calvin that Janet came to the zoo and got into the barn and whacked Wallace. So he confessed."

She looked at me sidelong. "Um, Iris…You don't really know he didn't do it."

"Yes, I do. If he did it, he'd have confessed right away. Why would he wait?"

"Because he wouldn't expect his daughter to be suspected."

"No, no, no. He didn't do it. He thinks she did it. He doesn't lose his temper, and he wouldn't plan a killing this poorly. Trust me." She knew Calvin. The idea was absurd.

Linda said, "Tell the police. They need to check this out."

"I was going to, until I realized it was kind of a betrayal." A penguin brayed, and I closed the door on them and sat back down. "Look, you're not a parent. I'm not either, not yet, but I'm in training. Calvin is doing what he thinks is right for his daughter. Is it my place to try to wreck that? He's already decided he would rather go to jail than see Janet in the slammer. She's raising two kids, did I mention that? One of them is autistic. I'm sure he sees this as the best option. It's not right for me to meddle."

Linda tucked her lips in and bit them. "You want a killer raising kids? She could flip out again. She needs to be locked up for everyone's safety, *especially* the kids. Calvin's not thinking clearly, and you aren't either."

"We don't really know that Janet did kill Wallace." This was getting even more muddled.

"Call the police and tell them what you think. Let *them* sort it out."

"Promise me you won't call them yourself."

"No promises. You let me know when you've done it."

And that was where we left it. I had no doubt she'd ask tomorrow whether I'd called. She could usually tell when I was lying. I stewed about it all day, but I didn't call Quintana again and he didn't call me back.

Dr. Reynolds found me cleaning parrot cages at the Children's Zoo in late afternoon. It was Arnie's day off, and there was no Calvin to do it. Happy Birthday, the red-crowned parrot named for his favorite phrase, was screaming at me for ruining his life. I'd locked him in the little den box while I scrubbed perches and plastic toys and set out his dinner. My real crime was being me, not Calvin or Arnie.

"Iris, I need to interrupt you for a minute."

"What's up?"

Visitors—families with strollers and toddlers—were all in the goat corral at the moment so we had a little privacy. Dr. Reynolds stood in her white lab coat with her arms crossed, looking worried. "Why were you asking me about Ian Sullivan? I found him asleep in his Jeep two doors down from my house this morning. I think he was there all night."

"Like a stalker?"

"Exactly. I woke him up. He said he was there to protect me. I told him I would tell the police." She looked more angry than frightened.

"Sam said he had a crush on you."

"Why didn't you say something?"

The parrot screamed, "Trick or treat! Shut up!"

"Because they dislike each other so much I'm not sure if Sam knows what he's talking about when it comes to Ian."

Dr. Reynolds said stiffly, "I'm telling you this because I am concerned about your safety, in case he was stalking you as well. You said he was acting oddly toward you. Please let me know the next time you learn something relevant to *my* safety." She dismissed me with a nod and started away.

"Wait. Dr. Reynolds, is that why the security guards have been escorting you to and from the parking lot?"

"Of course."

"But what tipped you off before finding him this morning?"

A pause. "I am not free to discuss that."

Why not? Bewildered, I set that aside. "I can follow you home to make sure no one is hanging out there."

"I'm sure that's not necessary."

How could I have screwed up by not sharing a rumor? This wasn't fair. I parked that notion also and tried to focus on the main issue. "Uh, Dr. Reynolds?"

Kids were pouring out of the goat corral, on to the next thing to catch their attention. A woman pushed a stroller between us, one kid running ahead, another following. I waited until they were occupied with rabbits. "If Ian has a crush on you, he had a motive for killing Kevin Wallace."

She looked at me in alarm, but not for the right reason. "Being stalked by Ian has nothing to do with Kevin. Calvin Lorenz confessed last night."

"I know. I don't think Calvin did it."

"If you have any evidence to back that up, you should share it with the police."

She gave me a troubled and wary look, and this time I did not interrupt her departure. My effort to protect Ian had left her feeling at risk, and she would be slow to trust me again. Discouraged, I returned to arranging chew toys for Happy Birthday.

Denny called forty-five minutes before my day's end and caught me in the middle of the afternoon penguin feeding, rushing to finish up. "Ire. I need to talk to you."

"Denny, busy here. Tomorrow."

"This new curator wants a tour of Reptiles today. What do we know about him, really? What if he's Thor's boss, and he's setting us up? What if he killed Wallace to get this job?"

Even for Denny, this was peculiar. So was his voice—tight and anxious. "That's crazy. What's wrong with you?"

"He could be anybody, and he'll be here soon. I want to understand the risk."

Something was not right. "I'm coming over. Sit still until I get there."

I got to Reptiles as fast as I could and found Denny holding a grass snake up to the light, studying its scales like they held the secret of the universe. The snake wasn't happy about this, and I made him put it away. "Are you stoned?" The answer was obvious. "Are you out of your mind? Do you realize what Neal's going to think?" Denny had to have history with drugs, all things considered, but I'd never seen him ripped at work.

"Didn't smoke anything." He looked at me closely. "Why did you say that? Is this some kind of a joke?" He stepped away from me.

"Did you take any pills?"

"No. I don't do pills. You never know what's really in them."

"What did you eat?"

"A brownie. It's giving me energy."

"Energy, my foot. Where is it?"

He frowned. "I told you, I ate it. It was a gift."

This was *so* not good. "A gift. From whom?"

"It was an apology." His mental light bulb went off, and he straightened up. He dug around in his uniform pants' pocket and handed me a folded piece of paper. "See? Gift."

I scanned it swiftly, expecting Neal to show up any second. The typed message said, "I am so sorry my boyfriend cut your tires. It won't happen again. Please take this as an apology."

"It was in my van, on the driver's seat." Denny adored his van, a dented panel truck that smelled of mildew.

Someone had left a doped brownie inside his van? "Don't you lock it?"

He thought about that for longer than seemed necessary. "No one ever bothered it before. Tires are so expensive and so not green. I hate buying them. Made me late to work twice." He blinked a couple of times and got back on track. "It was from the store, but it was good. Like home-made."

"Let me see the wrapper." I found it in the garbage can, the cellophane package from a cheap supermarket brownie. It was ripped open and crushed, but a close look at the seam showed where someone had cut and carefully re-glued it. This was some *bad* neighbor. "You would never survive in the wild. We've got to get you out of here."

"Can't. Need to find out who Neal really is. You already know, don't you?" He looked at me with deep suspicion and took another step back.

"He'll tell in a heartbeat that you're stoned on your butt. He will never believe this story. Come on."

"Why are you trying to get rid of me? What are you and he planning?"

So this was why he didn't use. Cannabis made him paranoid. He was minutes away from getting fired, and he wouldn't budge. I took a deep breath, stood up straight, and used a sober, serious voice, aiming for something between Sarah Connor in *The Terminator* and Obi-Wan Kenobi. "Denny, I have to show you something right now. It's in the parking lot. I've been waiting, and now it's time."

His eyes widened. "Oh. Okay."

It wasn't easy getting him across the zoo because he was uncoordinated, and he wanted to stop and look at everything, especially visitors. The visitors stared back at the two of us stumbling along. I smiled at them, hoping they would invent an explanation that didn't require notifying the front office. The radio on his belt buzzed twice. We ignored it.

Denny crashed in the back of his van, curling up on the mattress and pillows, my promise of a world-shattering revelation forgotten. I confiscated his keys and slammed the door on him. With luck, he'd fall asleep and stay that way. With luck, it really would be hash he'd ingested and not something else, something worse. No, I was sure it was weed. Pretty sure.

I rushed back to Reptiles and found Neal fuming. "Denny said to tell you he's sick," I said. "He's running a fever. I'm getting his girlfriend to drive him home. Could you have Arnie finish up here? He's supposed to know the routine."

"He didn't call. What are you, his mother? He should have contacted me." Neal looked ready to trample and gore something, anything.

"He was throwing up. And diarrhea. He's not making any sense."

Neal gave it up in disgust. "He never makes any sense. Tell him to call me."

My feet and belly ached as I trotted back to the parking lot. Would this be easier to deal with if I were a senior keeper? Probably not. Denny was still in fetal position. He whimpered a little. I called Marcie's office number on my cell phone. She showed up after an eternity, and I rattled off the short version, handing over the keys. She crouched over him in the back of the van with a definite tigress-and-cub attitude. "This is crazy. Why would anybody dope him? What's going on?" She pushed his arm away gently as he tried to get her to lie down with him.

Aliens took control of my mouth, and I told the truth. "He thinks it was an apology from his hostile neighbor, the one who slashed his tires. More likely it's because he was asking about alibis the night Wallace was clobbered."

Marcie reared up on her knees. "He told me he'd stay out of that, then he went ahead anyway? Did you know about this? Did he tell you he was doing this?"

"I have to finish feeding." I jogged off to avoid any more damning admissions, then hid and waited to be sure she got the van started. She had a little trouble, but got it going and pulled out. Later we would figure out how to get her back into her own car. Later I would figure out how to justify or apologize or whatever for my role in this.

I was exhausted. And, the more I thought about it, worried and angry. I had sicced Denny on Janet, and who knew better how to get a zoo employee fired? No one would savor it more. She wasn't getting away with this bullshit.

I slammed through the last of my work and enlisted Hap for security. He followed me on his Harley to Janet's house. I would guilt-trip her into going to the police and clearing Calvin. I would also tell her to back off from Denny or she'd be short more than a few tires herself. This wasn't much of a plan, but it beat simmering in fury.

She wasn't home. The house was dark, no car in the driveway. I knocked on the neighbor's door, and a chunky woman with frizzy hair opened it. I said I was a friend of Janet's and needed to talk to her about a job opportunity. The neighbor wasn't the least suspicious, possibly because of my zoo uniform and baby bump. She told me that she'd seen Janet loading kids and suitcases into her car the morning of the day before. No, she had no idea where they had gone. Janet wasn't neighborly. What kind of job was it? A good one? Her brother had been laid off from his cooking job, and if Janet wasn't available…

I backed away, mumbling explanations, and she gave up on me and shut the door. She never noticed Hap and his bike. I sat inside my car with the window rolled down so he and I could consult. What the hell was Janet up to? Hap agreed it was looking as if she really did kill Wallace and had lit out for the tall and uncut. Did she think this was her opportunity for a getaway, before the police figured out Calvin wasn't the killer? Or did she even know her father had confessed? We talked, gave up, and went home our separate ways.

As soon as I got home, I checked in with Marcie. Denny was recovering at her apartment and considered the whole event a misunderstanding. He was sure the neighbor was trying to be extra nice by loading the brownie. Marcie thought that he would be competent to drive her to get her car in a few more hours. She also said, "We have to talk. Tomorrow after work?" I put her off, saying I was supposed to be at my folks and would get back to her.

I hung up and sat wondering what my world was coming to that I would lie to my best friend to avoid talking to her. Before I came up with an answer, Linda called and I knew at "hello" that it wasn't good. I changed gears with an effort. "Calm down. Janet blew town with her kids. I need to think before I call the police."

"That's not why I'm calling."

Uh oh.

"Losa killed one of the cubs. The littlest male. Late this afternoon."

"Oh, no." Yet another bolt of dismay. "What happened?"

Soft voice, diamond-hard rage. "You know that guardrail in front of the cougars that the garbage truck ran into last month? Maintenance decided to fix it. They decided to jack-hammer the bent metal post out of the concrete so they could replace it."

"A *jack hammer?* Next door to the clouded leopards? What part of 'Do Not Disturb' don't they get?" My voice was shrill. I hadn't heard the racket because I was distracted by Denny or shut in the Penguinarium kitchen.

"It's been two weeks. They seem to think it wouldn't apply any more. Besides…," she paused, "Arnie signed off on the work order."

She waited until I ran out of bad words. "I was on the way to the Commissary to talk to Hap about the cow bones we haven't been able to get for the lions when I heard the noise. I ran back and yelled at the guys to stop. They shut the thing off. Couldn't have been on more than three or four minutes. But Losa brought the cub out and paced around and up and down the tree trunks, carrying it and banging it on branches. It hung there limp like they do when they're picked up by the neck."

"Couldn't you get her inside?"

"I tried calling her in for food, but she wouldn't come. I shut the den so she couldn't get at the other cubs and called Dr. Reynolds. She decided that trying to dart her would make it worse. Losa kept putting the cub down, then picking it up and pacing again."

It was all too easy to picture Losa panicky and unable to settle down. She was a nervous cat to begin with. Inexperienced and rattled, she sought a safe place for her baby and couldn't decide on one. Those super-long canines wrapped around a little cub…"She never took it into the second den?" We'd provided an alternative safe location for just this contingency.

"Not once. Finally she left it and went up to that high ledge and lay there, then she came down and licked it. I went inside and called her. She came and left the cub behind so I went in and got it. It was dead. Dead as a doornail."

I said more bad words through a thickened throat. "I am going to kill Arnie."

"No, I'm the Feline keeper. It's my right. You can watch."

"Is she back in with the other two?"

"Yeah. Dr. Reynolds gave me some kitty tranqs. I put it in a little bit of meat and she ate it. We waited to make sure it worked, and then I let her in the den. She lay down with them and went to sleep. I called a couple of Education volunteers who were on the pregnancy watch. They'll watch on the monitor tonight and call me if she's restless. I have to stay away for a little while." She went silent.

"Have you talked to Neal?"

"No, he was gone by the time it was over. Dr. Reynolds said she will." Her tone became iron and rust. "But I do plan to have a word with him myself."

"Shit."

"Yeah. That's about it. I'm going to bed. Oh, Iris…" She didn't say anything more.

After a bit, I gentled my voice and said, "I'm still here."

"Thanks for that. Okay, good night."

Chapter Twenty-two

When I clocked in the next morning, the note on the white board was changed. Now it read "*Neofelis nebulosa* 1.1, 1 DNS". One male. One female. One did not survive. Linda's handwriting. She had come in early and made the disaster public, for all to see and inquire about, as Hap and Denny both did. Denny looked no worse for wear. I told them what Linda had told me. Their reactions were more grim than outraged. We were all dragged down by disaster fatigue.

Denny said, "It'll keep happening. This isn't the third big shift, not yet."

Hap said, "A bad moon rising. I'm getting afraid to come in."

I needed an opportunity to talk to Denny in private, and this wasn't it. I didn't want Hap or anyone else to know he had been drugged into incompetence while on the job. Instead, I found Linda and we walked to the Administration building. She went in to have her word with Neal, and I paced outside in a bright, cool morning balanced between spring and summer. A house finch sang a meandering announcement in a rhododendron. Yellow-faced bumblebees worked over spikes of lavender. A ground squirrel rummaged under a dogwood tree. Life busied itself around me, greedy for the season of plenty. Yet only two cubs rooted at Losa's belly where there should have been three. No malice, only stupidity, but what did that matter? Dead was dead, and my heart was constricted by sorrow and anger and immune to joy.

On the asphalt lay a long, inky feather. Our crows begin their molt in June. I held the weightless thing, a primary, the biggest feather a crow has. The surface was split and dusty. I stroked it smooth and clean. The gaps in the vane closed as my finger nail duplicated the bird's bill preening, helping the tiny barbs link the feather together until it lay tidy and united, only a little frayed at the tip. Would life at the zoo ever close up again to a functional unit, the rips in our fabric mended?

Linda emerged, hands in fists at her thighs. "Arnie's not to blame," she said, flat-voiced, emotionless. "It might have died of a birth defect since it was the smallest cub. Losa was only disposing of it. It's instinctive, so she invests her parenting effort in the healthy cubs. We won't know until Dr. Reynolds does the necropsy. The jack hammer probably had nothing to do with it."

"If the right prince finds the cub and kisses it, will it come back to life?"

"Oh, yes. And chipmunks and happy peasants will dance all around."

We walked in silence, side by side, until Linda said, "Us girl keepers are *so* emotional."

"Tell me he didn't say that."

"No, but he was thinking it."

"I'm only an ignorant bird keeper, but this sucks swamp water. Wallace wasn't perfect but…"

Linda said, "Yeah. I know. This guy will be running the place for years."

Before our ways parted, I glimpsed Arnie heading from Bears toward Felines. His chin lifted when he saw us, and his stride wobbled. He stopped and then veered off toward Primates. I nudged Linda. "For some reason, Arnie doesn't want to talk to us today."

"That moronic tool. I am truly amazed he even understands what he did."

"We need to find out what spell of protection he's under and then break the magic."

"Count me in. Can we do boils and itchiness at the same time? Shrivel his proud manhood into a diseased little twig?" She smiled in a way I'd never seen before.

"Absolutely." A shiver snaked up my spine.

As it turned out, it wasn't only girl keepers who were emotional.

Later in the morning, Linda and I took our lunches outside to the benches near the zebras. We'd bought food at the café and chose this area as least likely to be contaminated by Arnie's presence. The old giraffe studied us from above while next door to him llamas lay in the dust like fluffy Inca carvings. We could smell the elephants, but they were on the other side of the giraffe yard out of sight.

Kayla and Hap had followed us, hoping to get the details on Neal's response to the cub's death. Linda delivered the same dead-pan analysis she'd given me. Hap and Kayla started to get excited and rebut this, when Denny found us and grabbed all the air time.

He bounced between rage and bewilderment, hands shooting off in all directions. "Animals do not disappear. That is not how it works. They die, they escape, they get moved elsewhere. You *find* them. Two healthy turtles in a perfectly good enclosure, a terrific enclosure—they do not disappear. They do not."

"They disappeared," I deduced.

"*Yes.* I'm out sick for one hour, I come back, and two animals are missing. My area does *not* lose animals. Reptiles does *not* lose animals."

"A boa got out on Rick one time. I almost stepped on it," I said.

"*Nothing* got out. The lid was on. The doors were locked. I took the place apart looking for them. They weigh, like, five pounds apiece. They're not *tiny.*"

"Did you tell Neal?" I asked.

"What's he going to do? Put out an all points bulletin? If anybody's going to find them, it's me."

Linda asked the obvious. "Who finished up at Reptiles for you?"

Denny took a huge breath and let it out. "Arnie."

"It's gone to his head," Linda said. "He's a senior keeper now, and he thinks he can do anything he wants."

"I asked him," Denny said. "He said they were all there when he left. I don't think he would outright lie."

"No," I said. "But he would outright be wrong. You better tell Neal."

"I did, I did. He said he wasn't surprised they'd vanished—he'd already seen everything here but a volcano erupting in the goat corral. I told him that I was expecting an earthquake, and he threw me out." Denny finally sat down. "Do I have to tell the guy who bred them? Is there a moral issue here?"

"It was those Asian tortoises you traded…" I caught myself. "…that got out of quarantine last week."

"Yeah. When I told Neal they were from a private breeder, he lost interest. 'Donated pets'. He has no clue how *significant* these turtles are."

We kicked it around, why two turtles would disappear and two remain behind, whether Denny had an obligation to notify the hobbyist who had hatched and raised them, whether they were stolen or strayed. The discussion took our minds off the dead cub and Calvin.

"It's like Rajah disappearing," Denny said, brooding.

"Except," I said, "that these are turtles and he was a tiger. And he was dead and these are alive. And he was hidden in a van and these were on exhibit. Other than that, yeah, a lot alike."

Denny ignored me. He sat on the bench between me and Kayla, staring at the ground, wrists on his knees, frowning. "Some evil force is aligned against Finley Zoo. A malicious entity at work behind a smoke screen. I thought it was one of those big shifts that happen, seismic, a new beginning after the old ways fail. But this is deeper, worse." He raised his head and braced his hands on his thighs. "We need to hire a shaman."

"Or a priest to perform an exorcism," Hap said.

Linda nodded.

"And a good attorney," I added. "TV news said Calvin was going with a public defender. That's not good. Not a word about setting bail and letting him out."

Denny said, "Calvin. Proof that the killer instinct is in all of us. When circumstances align—maybe directed by that malicious entity—the lizard brain takes over. We bury primal anger under the cortex, but it peels away in an instant when—"

"Oh, bullshit," I said. "He didn't kill Wallace any more than I did."

"You decided to go to the police," Linda said.

I shut up. I hadn't made up my mind, I was just annoyed with Denny.

Hap and Denny worried at me, Kayla chiming in now and then, like ravens picking over a road kill, until I told them what I thought Calvin was doing.

"That makes more sense," Hap said. "Calvin's not a hair-trigger dude. He wouldn't lose it and brain someone. I feel like a turd for ever believing it."

"Take it easy. We're all desperate for answers," said Linda.

I said, "I keep going back and forth on whether Janet actually could have done it. I talked to her, and I think she hated Wallace enough to kill him. She could figure out how to get into the zoo and the elephant barn."

Denny said, "It's not like Finley Zoo has changed much since her time."

Probably true. "But why would Wallace meet her at Elephants in the early morning? How'd she get the jump on him? It's possible, but it's a long shot. The important thing is that Calvin didn't do it, and that he thinks she did."

"It's not going to do any good to talk to the bacon," Hap said, "especially if all you have is a guess."

"What else can we do?" Linda said. "Pick someone, truss them up, and claim that's the murderer?"

Nobody had a better idea.

"Give it a try," Hap said. "This is bad. Calvin's not the right kind of tough for prison."

◇◇◇

Talking to Quintana. What did I have to offer except opinions and theories? No keen insider perspective, no stunning new information. Nothing to support the possibility that Janet was guilty, her or anyone else. Such as the rumored person possibly seen when and where they shouldn't have been, behind the elephant barn in the early morning. Which made me realize I hadn't been thorough, hadn't looked into that properly.

I hit the time clock a few minutes early and lurked until Denny showed up. We walked together toward the parking lot in relative privacy. "Look," I said, "that brownie was no accident. You need to be careful."

He stopped walking, surprised. "Nah, it was just a present. I should have noticed it was loaded, but I was busy working. An apology, like the note said. Nobody slashed a tire today."

"Denny, this person made a hash brownie, bought a store brownie, opened up the package, substituted the brownie, and re-sealed it. That's not how anybody apologizes. You need to be careful. Someone's trying to get you fired."

He stared into the distance with his head bobbing in a turtle sort of way. "Yeah, yeah. I see what you mean. The hidden force I was talking about. Something lurking. Like that Dale guy that hangs with Thor. I get really bad vibes off him."

Dale was indeed a possibility. "You'd better quit asking about alibis. Marcie's on the rampage about it, for one thing."

Denny's wheels turned. "It could still be the neighbor. I turned in this guy down the road for leaving his dog chained up outside with no shelter. That was a couple months ago, but he maybe found out recently it was me."

"Whatever. Someone's after you. Watch your back."

"Right."

"And make up with Marcie."

"It could be this guy from the comics convention in May. He was seriously misinformed about Dark Horse comics, and I told him…"

I sighed, got into my car, and left him standing alone in the parking lot still searching for possibilities. Instead of taking the direct route to the freeway and home, I took a back road, circling the zoo, winding among a patchwork of open fields, isolated houses, and new subdivisions. At a weedy field with a few scrubby hawthorns, I pulled the Honda onto a strip of mud rutted with old tire tracks and parked. The slam of the driver's door was loud in the quiet afternoon.

I stepped away from the car into the field and slowly turned 360 degrees. If someone had figured out how to break into the zoo from the back, he or she had to start from somewhere near here.

Between the zoo and the road lay a strip of land that was roughly plowed, with weeds pioneering here and there. Beer cans and a scattering of cigarette butts showed that people hung out here to drink, although the field had no amenities except a backside view of the zoo. The other side of the road was also a field, but it bore a for-sale sign indicating that the land was suitable for development. Beyond that, on a slope in the near distance, the bones of new housing jutted skyward, a row of ten identical roof peaks above ten matching skeletons waiting for sheetrock and siding. No one was working there on a Saturday. The afternoon sun filtered through an even cloud cover, the light vague and glaring. I didn't see another soul.

Hiking over rough ground brought me to the zoo's perimeter fence. Turning left, I walked along it a good distance until it intersected a barb wire fence with "No Trespassing" signs guarding a field plowed into neat, weedless ridges. Whether a crop was planted and not yet up, I couldn't tell. A robin called, distressed at my intrusion. In the distance the freeway imitated the sound of wind in trees. Scrubby clover bloomed yellow underfoot.

I'd never seen the aviary or waterfowl pond from this perspective. I hung my hands on the fence above my shoulders and studied the zoo from the outside. Trash had accumulated inside the perimeter fence where it wasn't obvious from the zoo side. Mallards quacked, unhappy to be stalked.

The fence looked tight except for a spot where water running off the field had undermined it. This was the traditional entrance point for hooligans. The gap was filled with a knot of barbed wire that would require gloves and heavy clippers to remove. Calvin would be pleased.

I turned around and walked back the way I'd come, past the car and along the fence until I was stopped again, this time by hawthorn trees infested with Himalayan blackberries. I was shunted away from the fence to get around the thicket. The ground was littered with a faded pizza box, wrappings from hamburgers, plastic bags of various sorts, and a sleeping bag. I checked out the sleeping bag, poking it with a stick. It was rotted and useless. No one was using it any more.

When I could get close to the fence again, I stopped and studied the tangle of invasive plants. I hadn't noticed the thick old cottonwood rising above the hawthorns, ridged black limbs stretching sideways, a relic of what this land did when it was left to its own inclinations. I'd walked beyond the elephant barn, closer to the Asian Experience construction. Concrete pillars rose to my right, I-beams and rebar poking out.

I was raised in the Northwest, and I'd picked feral blackberries most summers since I was old enough to walk. This thicket might be impenetrable, and it might not. I worked tight along the fence and found that only tender new growth blocked my way. The blackberries had been hacked back, perhaps the previous fall. New shoots of Himalayan blackberries carry thorns almost as wicked as those on old canes, but they can be bent out of the way, if you wear gloves or are careful where you grab them. It got easier as I worked my way in and under the cottonwood, where the berries were shaded out. I wasn't the first. The ground was trampled, the thin grass smashed flat. On the other side of the fence was the solid bulk of the manure shed.

At the base of the big cottonwood a thick, gnarled limb had snapped off, probably from its own weight and a little wind. One end had jammed itself into the dirt, the once-leafy end leaned against the trunk. Like any cougar, I walked up, boots solid on the rough bark. It was an easy climb to another big limb that had been cut off three or four feet from the top of the fence. The roof of the manure shed was less than a dozen feet away and the same height as the limb I stood on.

There was a secret here.

I stood in the tree ten feet above the ground and tried to figure it out. It took awhile because the system was dismantled and because I wasted time picturing how to jump to the fence, crawl through the wire, and drop to the ground. Maybe Delta Force could do it, but it would hardly be convenient.

An impression in the thick moss next to my boots showed me the method. A plank to cross the gap. It would rest on the cut end of the branch where I stood, slide below the lowest strand of barbed wire to rest on the top of the fence—metal pipe—and end up on the roof of the shed. Three strands of barbed wire impeded this elevated path. I favored a layer of carpet scrap to get over that. And a rope ladder to hook on the top of the fence for a quick return. Walk the plank, cross over the barbed wire, drop to the ground, and it was a short stroll to the barn's back door, which was keyed the same as the front door.

Perhaps Thor Thorson kept a rope ladder in his gray and blue backpack. Did Quintana even know that Thor existed?

This access was used once or many times? No way to tell. Remove the plank, carpet, and ladder and hide them in the blackberries or, better, put them in your car. Come and go, with the shed to hide your entry and exit. Risky, though. Better to do it at night. Or early in the morning before the staff arrived.

I slid carefully back down and crawled around in the thicket looking for the plank and getting thorns jabbed into my palms. No luck. I stood up and pushed out of the thicket on a thin little trail I'd missed. I stepped on an empty Camel's package and stopped to pick it up. Ian smoked Camels. The logo was a handsome dromedary, a beast inexplicably considered ugly and ungainly by many. I put the package in my pocket to think about later.

I walked toward my car, and turned back to scan the tangle of vegetation. The trail wasn't that hard to spot. My woodcraft failed because I was distracted by the decaying sleeping bag. I would bet my next paycheck that Detective Quintana had blackberry scratches on his hands. I got into my Honda and started home. I should come back in August to pick berries. No, come to think of it, I'd be pretty busy in August.

Chapter Twenty-three

I found a message on my home phone from Neal asking me to work though my weekend. No surprise. Sam had quit and Calvin was in prison. The upshot was that the zoo's animal department was short-staffed. I called back—he was still at his desk at seven o'clock in the evening—and agreed, but called him again after thinking it over. "I need to leave early if I can get the basics done. I need some rest." He didn't argue. I felt a faint sympathy for him, dependent on a keeper with belly and ankles both swelling.

So Thursday morning I was thinking lick-and-a-promise—feed, clean, go home. I was not prepared for an unscheduled keeper meeting. I'd learned better than to even consider skipping it. Keepers trickled into the auditorium, where I sat grumpy and low energy between Linda and Kayla, Denny a row back. This meeting could cost me an hour.

Mr. Crandall was not present. Neal Humboldt radiated tight-wound energy at the front of the room, pacing with quick glances at the audience. Dr. Reynolds also stood in front, off to one side, looking at the floor with her back rigid. I glanced at Kayla, wondering why the two weren't joined at the hip as usual. Kayla was stony faced and still.

"What's up?" I hissed at her. She pretended she didn't hear me.

I raised an eyebrow at Linda, who made a "beats me" face. "How are the cubs?" I whispered.

"At the hospital," she whispered back.

"*What?*"

Linda leaned close. "The Species Survival Plan coordinator for clouded leopards called and leaned on Dr. Reynolds about hand rearing. She changed her mind and pulled them."

"You didn't call me."

"I just found out on the way here."

"Wow."

Linda bobbed her head. "Dr. Reynolds said the SSP guys want to pair up the cubs before they're six months old. Give them a playmate that grows into a real mate. Cuts down on the male aggression. So we may ship them out in a few months."

I knew that the cubs wouldn't stay forever. The whole point of breeding Losa and Yuri was to help create a self-sustaining captive population and that meant coordinating with other zoos. Still, I hated to think of losing them so soon. I sat back wondering if I'd ever be able to keep up emotionally. Then I wondered why Kayla wasn't thrilled at getting to handle the cubs every day. She looked like her dog died.

"Okay, okay." Neal called the meeting to order. "I'm sure you are all aware of the big picture right now. The bottom line is staffing shortages as well as a number of process failures and other challenges." He took a breath and charged on rapid-fire. "I am resourcing staff as fast as possible, but we need quality as much as head count. I've got feelers out for experienced personnel and my expectation is to have temps on board in a day or two, next week at the latest, at least two FTEs. I'm also fast-tracking the hiring process for permanent positions, but fast turns out to mean slow given the existing human resource procedures. A senior keeper position is open and in-house applications are welcome. Any questions?"

Denny said, "What did you say? Can you diagram that on the board or something?"

Neal lasered him with intense blue eyes. He spoke slowly, enunciating carefully. "Two temporary keepers start soon. I will hire two permanent keepers. Keepers can apply for the senior keeper position." He paused. "Would you like me to go over this again, off-line?"

Denny shook his head. "No, I get it now. Thanks for the translation. English is my first language."

Neal's look indicated there would be consequences for lip. "In the meantime, I'll be talking to you individually about opportunities for overtime. I appreciate your flexibility."

Was this all the meeting was about? Could we go now?

Neal said, "Dr. Reynolds needs to speak to you also."

The slim veterinarian stepped forward and faced us. Short white lab jacket and brown pants, brown hair falling straight behind her shoulders, a plain green shirt—she looked like somebody's lab assistant. Neal faded to a back corner. She scanned the room—keepers, Hap, gardeners, maintenance guys, even George the security guard. Neal's announcement was of interest only to keepers. Why were maintenance and gardeners here? Why George?

Dr. Reynolds clasped her hands together in front and spoke in a voice not at all like a lab assistant, more like the lab's top director. "Recently we've faced some terrible challenges. Kevin Wallace was murdered. Calvin Lorenz is in jail for the crime. Sam Bates has left. We have had to perform our jobs to the best of our abilities despite the emotional toll these events have taken."

She looked strained. And something else. Anger?

The vet continued. "No matter what else happens, the welfare of the animals under our care is our most important responsibility. I think we can agree on that." Her glance around the room dared anyone to differ.

"What I have to say applies to only a few of you. As for the rest, please be assured you have my respect for your excellent work." She crossed her arms over her chest and spoke in a voice that could etch steel. "Be aware that I will not tolerate any action that impairs my ability, our ability, to maintain animal health. I've discussed this with Neal, and, while he reserves the power to terminate staff, he supports me in this. You cross these lines at peril of your job."

Yipes. Yes, anger. Her audience was silent as death.

"*No one* will ignore my orders that animals are not to be disturbed, not keepers, not maintenance staff. Communications broke down in regard to the clouded leopard. That will not happen again." Her head bobbed. Her gaze fixed on us. "Maintenance and Security departments will do their jobs so that a zoo van *with a tiger in it* will not vanish without a trace. The physical boundaries of this zoo *will be* secure." Head bob and a pause. "Security and keeper staff will ensure that *all animals are accounted for at all times.* Two turtles disappeared from their exhibit and presumably left the grounds. This will not happen again without serious consequences." She looked around the room. "And *no one* will enter the necropsy room without my permission. The locks will be changed *today* and, for now, I will have the only key." Her voice wavered with suppressed fury.

I glanced at Linda and caught similar twitches through the room. What was this last ultimatum about?

Dr. Reynolds said more quietly, "You may not have heard yet. I cannot perform a necropsy on the clouded leopard cub that died. The cub has disappeared. It presumably was discarded into the trash and removed to land fill. No one can tell me how this happened. There is no possible justification for *anyone* to move that cub." Hard brown eyes raked us. "This is not your personal animal playground. This is a professional zoological institution that will adhere to the highest standards of care. That is all. Go back to work."

She and Neal left by the door at the front of the auditorium. The rest of the audience filed quietly out the double doors at the back. I stood to leave, but Kayla was still in her seat, blocking my way. She was doubled over with her face in her hands. "She thinks I did it. She thinks I threw out that cub. I didn't *do* it," she sobbed. "I don't *know* how it happened. It wasn't *me*." Of course. She had access to all the rooms at the hospital. She would be the first person suspected. Linda patted her on the shoulder. Kayla finally rose. "Should I quit?" she asked us. "What should I do? We were *friends*."

I shook my head. "Do your job. That's all you *can* do. Maybe the cub will turn up."

Kayla edged out of the aisle and we followed. Linda grabbed my arm and pulled me away from the others, toward the front of the room. "Did you know about the cub disappearing?"

I shook my head. "Nope. I feel like I've been punched in the mouth."

Linda gazed into the distance, biting her lip. "Arnie. He took that cub because the necropsy would show it was perfectly healthy and his fault that it died."

"Whoa, Linda! You can't be sure of that. Arnie is used to problems solving themselves without him lifting a finger. Would he even think of that?"

"Don't defend him! He's left Kayla taking the heat. I'm talking to Dr. Reynolds."

I watched her dodge past slow-moving Kayla and stride toward the Administration building, where Dr. Reynolds might have gone with Neal.

I stood in the auditorium as it quieted, listening to the echoes of the meeting. Was Denny right? A malicious intelligence at work? That sounded like a low-budget horror flick. Weeks after Wallace was attacked, we were no closer to understanding what had happened. The police were still holding Calvin. Maybe they truly believed he was guilty. That was what I needed to focus on now. Calvin. The rest would have to wait.

After lunch, I phoned Detective Quintana, who was, as usual, not in or at least not answering. I left a message that I'd remembered some information I wanted to share. "But I don't like police stations and I'm going to be starved, so let's talk at a restaurant." I said I'd be at the Thai Orchid on Washington Street in downtown Vancouver at six o'clock. Neutral territory.

By that point, it was clear that I would not be clocking out early. In fact, I accurately predicted that I would leave work an hour late. I departed weary and bitter that I'd barely managed the basics despite showing up on time and avoiding distractions.

The Thai Orchid was pretty and soothing, full of lovely pottery and paintings. Even better, they had food, which was far more important than whether or not Quintana showed up. I was inhaling spring rolls when he slid into the other side of the booth. I stopped in time to leave him half a roll, shoving the plate toward him. He shook his head, so I pulled the plate back and ate it.

"Let's hear what you've got," he said in his gravelly voice. "Friends are coming for dinner, and my wife won't be happy if I'm late."

My chicken Pad Thai showed up before I could say anything, and my verbal abilities shut down until I'd eaten most of it.

"That waiter nearly lost a finger," he noted. "Do they normally feed you from a forked stick?"

I sat back and sighed. "I'm eating for two, and one of us is a wolverine. I can't help it."

Cups of jasmine tea had materialized on the table. We sipped. He shooed away the waiter.

"So," he said, and fixed me with his penetrating, already-disappointed stare.

"So. Calvin Lorenz. You know he's trying to protect Janet, his daughter."

No reaction.

I went on. "You're not stupid. You must have figured out that Calvin believes his daughter offed Kevin Wallace. Maybe he heard about that nasty email Janet sent Wallace, and she told him something about being happy he was dead. She really does hate him. Maybe Calvin figured out she could have copied his zoo keys. I think you started that rumor at the zoo that an arrest was about to be made, that you set it up to see who bolted. I passed it on to him, Calvin panicked and confessed, and you're holding him until Janet shows up."

Detective Quintana looked bored.

I soldiered on. "I figure either *she* panicked and ran away because she thought the email made her a suspect, or else she took the kids to Garibaldi to go crabbing and hasn't heard that her dad fell on his sword for her." Come to think of it, I might have helped trigger her flight by my original visit. First the cops, then me might have been too much for her nerves. I didn't see any reason to mention this. "Have you found her yet?" I waited a bit and sighed. "This would be easier if you said something now and then."

"It's your show. I'm still hoping that you'll come up with something useful."

I'd decided not to mention Denny's cut tires and loaded brownie unless I had to. That was likely to backfire. Instead I said, "Pull up your sleeve." That surprised him. I pushed back my own sleeve. He frowned, but he unbuttoned the cuff of his blue shirt and slid it up, pulling back his dark jacket sleeve as well. I leaned forward and inspected the back of his hand and wrist. They looked much like mine, except for being hairy and bigger. "I'd say you've been messing with blackberries and got scratched up a little. You found the route into the back of the zoo. I'm not sure what that tells us. Janet couldn't have gotten in that way, and Calvin had no reason to."

He pulled his cuff back down and rebuttoned it. In an uninterested, neutral voice he said, "Why couldn't Janet have used it?"

"Ah. You *haven't* found her. She's really big. Not a climber. So if Janet did it, she came in some other way. I should have seen her when I ran to the elephant barn. I'm not saying she didn't do it, just that I can't figure out how."

A mistake. I'd accidentally tricked him into revealing information, and now he was mad. "Ms. Oakley, withholding information about a homicide is a crime with serious penalties. If you have information you have not yet shared with us, this would be the time to do it."

"You should eat something. The shrimp cakes are good." I meant well, thinking it might improve his mood, but my suggestion fueled the ire lurking in his sagging face. I said, "Look, I called it wrong at the beginning and led you astray. I really thought Damrey had trampled Wallace to death. I'm not an elephant keeper, and I didn't understand what she was doing.

I'm trying to work with you here, trying to give you information that you can only get from a zoo employee."

One side of his face winced in a skeptical way.

"My father does that silence thing, but it works out a lot better. I think you should talk to me. Like about whatever Dr. Reynolds' big secret is. Was it enough for her to kill Wallace if he found out? You know they were dating…"

This didn't cut any ice. "Let's make this clear, Ms. Oakley. There is no way I'm going to share confidential information with you. In fact, all this scrambling around you are doing makes me think I should take a much closer look at *your* relationship with Kevin Wallace."

"Waste of time. You can't prove I did it because I didn't." I took a breath and persevered. Ian's crush on Dr. Reynolds was also in the skip-unless-essential category, but I could come at it from another angle. "Ian Sullivan smokes Camels, and yesterday I found an empty pack near the cottonwood tree behind the manure shed. I think it's a plant. Somebody's trying to implicate him and must have left it recently because you didn't find it and you were there before I was, right?"

I didn't get a nod. I moved on. "Why would Wallace be at the barn alone so early except to catch an intruder? And the first people who come to mind are these animal rights activists who've been making pests of themselves about the elephants. This Thor Thorson pops up everywhere at all hours. He's sort of a reverse Houdini, good at getting into places." I explained about his backpack, which could hold a rope ladder. "He's got this creepy sidekick, Dale something, who was following Sam around. He tried to scare me, too." I explained Dale's suspicions about Nakri's wound. "If he or Thor broke into the barn to take pictures, Wallace might have caught him. Maybe they fought, one of them nailed Wallace, and they left out the back, and I never saw them."

"Is that it?"

"Well, yeah. I think you should look at Thor and Dale." I hesitated, not sure whether pushing would help or hurt. "And then you could turn Calvin loose. I've known him for years. He wouldn't hurt a fly. He and Wallace worked together for years after Janet was fired. No reason for him to fly off the handle now. He's a good person. It's just that he's a *parent*."

Detective Quintana sipped his tea and studied me. He set the cup down. "What I'm hearing is a load of creative speculation and a lot of nosiness. It's also clear you've been messing around with the evidence in this case, which is more unacceptable than you can begin to imagine. Let me put it this way. I'm willing to stipulate that you're a pretty good zoo keeper. I know for a fact that I'm a pretty good cop. This investigation will work out best for both of us if we stick to our own jobs. I won't screw with the birdies, and you stay out of this from now on. Otherwise, you may be contaminating evidence and getting people stirred up who don't need to be stirred up. Do we have a deal? Because otherwise I'm going to have a chat with your boss or else charge you with obstructing justice." His face was not friendly.

"Don't be so *mean*," I wailed. "I work there, and I know stuff you don't. Did you even *know* about Thor?" Once again I felt like crying. Another pathetic side effect of pregnancy? "You're never going to figure this out because the elephants wrecked the crime scene, and it was days late before you found out it was a murder. Calvin's knees hurt, and jail isn't good for him. And lots of other bad stuff is happening at the zoo."

"Such as?"

"Animals disappearing, and the wrong people being promoted. Tire slashing."

It was his turn to sigh. He spoke as if I were dimwitted. "We have a confession from a person with motive, opportunity, and means. He's a friend of yours. You're trying to help him. But you are doing more harm than good, and you are straying into fantasy when you try to link unrelated events to the murder. Stay out of this or I am going to come down on you like the hammer of Zeus."

"It's the hammer of Thor," I said. "Thor Thorson. Not his real first name, which I forget. But I—you—could find out."

"I am not kidding," he said. He slid out of the booth and stood up. He shook his head at me like a bloodhound with ear mites. He left.

All I had gotten out of this was Pad Thai and a dent in my budget. He knew everything I knew, had the same suspicions, had hit the same walls. Or else he didn't believe me or didn't care. I had no magic abilities with Sam or Ian, no special perceptions, and I had learned nothing useful about why Kevin Wallace had died. I couldn't save the friend I knew was innocent.

I flagged down the waiter and ordered the shrimp cakes. Fiscal irresponsibility was better than bawling.

Chapter Twenty-four

Saturday morning, two bleak, exhausting days later, I shut the alarm off in my sleep and showed up for work an hour and a half late. I called Neal to tell him I'd made it in. "Don't make a habit of clocking late," he said. "I have to approve schedule changes, overtime or not, and you need to manage your time. Incidentally, I noticed a lot of trash around the pond. Let's get that cleaned up."

I was within a microsecond of hanging up on him when he added, "I have some help for you today. Should be in around noon. His name is Pete Latimer. An experienced bird keeper. Let me know when you think he's ready to solo. I'm guessing three-four days of training."

I'd be dead by then.

All our schedules were disrupted, and Linda was off today. I could imagine what it felt like to leave Arnie in charge of Felines for two days. I hadn't heard how her meeting with Dr. Reynolds had gone. If I weren't too tired to think, I'd remember to call her and ask. I hoped she'd stopped Dr. Reynolds from making Kayla's life miserable.

After seven work days in a row, I had no brain power available for thinking about Calvin or Janet or Thor, only a nagging sense that yet another disaster lurked, waiting for me to relax. Someone had tried to stop Denny. It was logical to go for me next.

I no longer had my elephant chore, but this was weighing day for the penguins, a monthly ritual. I set the electronic bathroom scale down on their island. The birds gathered at a safe distance and regarded it as if aliens had dropped off a portal to an unknown planet.

This was normal. I stuffed vitamins into fish gills and, when that was done, checked how the group process was going. The birds were now clustered around the scale pecking at it and braying about their courage. I stepped over the baby gate with a clipboard and a bucket of fish. Mrs. Green, ever the opportunist, hopped on the scale and collected her smelt. I put the bucket down, fastened the lid, and wrote down her weight using the clipboard. Mrs. Yellow did her best to work the lid off the bucket. Mrs. Green insisted on being weighed again. Mr. White brayed long and loud and then pecked the toes of my rubber boots.

This was much easier with two people. After a good amount of frustration and an extra half hour, almost everyone was weighed and had eaten a vitamin fish. The exception was Mrs. Brown, who declined her smelt and even refused a particularly choice herring. Calvin's absence was a bitter ache. I couldn't even call him at home for advice. Instead, I left a message for Dr. Reynolds that Mrs. Brown was again off her feed.

Word got around, of course, about the new person arriving. At lunch break the café had a brisk business in keepers who showed up hoping one of us had real information. We pushed two tables together, although Arnie chose to sit at a third one nearby. A couple of visitors wandered over once we'd all settled. "Hello there!" the woman said with a big smile. None of us was particularly welcoming, but I was raised right and made the effort. "Can I help you?" The last thing we wanted to do was answer visitor questions during our lunch.

"I'm Cheyenne Courtenay, and this is Pete Latimer. We're not from the government, and we're here to help."

"The temps!" I said. "Save us!"

We established that they weren't hungry, found room for them at the tables, and introduced ourselves. Cheyenne looked tanned and fit, mid-thirties, dressed in jeans and a t-shirt for the warm day. No makeup or jewelry, wiry brown hair cropped short and thick. Pete was dark-haired, darker skin, also jeans and t-shirt. His arms and chest were muscular, tattoos twining around his fingers. Linda, Denny, and Hap took turns grilling them while I ate. They turned out to be partners and had worked at a major zoo in the Northeast. They quit to spend a year in Thailand looking at wildlife and working in little Southeast Asian sanctuaries and zoos. Neal had somehow gotten their email address and set up the gig while they were still overseas. They'd gotten off their return flight in New York yesterday, landed in Portland a few hours ago, and were delighted to have jobs. If they were jet-lagged, it didn't show.

Pete's experience was in marine mammals, cheetahs, and birds. Cheyenne was an elephant keeper and remembered that she'd met Ian before. Ian managed a nod and brief smile.

"What, is there an underground network of elephant keepers?" I asked. Turned out there was. They knew each other from a conference and visiting other facilities.

Pete and Cheyenne asked for suggestions for a place to stay while they found more permanent housing. I caught their expectant look at Ian, who kept his eyes down. After a moment's consideration, I said, "You can crash with me for a few days. I've got a spare bedroom." They were grateful. "My house is in Portland. Have you got a car?" They did not. I wondered what I'd gotten myself into.

Pete followed me around for the rest of the day. He seemed to grasp the routine easily and didn't sneer at our exhibits or offer a boatload of suggestions or question my face mask. He provided an energy boost that made up for the extra time training. We even got the trash at the back of the pond cleaned up.

We met Cheyenne at the time clock, rounded up their duffle bags from where Jackie had stored them in the office, and loaded ourselves into the Honda. As I drove by the front of the zoo, I pointed to the sole picketer on duty, a woman. "You guys wouldn't happen to know a Thor Thorson, would you? He's in charge of a bunch of people making trouble about the elephants."

Cheyenne, in the seat next to me, said, "Ohhhh-*yeah*. So it's your turn. We had him for months."

I filed that away. We stopped by my parents, who I'd warned in advance, and picked up a foam mattress and bedding. My mother thrust a meatloaf on me, solving the issue of dinner. I nearly wept.

At my house, I left my guests to set up the second bedroom, once I shoved baby gear into the closet. This was one more opportunity to be glad I'd made Denny take Rick's iguana, Bessie Smith. Her big glass habitat would have taken up half the room. The third bedroom was hopeless, full of boxes I hadn't yet dealt with. I threw potatoes into the microwave. Frozen peas made it a complete meal.

Over dinner, Cheyenne asked how long Neal had been with Finley Memorial Zoo, which led to me explaining about Kevin Wallace's demise. They'd spent a month in a little village without Internet access and had somehow missed the news.

Pete put down his fork. "What? Neal never said a word about a murderer on the loose." His eyes flashed. "He's sending Cheyenne to Elephants without a word of warning? Who the hell knows what might happen in there?"

"I'll be fine," she said. "Ian will be with me most of the time, and Neal's looking to hire another elephant keeper, so then there'll be two of us all the time. Whoever did this is probably long gone. I'm not in any danger."

Pete wasn't so sure. I had no idea.

"My job's enough," Pete said. "You don't have to work there. You could quit." But it was clear from her tolerant, stubborn face that he'd lost before he started. She got up and put a hand on his shoulder before rummaging in the freezer for ice cream.

"Tell me about Thor," I said as we polished off the chocolate swirl.

Pete and Cheyenne looked at each other, one of those couple things I'd almost forgotten. "He's sincere as all hell. He never quits," Pete said.

Cheyenne nodded. "He loves elephants, but he's got a blind spot about zoos. He thinks we can never provide good conditions. He's stuck on having hundreds of acres, like that's all that matters." She explained that Thor enlisted Ian to help establish a new elephant sanctuary. Ian had elephant experience with a couple of zoos and a circus and was an eager convert. But he changed his mind. She said, "One of the sanctuary volunteers is a friend of mine. The vet had no experience with elephants. The safety procedures for staff and volunteers weren't good. They didn't approve of breeding more elephants, and Ian thought that was cheating the cows out of having a family. He told Thor and the director about all this—you can imagine him trying to say anything that complicated. Everybody yelled at him, and he ended up walking five miles with his suitcase to the main road so he could hitchhike out."

"He came here," I mused, "thinking he could be part of building a really good elephant facility. Then he found out that the project hasn't gotten off the ground."

Cheyenne nodded. "He'll probably stick around until a decision is made about what to do with Damrey and Nakri."

"We're all worried about that," I said. "Sam, the elephant keeper that quit, thought Wallace planned to ship them to another zoo instead of improving the exhibit. Thor is pressuring the zoo to send them to a sanctuary."

Cheyenne said, "Sanctuaries can be a good option, but it's not just about acreage, and it's not just about hanging up the ankus forever. Nutrition, veterinary care, foot care, managing their friendships and feuds, lots of things need to be in place. Oh, and stable funding. Elephant care isn't cheap."

"You've talked about this before," I said.

"Well, yeah. I had practice at our old zoo."

I said, "Sam said that sanctuaries usually limit public access, so problems can be hidden."

Cheyenne shrugged. "Possibly. I'd like to see them have a strict accreditation program, like zoos do."

"Which aren't all accredited. Finley isn't there yet."

Pete said, "And won't be until you solve the elephant problem."

Cheyenne said, "On the plus side, Ian's good at training and enrichment. Their feet look okay. The girls are good friends."

"Tell me more about Thor. Did he ever get violent? What sets him off?" I asked.

Pete shook his head. "He's totally under control. With the press, with pissed-off keepers, with teenagers mouthing off. He started a media circus at our old zoo that lasted a month, and he enjoyed every minute."

"There was a story," Cheyenne said. "Nothing I saw myself."

"Tell me," I said.

Cheyenne looked uncomfortable.

"I need to know about Thor and how he operates." I wasn't letting this go.

She said, "It's not just about Thor…It's about Ian, too. I'm going to be working with him. I don't want to be telling tales."

Pete said, "I think you should. It might matter."

She gave that a thought, then she told me that Thor had a girlfriend who also worked at the elephant sanctuary, although "she wasn't an animal person. She did the web site." Ian had developed "a crush" on the girlfriend, which eventually annoyed her. She told Thor, who asked Ian to back off. When Ian kept staring at her, the girlfriend lambasted Thor for not being man enough to punch him out. This led to a protracted argument about whether there was an appropriate role for violence in personal or public life. In the end, she broke up with Thor and left.

"The only problem I've had with Ian," Cheyenne said, "is that he'll barely speak to me. He acts like I'm poison ivy."

"Yeah," I said, "For awhile he was almost normal around me, but no more."

Cheyenne didn't know anything about Dale, Thor's black-haired shadow.

Pete said, "I am liking this gig less and less."

Later, getting ready for bed, I felt Thor fading as a suspect. Dale stayed in play. Ian seemed too ineffective for violence. Calvin was still in jail. Janet was still not answering her phone. Detective Quintana had not called me to suggest we work together.

My options were boiling down to one: stick to my birdies.

The next morning we munched our granola in sleepy silence. Pete was a tea drinker, Cheyenne was as addicted to coffee as I was. Having people around was surprisingly pleasant, even if they couldn't solve all my problems. I ferried them to the zoo.

Pete stumbled a little with the penguins, rushing them while they were still shy of the stranger. They wanted Calvin, would tolerate me, and thought Pete was a shark in disguise. We got through it. Dr. Reynolds had us catch up Mrs. Brown. I wrestled her into an animal carrier and left her for the moment. Pete did well with the aviary, reading the feeding charts carefully to prepare the food bowls. When we set them out, a Brazilian cardinal landed on his head without hesitation and accepted a meal worm from his fingers as her due.

I left him cleaning the aviary and arranged for the security guard to take me and Mrs. Brown up to the hospital in one of the electric carts. Penguins are heavier than owls. Dr. Reynolds wasn't there, probably out on the grounds, but Kayla was, in a red camp shirt, a cluster of little red gems in each ear. I thanked the guard and handed the penguin over to her. "She likes the little bait herring," I said. "Try that if she won't eat. Hap can get them on special order, but they're expensive."

"I'm all about gourmet treats," Kayla said. "My tartar sauce is to die for." She waited with the animal carrier at her feet outside the quarantine room.

I stalled, not sure how to avoid sounding totally intrusive.

"What's up? I need to feed things," she said.

I said, "Has Dr. Reynolds calmed down? Did Linda get her to consider that someone else might have taken that cub?"

"It's fine." Kayla didn't want to talk about it.

I blurted, "What was her married name?"

Kayla looked at me sideways. "Why do you care?"

"I overheard Neal call her Jeannie Franklin." I'd tried an online search under both names and found nothing useful.

"So? She changed back to her own name. I guess you did, too?"

"She seems to be keeping quiet about something in her background. You wouldn't know what that is, would you?"

Kayla made a face. "If I did and if she's my friend, which she still is, why would I spread it around? What's up with you? This is kind of weird."

Way to go, Iris. Replace Jackie as the zoo's czarina of gossip. "Just wondering. Lots of strange things going on around here."

"Well, if she has some big secret, she's keeping it from me, too. And I'm sure it has nothing to do with Calvin or Kevin Wallace." She picked up the carrier and opened the door to the quarantine room.

I took the hint.

Pete and I finished a little early, with the penguins more accepting at the afternoon feeding. I put him to work cleaning the cricket box while I did reports and then watched with my feet propped up on an overturned bucket. He seemed to have plenty of energy left over and once we were home, he stepped up to cooking dinner.

It had become clear that my visitors were stony-broke. I would be on the hook for housing, food, and transportation until Neal coughed up advance pay checks for them. Pete and Cheyenne seemed untroubled by this and slid smoothly into the household. Pete cooked and Cheyenne did the dishes. I began to think of them as bright-colored birds that had wandered outside their normal range, exotic strays that obeyed different laws. This made me a trifle uneasy, but it didn't keep me from sleeping. Without nightmares.

I did not share the zoo's troubles with them, much less my surmises and suspicions. Pete might insist they quit for Cheyenne's safety, and his help with Birds was saving my rear. Having them in the house let me relax, impossible at work.

Monday, with Neal's permission, I clocked out after the morning penguin feeding, leaving my guests to the mercies of the bus system for a ride home. I swung by Felines on my way out, hoping to catch Linda. She wasn't around. Both servals were in view, small, leggy, spotted cats from Africa. Pele, the male, secured the perimeter by squirting as he paced. His mate, Spot, drowsed under a sword fern. Their elegance and grace seduced naïve people into buying them as pets. *The Oregonian* had run an article on how badly that turned out. Hyper-sensitive predators do not good house pets make. Dozens of them were abandoned by their owners and ended up in rescue centers.

I stalled at the empty tiger exhibit, leaning against the guardrail that separated viewers from the shrubs that bordered the moat. The pool was drained and dry to prevent mosquitoes from breeding. Grass in the exhibit was tall and lush, healthier than it had been with Rajah chewing and trampling it. Grass or no grass, it was a desolate scrap of land without Raj.

The lost tiger. Not a hair had turned up. Insurance would replace the van, Neal would find animals to fill the exhibit. Rajah was obliterated. Not even a skeletal mount at a university remained. "Ah, Raj. I miss you," I whispered.

Like a virus or fungal infection, the disasters had started with Wallace in the elephant barn and had spread to two senior keepers, Felines, Reptiles, and the hospital. Had Janet set off this string of misery? I could picture her clobbering Wallace, no problem. She nurtured her rage and kept it close. If she killed Wallace, that meant a friend of mine hadn't. But the possibility was breaking Calvin's heart.

How, exactly, could she manage to do it? She had not come over the fence behind the barn. She had to know the combination to one of the vehicle gates, then enter the barn through one of the keeper doors and encounter Wallace off guard. The elephants began their uproar. How had she left? The exit turnstiles at the visitor entrance were locked. She wouldn't fit through a turnstile anyway. So she had to use the employee gate into the Commissary/Hospital area, then through the outer perimeter fence using the delivery gate or the gate to the employee parking lot. Whichever, her car had to be parked nearby.

This was reaching deep into the realm of improbability. Keys, gate combinations, me not seeing her…And she would have no reason to find Wallace at the elephant barn unless he'd arranged it in advance. I couldn't think why he would want more contact with her. It hadn't exactly worked out for him the last time.

A pair of blackbirds foraged in Rajah's grass, the gold eye of the male gleaming in his black head.

Why had she vanished? That was the most damning thing she could have done. I set Janet aside. I was sure that Wallace came to the barn early to get the jump on someone sneaking around. That would be someone using the secret access behind Elephants. An outsider. No one who worked at the zoo had any reason to use that.

Yes, they did.

They did if they wanted to come and go without anyone seeing them at Elephants when they had no business being there.

Something about the elephants themselves didn't seem right. I'd have to think about that.

What had happened to Dr. Reynolds in a previous life that she wanted kept hidden? Something that Quintana had found out. That had the feel of trouble with the law.

I felt explanations floating just out of sight, drifting away when I turned my attention toward them. I pushed away from the guard rail in frustration.

Chapter Twenty-five

"Come on up, Oakley. It's not a party without you. I'll buy your soda pop." Hap, in his cheer-leader, team-builder role, called me at home to announce that he was initiating Pete and Cheyenne into the Vulture's Roost. My guests had assured me they were world-ranked experts on urban transit and had left at some early hour to take the bus to Finley Memorial Zoo, another state and fifteen miles away. Apparently they had survived the journey and their first week in good enough shape to party. I felt better after a day off, but still, a tedious drive and a beery gathering was a stretch. On the other hand, I wanted an update on the cubs and Dr. Reynolds' progress down the warpath. Linda and I hadn't had a minute to talk for days. I should have asked Hap if she was there…

She was, also Denny, Kayla, Ian, and Arnie. The place was close to full, with more people coming in. Hap had scored our usual table, the big corner booth. The music was loud zydeco and Tex-Mex, spreading positive energy and impairing conversation. Foosball and pool tables were busy. Two bartenders sailed through the crowd with big trays of pitchers and glasses. I didn't recognize either and missed the powerful blond woman. Arnie held the floor with stories of mules he had known and their ornery antics. No one was paying much attention, and they looked relieved to see me.

"That little stranger is growing like a weed. Nah, like a water-melon!" Arnie chortled. I started to take the end of the bench, and he reached out to pat my belly. I stood back up to avoid him and felt my lips draw back to show teeth. Denny rapped his wrist. Arnie looked astonished. I settled in at the other end of the bench, and ordered a lemonade and a burger.

"I tried to get Sam," Hap said. He was summery in a black t-shirt with the sleeves cut off, the long cobra tattooed on his muscled arm once again on display. "No answer on the house phone or the cell. I left messages."

"He's probably on vacation somewhere exotic and wonderful," I said. "Are we expecting Thor?"

Pete and Cheyenne, both still in uniform, looked interested. Ian, shrinking in a corner, flinched.

Hap said, "He butted in last time we were here. I guess he thought beer would make his pitch sound better."

"He's not a bad guy personally," Cheyenne said, tracing lines in the fog on her beer glass with a finger.

Denny, hunched over the nachos, said, "I still haven't found out where he was the night Wallace was attacked."

"I don't think he did it, so don't bother," I said. "Too much of a pacifist, right, Cheyenne? Anyway, Marcie's on a rampage, so you'd better let it go." I'd finally talked to her, but so far I hadn't had to come clean about inciting Denny to research alibis.

Kayla said, "Calvin or Janet did it." She had also adapted to sunshine—teal Capri pants and a white blouse with a pattern of little green glass gems on the front.

"Doesn't hold up." I explained why neither made much sense. "That leaves Dale, as far as outsiders go. Anyone know his last name?"

No one did.

I said, "I'll ask Thor. I want to hear what he has to say about that missing van."

Denny started in about security at the zoo and visitors breaking in after hours, which led to no one caring about Asian turtles, all they cared about was a missing dead cub. Linda stiffened at this last, but she didn't say anything.

When Denny ran down, it seemed like a good time to change the subject. I asked Kayla, "How are the cubs? I am so jealous you get to feed them."

"Also I get to rub their bottoms to make them pee and poop."

"Like a real cat mommy," I said.

"All at once they're in quarantine," Linda griped, "and I'm not allowed in the hospital. I miss them."

"They *are* adorable," Kayla said. "Bigger and stronger than I expected. They've got their eyes open, and they crawl around a lot. Good nursers. They meow." She meowed. "Mr. Crandall let a couple of board members name them. Ning for the girl. It's Chinese and means tranquility. Nimbus for the male because of the coat pattern."

Not bad. I especially liked "Nimbus."

Kayla was subdued tonight, no flirting with Hap or Arnie. Was she still on Dr. Reynolds' shit list? I didn't dare inquire. "Losa?" I asked Linda.

She said, "Calmer. She'll be back in with Yuri soon."

To have babies and lose them. Not unusual in the wild, and she probably *had* managed to kill one. But still…I caught myself assigning my own emotions to her. "We'll breed them again? I thought we only got her and Yuri because they weren't prime breeding candidates."

Linda half-stood to reach the pitcher and refilled her glass. "Species Survival Plan people re-ran the genetic calculations and changed their mind. Another litter would be good. I don't know if I have the nerves for it. Think I'll switch to Children's Zoo or get Kip to take me on at Primates."

This was horse puckey. "Working in the office might be better. You could sell tickets. Or maybe become a gardener. You're good with a rake."

Linda slugged me in the shoulder, not too hard. I looked around for other amusement. "How's your first week?" I asked Pete. "You coming back for more?"

"Oh, sure," he said. "Neal got us an advance on our pay. He looks like ten pounds of shit in a one pound can. The man needs Prozac."

No one looked all that sympathetic.

Arnie piped up. "We had a senior keeper meeting today, and he said he's waiting for a day when no one has a mental breakdown. I told him everything used to work pretty well under Wallace."

Easy to imagine how Neal took that. "Not going to settle down until we find out what happened to Wallace," I said.

Kayla made leaving motions, and Denny got out of her way. "Too depressing to keep talking about this," she said. "I'm out of here."

"Kayla, I'm sorry," I said.

She shuddered her head and shoulders, brushing me off. "See you all later," and she was gone. Ian followed without a word.

I felt like a jerk. This was supposed to be a welcome for Pete and Cheyenne, and I'd let the air out of it. "I should go, too," I said, and remembered my guests. "If you guys are ready?"

"I'll take them," Hap said. "But hold up a minute. My new African greys just want to be pals. No love, no lust. You and Pete, help me out."

Hap knew most of what there was to know about African grey parrots, but Pete and I worked it anyway, starting with whether the birds were sexed correctly and ending with diet options, including evaluating the calcium/phosphorus balance. Pete knew more than I did and suggested wood chunks for chewing and providing parallel perches to help the female balance during copulation.

Denny said, "Try red palm fruit oil. I'm testing it on two groups of juvenile garter snakes. The treated ones seem a little bigger. Ian's trying it on the elephants. It's recommended for birds, too."

"Don't even think of telling me to eat it," I said.

Linda said, "Is it from palm oil plantations? From Indonesia? Where they're cutting down jungle to plant palms, and it's ruining orangutan habitat?"

None of us were sure whether this was the same kind of palm oil. We chewed on the irony of tropical forests being destroyed to grow bio-fuel. Arnie said he had to go and left. My houseguests decided to stay, and Hap said he would bring them home. They had a house key.

Outside was pleasantly warm, a breeze tainted a little by automotive smells from the crowded parking lot. No one around, no sign of Dale. It was about ten-thirty, late for me on a work night, but I felt pretty good. I squeezed into the Honda, wondering how this was going to work in another month or two. The seat could go back one notch more and that was it. A least the seat belt seemed ample.

I pulled out onto a deserted street. The surrounding businesses were long closed. At the first cross street, the corner of my eye caught a big pale flicker of motion. I looked left and slammed on the brakes, way too late. A hollow boom wrapped around me. The Honda flew sideways a timeless instant. Slammed itself against something solid. The world went dark.

The night filtered back in fits and starts, with bright lights and incomprehensible sounds. I closed my eyes again, which didn't help.

Someone called my name. I opened my eyes. Hap. Hap right outside my window. Window with air coming in through a crazy-glass frame. Pain all over my left side. Other voices. Denny. Metal noises. Hap: "On three. One. Two. *Three*" and the driver's door screamed and went away. For a confused moment, I thought I'd fall out onto the pavement, but the car was tilted the other way.

A hand on me. A lot of questions and demands. Pain weaving in and out. A siren, flashing lights. A light in my eyes. I batted at it with the hand that worked. A woman I didn't know asked questions I couldn't answer.

Clarity arrived in one white-hot piercing beam: *"My baby."*

Chapter Twenty-six

At last the world was quiet. Quiet and painful. I lay curled up in a hospital bed with a fresh splint on my left humerus. I'd never been able to remember the name for the upper arm bone. I wouldn't forget it again. Humerus with two "u"s. Not humorous. My left wrist also throbbed but wasn't broken. Neck not good, wrapped in a collar that prevented nestling into the pillow properly. Exhausted from questions, MRI, people messing with every part of me. Everything hurt but my heart. My heart soared, its tether snipped loose from dread.

My boy swam his laps, pushing off from my bladder, colliding against the cracked rib, jamming his small self against my diaphragm, tumbling in the tight watery confines of my body.

"She doing okay?" My father's voice.

"I think she's asleep." My mother.

I was facing the wall and couldn't turn over. I meant to say something to them. Safe, both of us safe. I slept.

Nurses woke me time after time, all night long, and nattered stupidities at me and made me open my eyes. I snarled at them and endured pain until sleep snuck up on me again. I awoke for real at some uncertain time of day, no clues from the lighting. After careful consideration, I decided to try sitting up. My mother flurried over and helped stack pillows behind me. She looked tired and worried.

"The baby's okay." I wasn't sure if I was asking a question or reassuring her.

"Yes, they think he's fine. The doctor said he would probably survive anything you would."

"Am I surviving?"

"Yes, dear. How's your head? Is your neck okay?"

The bladder seemed to be the most urgent problem. I rejected the bed pan option, which meant I had to stand up and walk to the little bathroom, then a really tricky series of maneuvers—sitting down and standing up again. Most of me resented this activity with a deep and bitter intolerance. Back in bed, I dozed sitting up.

Nurses and doctors came and went, apologizing for the wimpy pain meds, in deference to my fetus. I sought my inner warrior, the one who was indifferent to pain. She had flicked it in long ago. I got to eat lunch—tomato soup and a thin, pitiful toasted cheese sandwich. My mother left for work, leaving my father on guard duty. My dad read *Sports Illustrated.* I found the TV remote.

Late afternoon, I carefully turned my shoulders toward Marcie and Denny's voices and clicked off the TV. Marcie fussed at me, including a floral-scented feathery hug. She was still in office clothes. Denny, in civvies—jeans and a beat up bomber jacket—stood fidgeting by the bed. He said he was representing the entire zoo, which my mother had forbidden to come. Having them there was a good distraction. The part of my brain that did pain eased up a little.

"You look like every move hurts," Marcie said.

I didn't nod. "Yup."

"And Rick, Jr. is okay?" Denny asked in a voice that tried for casual and failed.

"Yeah, the baby's fine. Better than I am."

A belly-deep sigh. A squeeze of my right hand, blinking and looking away. This was not the Denny I knew, whose emotions ranged from wild enthusiasm to frustration and despair. Not this shuddering relief that sounded as deep as my own. A memory floated up. "You rode with me in the ambulance. You were really upset." Silent and terrified. He'd held my hand then, too, his face white and still.

"It looked bad."

This reticence was also strange. Sure, he would worry about me, but still…"What? You thought I'd die?"

He didn't meet my eye. "I wasn't there when Rick needed me. I promised him I'd take care of you and Rick, Jr. Not doing too good at that."

A promise made to a dead friend. "Goji berries," I said. Raspberry leaf tea. Endless warnings and worries. Intrusive and controlling, but for a reason I had underestimated. The baby was all he had left of Rick, too.

"Full of antioxidants," he said.

"Yeah. Good stuff. Thanks for them." I studied him, chewing on this little revelation. I glanced at Marcie, who stood pale and frozen, one hand gripping the other so tight the knuckles were white. But she wasn't looking at me. She was looking at him. She shifted her gaze to me, and her face changed. The calm slipped back in, and she said, "Do you need me to do anything at your house?"

Denny paced away and back. "Pete and Cheyenne are feeding your dogs." Yes, they would walk the dogs every day and throw balls in the back yard. Pete had Birds covered, no worries.

"What about whoever hit me?" I asked. "Were they hurt, too?" No one had been able to tell me.

Denny shook his head. "Hit and run. Hap's driving around looking for a smashed-in car. He's sure it was pretty damaged, too, so it ought to be close to the Buzzard."

"Was it my fault?"

"I don't see how. They had a stop sign and you didn't."

A relief. "Was mine totaled? I was starting to like it."

My dad spoke up. "It's been towed. We'll know in a day or two. Don't worry, we'll find another one with the insurance money."

The room phone rang. Marcie picked it up. No way was I going to reach over to the little table alongside my bed. It was almost two feet away.

She handed me the phone. "It's your boss."

Not Mr. Crandall. Neal said, "How's it going? I hear you got banged up."

"Yup. Broken left arm, cracked rib."

"I'm sorry to hear that. Good thing the temps can stay on awhile. You're right handed, right? Do you know when you'll be back?"

"Nope. Doctors haven't said when I'll be released for work. Maybe a few weeks."

"Let me know so I can set up the schedule."

"Yeah, I'll be in touch when they decide. Thanks for calling." Thanks for all the slack.

"One other thing." A change in his voice.

"Yeah?"

"Tell me about the turtle in the cardboard box. The towing company found it in the rear of your car. Lucky thing somebody noticed."

"Huh?"

"The turtle. In the box in your car. They knew you worked here so they called me." Patient voice, but with an edge.

"What?"

This was going nowhere. I put the phone down on the bed. "Denny, what is Neal talking about? A turtle in my car?"

Denny came around the bed and picked up the phone. We all listened. "No, both of them were there when I left today. Does it look okay?" A pause. "Sure, put it in quarantine. All of them were chipped. I'll get the chip reader from Dr. Reynolds tomorrow and check." He hung up.

Before we could try to decipher what this was all about, my father spoke up. "You are not going back to work until that baby is born. That's final."

My father never gave orders. I looked at him in astonishment. He said, "That's enough zoo business for today. Thanks for dropping by."

Denny and Marcie took the hint. I wondered if I was brain-damaged and imagining an entirely new father, as well as dream-turtles popping in and out of existence. A nurse arrived and insisted I get out of bed and walk up and down the halls. I did, too confused to protest, and then I slept.

At seven-forty the next morning, Denny called to confirm that one of the stolen Asian tortoises had really, truly been found in my car after the accident. Dr. Reynold's scanner had read the microchip implanted under the turtle's skin, much like the chips that Range and Winnie had under the skin of their necks. The dogs' chips carried a code linked to my address in case they ever got lost. Denny said the turtle was hungry but healthy. He had no theories of how it got into my car. I hung up before he did. But not before saying, "Denny, remember the brownie. Be careful. Bad stuff happening."

My mother showed up a few minutes later with a cup of Stumptown coffee for me with real half and half. After that, plus hospital eggs and French toast, I settled back against the pillows and found an almost-comfortable place to stash my left arm. We waited for the discharge process to wrap up. In the silence while my mother whipped the Sudoku in the *Oregonian*, I concluded that somebody had panicked. Panicked and made a mistake. Two mistakes. The turtle was one. Threatening my baby was another.

It *was* all connected. Now I had to figure out why. Then who.

Chapter Twenty-seven

"I think I found it," Hap said over a fitful cell phone connection. "Front end is smashed, and the paint scrapes look green, like your car. It's face-to-the-wall in the parking lot of this little strip mall by the freeway."

I was home from the hospital, sitting on the sofa in my green sweats, mid morning on a gorgeous day. My mother was outside weeding my shrub border, a task that had never once made it onto my own to-do list.

Hap said, "And you'll never guess—"

"It's the zoo van."

"You did guess. Damn. How'd you do that? I'll call the cops."

"Hap," I said. "Don't. Leave it there. Don't tell a soul. Please? We need to find this person, and I don't want to spook them."

He said, "You didn't ask if the tiger was in there."

"He's not."

"Tarp's gone, too." Traffic sounds. "Cops are actually useful for this. They can run the fingerprints. Whoever stole it might have been careless and might be on file."

"Hap, I think it's one of us. All our fingerprints are in it, so we've got nothing to gain. We can turn it in later. Don't report it yet, Hap. I'm asking you."

A pause. "Who was it?"

"I don't know yet."

Silence.

"Hap, the van wasn't stolen. The *tiger* was stolen."

"Spill, babe."

"It's way complicated, and I haven't got it figured out yet. Give me a day or so. Please?" I considered sharing more and decided against it. The fewer people knew, the fewer could leak it.

Traffic noises and something like a leaf blower. Hap said, "Not if someone might try for you again."

He wasn't that far behind me.

"How could they? I'm not alone for a minute. My parents are terrified my brain will bleed, and they'll find me dead on the floor."

"Not persuasive. I'll think it over."

"A couple of days. No, I need until next week."

Another pause. "I don't like this. Later." He disconnected.

I sank back on the cushions, hoping Hap would, one, not call the police, and two, forgive me for stonewalling him. I could always plead brain damage.

The aches had let up enough that I could think a little. Detective Quintana had scoffed at me for trying to connect all the zoo's current ails into one thread. Now it looked as if I was blundering toward an explanation that did just that. If I had the outline right, each disaster had triggered the next. An hour at the computer left my neck and shoulder muscles in spasms, but confirmed much of my theory.

My mother said she would depart when Pete and Cheyenne arrived after work, leaving behind the rosemary/tomato chicken stew she had simmering. I called Linda and invited her to dinner.

That was the easy call. The second was tougher. The best plan I could come up with was weak. I dialed and lucked out. Dr. Reynolds answered from her office. "This is Iris. Look, I know this is unusual, but I need to talk to you in private right away. It's about the stolen turtle that showed up in my car. You're the only one I can talk to." I wanted privacy and a neutral territory for this conversation. "We can't do this over the phone, and I can't drive because I was in a car accident. There's a coffee shop near my house. I can meet you in an hour." Awkward and chancy, but she finally agreed.

I needed shoes. Tying laces was impossible. I found a pair of fleece-lined leather bedroom slippers that looked like moccasins and slipped them on. I put a ten into my pocket and tidied myself up. How had the right side of my face gotten bruised? It was the left side of me that was busted. I practiced walking around a little. Now for my escape.

I stepped outside and found my mother yanking morning-glory vines off the bank fence. "Mom, I'm going for a little walk. I'll be back soon."

She brushed graying hair back from her forehead. "Let me wash up, and I'll come with you."

"No, you're doing good work there. I need to think. I'll be back soon."

She called after me, "Are you sure you're up to this?"

"No problem. I need a little exercise."

I was dragging by the time I walked the four blocks. It was farther than I remembered. I got my mocha and worked the pity angle to score a table, offering a wounded and grateful smile to the older man who vacated the spot. People sat with textbooks and laptops, mostly one per tiny round table. Dr. Reynolds stepped in a few minutes later, head high, alert. She pulled over a chair and sat down. "Coffee?" I asked. "Tea?"

"No. I have to get back. What's this about the stolen turtles."

I was still in my sweats instead of a uniform, and she had removed her lab coat. That somehow changed the dynamic, made us closer to equals. I inhaled and was reminded about the rib. "This isn't really about turtles. I don't know who planted it in my car. This is about something else."

"What." She sat stiffly in the chair. Her eyes were cold.

"Dr. Reynolds, is someone blackmailing you?"

The eyes went wide. "Whatever gave you that idea?"

"You're trying to keep something secret, something from before you started at Finley. I think it's related to Kevin Wallace dying."

She pushed back the chair and stood up. "That's absurd. You dragged me out here for that?" She stepped toward the door.

"Someone tried to kill me. And my baby." I didn't raise my voice. "I don't think it was you."

She turned and stared at me and went a little unfocused. "Neal said you were banged up. I didn't realize you'd been so badly injured." A pause. "Is your baby okay?"

"He's fine, but it could have been bad. It was enough to break a rib and my humerus." I remembered the name of the bone.

"Why do you think someone hit you deliberately?" Her voice was puzzled, not challenging.

"It was the stolen zoo van."

She came back and sat down. "What you're asking me about has nothing to do with Finley Zoo or Kevin's death."

"I need to know." I waited.

She ducked her head and brown hair flowed forward, almost hiding her face. "One bad decision, one bad choice, and it follows you forever." She raised her head and shook the hair away, in focus now, crisp. "Okay. I married a guy. He liked to scramble around in a four-wheeler. He took a bad fall and broke bones. The recovery was slow, and he got addicted to pain medications, started buying them off the street. I found out, and he went through a program. I thought he was done with that. Months later, I discovered he was stealing ketamine and other drugs from my veterinary clinic. He used them himself, and he sold them to others. He got caught, and I nearly lost my license."

Not what I expected, but not too far off. I remembered something Kayla had said. "That's why the team came to do the drug inventory."

"I'm being watched. One bad choice and it never ends."

"Is someone blackmailing you about this?"

She gave a dark little laugh. "No. Mr. Crandall knows. That's how he got a bargain, a wildlife vet he could afford. I'm damaged goods. Neal knows because he used to ride the dunes with my ex. He recognized me, and I had to tell him. I didn't want the entire staff to know, and Mr. Crandall agreed it would undermine my authority. But I see I can't keep it quiet for much longer. The police found out right away."

"Did Kevin Wallace know?"

"What, you think I killed him to keep my tawdry little secret?"

"I had to ask."

"Yes, Kevin knew from the time I was hired. I had no reason to kill a man I liked. You actually thought me capable of such a thing?"

Hot blood rose in my face, and I looked away. She pushed her chair back as though we were done. But we weren't. "At first, you really wanted me to help you find out who killed Wallace, then you changed your mind and warned me off. Why?"

She hesitated. "The police don't want me to talk about it." She thought it over. "I don't see what harm it can do now…I received a letter the same day Kevin died, after I talked to you. It was anonymous. It said something like 'I did it for you. I'll do anything for you.'"

"Wow. That is so ugly." I digested this for a bit. "What did the letter look like?"

"Typed on white paper. No signature."

"Do you have it with you?"

"No."

I didn't have the apologetic letter that Denny found with his brownie. "Was that the only one?"

"No. One more came. It said something like, 'I'll always be here. You can count on it. I'll do anything to be with you.'"

"Yuck. So you had the security guard escort you to and from the parking lot. Do you think Ian wrote them?"

She shrugged. "The police questioned him and a man in my neighborhood with a prison record. There's no fingerprints, and they both denied it."

No wonder Ian had become so unapproachable. He was probably afraid to be anywhere near a woman. I told her about Denny's tires and the "apology" he received. "I wish we could compare the letters. It wouldn't surprise me if the same person sent them."

She gave me that subtle "are you nuts?" look. "Why would you think that?"

"Denny was asking about alibis for the time of the attack. Nobody has one, so Denny is no threat, but the person who attacked Wallace wouldn't know that. He or she tried to stop him by getting him stoned and fired. Someone is muddying the waters. And trying to implicate Ian."

"Ian *was* parked outside my house all night. It seems extremely unlikely that all these incidents are connected."

"Yeah, that's what Detective Quintana said. I'm sorry about putting you through all this. I won't tell anyone about the old drug issue or the letters."

"We're done?"

I nodded to the extent my brace permitted.

She stood up. "I tried to call you off for your own safety." She left without another word.

The price for this conversation was high.

It was a long walk back, and my mother was anxious. I lay down on the sofa, worn out with nothing to show for it. No, not true. I'd eliminated a complication to my main theory. Dr. Reynolds' secret was irrelevant, but the letters she'd received were not. I slept.

Cheyenne and Pete showed up soon after work, sooner than I expected them to make it home by bus. They came in grinning and full of energy, a contrast to the gray anxieties that dragged me down. They urged me and my mother to take a look at my driveway, now inhabited by an enormous cream-colored Lincoln Continental with a peeling landau top. According to Pete, Hap had wearied of chauffeuring. He acquired or discovered this ancient vehicle, dropped in a battery and a radiator, and handed it off as a loaner. We admired it at length, and my mood lightened.

Cheyenne waited until my mother was occupied at the stove, then told me that she loved the car, but was a little perturbed by Hap's instructions. "He said never go over the speed limit and always use the turn indicators. No getting stopped by the police." She wrinkled her brow. "Would Hap give us a hot car?"

"No, no," I said. "Well, maybe a little warm. The registration might be unclear. I wouldn't worry about it."

She did not seem reassured.

I said, "The vacuum cleaner is in the closet in your room."

Cheyenne said, "It's not dirty. The upholstery is spotless. It's a really classy ride."

Pete blinked twice and said, "Uh-huh, you betcha," and pulled out the vac. My mother found the extension cord, and he scoured out the land boat until not a seed or a leaf or a dusting of powder could possibly remain.

My mother left to feed my father, and Linda showed up. We ate with Winnie and Range sitting on alert nearby, ready to assist with any spills the instant they occurred. Congenial, tired, hungry people eating a great dinner. In my house. Despite everything, it felt good.

After dinner, Pete and Cheyenne caught up on American television in the living room. I took Linda upstairs and sat on my bed with the door closed, leaning against the headboard with pillows behind me. She lay sideways across the foot of the bed. Her hair was still bi-color, red roots and blond tips. She wore a black sweater, jeans, and heavy boots that she stuck out to keep them off the bed. Her ears looked barricaded, loops like chainmail marching up the rims. She said, "Your forehead is all wrinkly with big thoughts. What's up?"

"Linda, I think all the disasters are connected, and the link is money. Not flash anger or jealousy or careers or embarrassing secrets. Wallace, Raj, the cub, the turtles—it's all the same thing." I was still in my trusty green sweats and slippers. My arm hurt, and I rearranged pillows.

Linda said, "Try me."

"The common thread is traditional Asian medicine. It's a huge market. Millions and millions of dollars. That's what's behind this. An opportunity to make some bucks."

Linda tucked her lips in and bit them. "Rajah. The van."

"You got it. Cut and wrapped tiger parts. Bones, fat, meat… It's all used."

She sat up. "The cub?"

"That too."

"Was the cub's death deliberate?" Her voice had that deadly edge.

I considered. "No, stupidity, like we thought—and then someone took advantage. It wasn't that hard to sneak in and out of the quarantine room until recently. It's all about taking advantage of opportunities."

"Somebody inside the zoo."

"The turtle in my car pretty much proved that. Whoever took the turtle knew where I was and decided to implicate me in the theft. Insurance in case the crash wasn't enough to stop me."

"Cold. But it fits." Her eyes narrowed, fists bracing her on the bed. "Asian wildlife exterminated, bears tortured for their bile in tiny cages, all for quack cures, and if you're right, it lands in our laps in Washington. Why do people still take that junk?"

I'd had more time to think about this than she had. "You know plenty of people distrust Western medicine, and plenty can't afford it. People have been using wildlife products and herbs for thousands of years. And most of us still are."

"Not me!"

"Think again. Denny's forever pushing herbal teas at me and those goji berries. Calvin eats raisins soaked in gin for his arthritis. The stores are full of remedies that didn't come out of any pharmaceutical lab or white-coat research institute."

"I don't eat dead tigers. The plant stuff is different."

"Not to the botanists who watch whole species get wiped out. Like ginseng. It's been hammered in the East. The United States East. Yeah, the whole business is unsustainable and often criminal, but it's big money, especially the wildlife."

"If we have our very own scum sucker, taking dead animals is bad enough, but it's escalating. Those turtles were alive, and the one they still have won't be for long."

"Linda, it's not a crook we're after. It's a murderer."

Her voice was doubtful. "You are losing me. I am not seeing this connecting to Wallace. Trying to steal an elephant? Last I saw, we still had two, and they were both healthy."

"Wallace confronted someone in the barn and that's how he got killed."

"Murder to cover up theft? Rajah hadn't been stolen then."

I explained how the elephants were alive but part of the scam. "This person probably panicked when Wallace caught him in the act." I told her about the brownie and about the zoo van turning up with green paint in its dents. "So there's a real mix here of planning and impulse, scheming and grabbing opportunities on the fly."

"You know who it is, don't you?"

I thought about what to say. "Maybe. Whoever it is, it's going to be hard."

"Tell me."

"I could be wrong. I have a plan to find out for sure."

I described what I wanted her to do. She argued. We kept at it until she agreed, and we were both exhausted. I started it up by calling Denny's house. No answer. He was probably at Marcie's, which complicated things. We decided it couldn't be helped. Marcie answered and we chatted about my recuperation, then I asked for Denny.

He had dropped the guardian angel role and didn't waste time with inquiries about my aches and pains. "Look. I think that turtle was a message. It means you're supposed to do something, and then we'll get the fourth one back. Have you gotten anything in the mail? Over the phone?"

"Denny, the message was that I stole the turtles."

A pause. "*Did* you steal them?"

"No, you idiot. It was a plant. Now listen. I want you to do something."

"I didn't think you did. Never hurts to ask, avoid assumptions. Start with verifiable facts, that's what Marcie says."

"Shhhhh. Stop talking…Listen."

"Okay, okay."

Eyeing Linda in case she wanted to fine-tune the instructions, I said, "Starting tomorrow, brag to everyone about that red palm nut oil you're using. Recommend it for everything. And, this is the important part, be sure to say how great it's working for the elephants." I emphasized the crucial parts.

"Is it true?"

"You're the one that said Ian was trying it on them, and yes, it's true."

"Why am I doing this? What has palm oil got to do with the fourth turtle? Does it leave a signature under ultraviolet light or something?"

"Whoa! Come back! Just do what I say and keep in mind this works only if you act normal. Your normal."

Linda rolled her eyes.

"What exactly is the plan here?" he asked, "'cause I hate finding out what you're up to when it's too late to duck."

"If it all works, this will get the fourth turtle back." This was unlikely, but it seemed the best way to keep Denny on the rails. "Call me tomorrow and let me know how it went." I almost hung up. "Oh, and tell everyone Janet killed Wallace, and I'm stupid and crazy not to think so."

I hung up and Linda said, "What's that bit about Janet? Why does that matter?"

"So no one will try for him again."

Linda looked at me funny. "You know, you two have the weirdest relationship ever. I don't know how Marcie stands it."

"Let's finish this up. Practice Part Two on me."

"Starting Friday afternoon, I tell people that I overheard Neal talking on his cell phone. He's going to ship Damrey and Nakri out on Monday. A truck is on its way to take them somewhere else, I don't know where. He doesn't want anyone at the zoo to know so that Thor and his gang can't interfere." She stopped. "But Thor and his gang *want* them shipped somewhere else. Did you forget that?"

"No, it works. If Neal doesn't want them to know, it must mean he's shipping to another zoo and not a sanctuary. They'd want to block anything else. I mean, that's the rumor. Wait until late Friday so Neal won't have a chance to deny it until Monday.

We're gambling he won't come in over the weekend and that no one will call him about it."

"People are going to be stirred up." She got off the bed, frowning.

"That's okay, as long as they don't do anything. Discourage any action."

Linda nodded and wandered around the room. She looked tense and still doubtful.

I plowed on. "Don't tell Thor. Leave him out of this. He really will react, and I don't think he's who we're after."

"Ian might tell him." She studied a picture of Rick on my dresser.

"We can take that chance. I don't think he will."

"What about Pete and Cheyenne?"

"Skip them, too. They aren't relevant."

"I'm going to look like a nut case if this doesn't work."

"It might *not* work. But I will come up with another plan in that case. This is like fly fishing. We've found the pond. This is our first cast. Maybe the trout will take this fly, maybe we'll need to try another one. But we will catch this fish. Worst case, I'll find a way to dynamite the pond." Linda stood at the window looking into the dark, her face unreadable. "You'll do this?"

"Yeah. It's worth looking like a nut case."

"The technical stuff," I said. "We need it in place Friday night, but no sooner. Can you handle it?"

"Yeah, I just need an electrical engineer. Got one?"

"I don't believe so. You can do this. The important thing is that nobody notices."

"The important thing is that I don't get caught."

"Same thing," I said.

"Not quite." She put her hands in her pockets. "If this works, we'll need the police."

"If this works, we'll have them."

Chapter Twenty-eight

On Friday, I had an hour after breakfast of fretting about The Plan. I worked through all the ways it could go wrong, which were many, and the changes that should be made so it wouldn't go wrong, which were none that I could think of. The rest of the day was devoted to health care, with my father serving as chauffeur. My mother had set up a medical marathon and our tour began with the dentist. Pregnancy can be hard on the gums, and my mother wouldn't hear of me cancelling. Dr. Chen lectured me yet again on the supreme importance of flossing.

Over lunch at my father's favorite taqueria, feeling a trifle bad about crudding up my immaculate teeth with a tamale, I told him I needed a replacement car pronto. He said he'd been busy and hadn't had a chance to work on it. Maybe in a couple of weeks.

"Oh, I get it," I said. "You want me stuck at home."

He chuckled. "Pregnant, barefoot, and in the kitchen. That's what they used to say about a woman's place."

"How amusing. I want a car. If you don't want to do it, I'll buy one on my own."

He casually sopped up fajita sauce with a scrap of tortilla. "Have you got the insurance money yet?"

I did not. What I had was a ripple of panic. Being without wheels would complicate my life further, and my once-reliable father was not going to help.

Next on our medical tour was a follow-up appointment on my accident injuries. I was getting tired, and The Plan was a knot in my stomach quarreling with the tamales. I asked the doctor when I would be released for work, which led to a stand-off between him and my father. They compromised on no decision, something that could wait a couple of weeks. I felt like a horse at the vet's, the participant without a vote. Back in the truck, Dad said, "Your arm won't heal for six to eight weeks. And then you'll be, what, eight months pregnant. So forget about going back to work."

"I can do light work with one arm, and I need the hours. I'm using up sick leave I want to use after the baby's born."

"Charge those free-loaders room and board and take unpaid leave."

I bristled and explained that, once they had some money, Pete and Cheyenne had bought a mountain of groceries and given me cash for gas and utilities.

"Then what's the problem? Relax and enjoy the summer. You'll be busy enough real soon."

Better to drop the subject.

After the clinic, Ob/Gyn took a crack at me. I contributed blood and pee and signed up for birth classes. Dr. Regan let Dad watch the sonogram of a sleepy but healthy ghost creature. "You need to slow down the weight gain," she said. "No ice cream or cakes. Eat all the vegetables you want."

Sweets? I craved food in whatever form was closest. Cake or kale, it was all the same when my body screamed, "Feed me!" I tried to explain this and received a helpful brochure.

My dad dropped me off at home, a rare and brief period alone, and I napped. After Pete and Cheyenne finished cleaning up from dinner, I called Linda from the kitchen phone. "I don't have wheels. Sorry to put you to the trouble, but I need you to come get me this morning. Four o'clock should do it. I'll be out front."

"Iris."

"Yeah?"

"Denny and I talked about it. We don't need you here. You might as well stay home and rest. It's not like you're in tip-top shape."

"Excuse me? You talked it over with Denny? We were going to keep it to the two of us, were we not?"

"You were. I decided this was better."

"And you are writing me out of the script?" I was getting hot.

"You wrote the script. You figured it out. Maybe. Anyway, you don't need to be here. I mean, look at you. Sling, neck brace, bruises—you look like a crash test dummy gone wrong. We can cover this."

"Linda. Do not screw with me. I *will* be there. We can do this the easy way or the hard way. Pick me up at four in the morning."

"Sleep well. I'll call you as soon as anything happens." She hung up.

I was speechless. Except for the swearing.

Cheyenne came out of the living room to ask if everything was all right. She and Pete had been watching *Monsoon Wedding*. I swiveled my body the better to see her. My neck was still off-duty. "I need to borrow your car later tonight. I'll have it back in time for you to get to work." This was almost certainly untrue, but what choice did I have?

Her eyes shifted toward the kitchen sink and her shoulders hiked up toward her ears. "Um, Hap said you might ask. He's worried about the car getting wrecked because of your neck and so on. He said it would be complicated. He said it wouldn't be good for you, and you might get hurt even more."

"Hap said not to let me borrow the car?" I was stuck between outrage and amazement. I smelled Linda in this.

"Um, yeah. And…it's, um, his, and we have to do what he says…"

Linda, Denny, Hap, my parents. A conspiracy to keep me at home. I climbed the stairs to my room. After a few minutes, Cheyenne said through the closed door, "I'm really sorry. Don't hate us. You've been so nice."

I lay on the bed on my good side and considered the bus. They ran infrequently at night. I could take a taxi. I'd never done that, but there's a first time for everything. Irritation faded slowly. This was simply a problem to solve. I decided what to do—the Plan now had a preface. I set my alarm for four o'clock and opened a book on Asian birds. Sitting in the quiet, I followed Pete and Cheyenne's evening. Loud intro to TV news, quickly hushed. Later, steps on the stairs. Water noises from the bathroom. Pete calling, "Are you coming or not?" Low murmurs of conversation from the bedroom next door, then a surprising giggle. Louder murmurs, abruptly cut off. Silence for several minutes, then a stifled groan, followed soon by a muffled gasp.

I put the book down and, out of emotional exhaustion or envy or just because it was time, dropped the barriers that took so much energy to maintain. A desperate yearning for sex swept in, for bare skin on mine, for eager hands and mouths creating pleasure. I ached with frustration and defeat until desire ebbed and left simple loneliness behind.

I probed for grief and found that the anguish of Rick's death, renewed when Wallace died, had eroded and changed, the glass shards tumbled and blunted in the waves of recent troubles. The explosive anger that flared up when grief was awakened the wrong way—I hadn't known it was there, and I couldn't tell if it had gone out. I slumped limp and aching in mind and body as a weary, tentative peace moved in. I could think of Rick, of being partnered again, of sex, without the sense of bitter loss. That was new. Damrey still tugged at her invisible chain, the chain that had scarred her leg. My chain had begun to fall away. I could imagine that someday the scar might fade.

The alarm woke me at four, cutting off a dream of elephants stalking me through a junkyard overgrown with tangled vegetation, elephants ridden by people who meant me harm. I fumbled the clock radio off as fast as I could to keep from waking Pete and Cheyenne. No telling what they had been instructed to do to stop me. I lay back in bed and gathered myself. I could do this. I lurched to my feet before sleep could reclaim me and stood digging my nails into my palm to wake up, trying to think.

I was dressed and had my cell phone. I could walk out of the house and call a cab from a block or two away. No, I'd made a plan and a taxi was only the fallback.

Awake now, I stepped out of my room and patted the dogs, who slept in the hallway. They followed me downstairs. I found the flashlight in the kitchen junk drawer and crept back upstairs and into my guest room, letting the light peek through my fingers. Winnie and Range wanted to come in, too, but I shut the door in their faces.

Pete and Cheyenne were spooned together on the mattress on the floor, bare arms relaxed on the light blanket. Pete had kicked the covers off his feet. I found his pants. No keys in the pockets. I found Cheyenne's pants. No keys. Pete snorted and moved a little. He shrugged off the blanket part way. A narrow band of dark hair made a line from belly button to sternum and feathered over his chest. Cheyenne's arms were pale and soft in the dim light. What if they caught me prowling? I couldn't guess how pissed off they would be, but for sure it would mean trouble.

I turned off the flash and thought. Where would they hide the keys? The easiest place to look, now that the pants had failed me, was their boots. The third boot did the trick. Triumphant, I backed out and eased the door shut. I whispered to the dogs to be good and locked the front door behind me.

The Continental started better than I feared, and I backed it down the driveway. I glanced back at the house. Pete stood at the kitchen door, the lights on behind him, jeans sagging on his hips, shirtless and defeated. I drove away wondering if he would call anyone.

The Lincoln was no picnic to drive, wavy steering and poor visibility. The fact I couldn't turn my head didn't help. I pulled over before the freeway entrance and fussed with the side and rear-view mirrors until they could give me at least a clue as to what was behind and alongside. I didn't ask anything tricky of the car, and it plowed out of Portland, floated over the broad Columbia River on the Interstate Bridge, and swooned off Interstate 5 onto the zoo exit.

I couldn't see any reason not to leave it in the employee lot. No one would recognize it yet. I walked through the employee gate into the zoo proper in darkness, twitchy and hyper-alert.

It was cooler than I expected, a breeze kicking up. I kept an eye out for the security guard, who wouldn't be leaving for a couple of hours.

The Education offices were a disappointment. No Linda, no video cameras set up as discussed. I stood in the dark wondering what was going on. I headed toward the elephant barn. Shivering a little, I used the flashlight now and then, but mostly could manage without it. I stepped carefully—falling down would be ugly. The paths around the elephant exhibit looked empty. I took a risk and shined the flashlight around the undercover viewing area and found no one. Damrey and Nakri stared at me through the window, reflections bouncing around.

I walked back out. The clouds relented and an almost full moon gilded the shrubbery and the rail around the exhibit. The soft hum of the electric cart warned me. I stepped back into darkness until the guard passed. What was going on? Where was Linda? Flummoxed, I came back out and stood on the path, wondering what to do.

A voice hissed, "Iris!"

I startled in a way that sent stabbing pain through most of me.

"Here, giraffe barn."

Linda. Relief flushed away terror and confusion. I hustled across the path and through the door into the shelter of the giraffe kitchen. She shut the door, and we whispered in the dark.

"You are crazy, you know that? How did you get here?"

"Stole a car. You are so going to pay for this. Why aren't you in the Education office with the video monitors like we planned?"

"I am not invisible, and I am not an electrician. No way could I get a camera set up at Elephants without the entire world knowing it. Trust me. This is better."

"We can't see a thing."

"Iris, when we are done yelling at each other, we will open the door and stand here and watch."

"Oh. Let's do that."

She opened the door, and we stood inside and stared toward Elephants. After about thirty seconds, I fumbled around until I found a chair and pulled it quietly to the doorway and sat. She stood and I sat, watching darkness.

My eyes picked out a shape moving swiftly toward us. Heart thudding, I elbowed Linda. She said, "He's late." Denny found us, we shushed him, and he moved off to the Asian Experience construction site. Linda whispered that he would sit on the ground by the backhoe and watch the manure shed and the back fence.

We waited. A faint descending warble might have been a screech owl or my imagination. A lion coughed to announce that he or she was awake. The air was cool and fragrant with animals, full of night secrets. I shivered, but not from cold. We waited.

The corner of my eye caught movement from the construction site. Denny, jogging toward us. I was surprised and then angry. If he wrecked this…

He veered close to us and said, "Reptiles."

I grabbed his arm before he could lope off. "What?"

"I set up a motion sensor. It sends my cell a text message when the door's opened. Someone's after the turtles again."

Linda said, "Stay here," and the two of them trotted away.

I made a half-hearted start after them, but running was out of the question. Linda was right. I was in no shape to tackle anyone, and they didn't need me. I turned around on the path and looked toward Elephants. There was still a possibility…I returned to the doorway of the giraffe barn. Probably I'd guessed wrong and stealing turtles was the target. Probably I was wasting my time freezing in the dark while staring at a dark barn. I thought I saw movement in the strip of land outside the visitor perimeter, but it wasn't repeated. I listened and heard only an insomniac mallard from the waterfowl pond. The lion coughed again, but didn't escalate to roaring. The sky had lightened a little. Small dark birds flew overhead, unidentifiable.

And then the elephant barn wasn't so dark. I didn't trust what I was seeing. The dawn sun shining through a window in the back door, dimly illuminating the front stall? There *was* no window in the back door.

I slipped into the visitor area, keeping well back in the shadows. One light was on, in the back of the barn. I pictured it filtering over and around the stacked hay bales. Large dim shapes moved in the front stall, long rolling snorts echoed. I caught the pink blotch on Damrey's trunk as she strode past the open door to the back stall. The other shape—Nakri—moved through the door, and I could see her backing up to the bars by the back hay rack.

I'd been right after all.

I flipped open my cell phone—bright in the darkness— turned to shield it with my body, and dialed Linda as fast as I could. It cut to voice mail immediately. Turned off. I dialed Denny. After way too many rings, voice messaging answered. "Come to Elephants right now," I whispered, and clapped it closed. He had the volume turned off. Why, oh why, didn't we all have our radios? Because radios were part of our work uniform, and we weren't in uniform.

Whoever was in there had a choice of three doors to exit: through the viewing room where I stood, the back door in the work room, and the back door at the far end of the barn beyond the hay. No way could I cover them all.

I couldn't take risks. I was in no shape to protect myself or my baby. But if I didn't identify this person, someone was going to get away with murder and attempted murder. I knew the barn pretty well. I could get close enough to see who it was and then hide until they were gone. It felt reasonable.

I put the key into the door at the end of the visitor window and stepped into a warm fog of elephant smells, closing the door softly behind me. Next, the door to the work room. I eased that door shut and felt my way slowly through the narrow room toward the hay storage, toward the light bulb and the backside of the second stall.

"Hold still," snapped a voice, and I juddered to a stop, adrenaline spiking. "Good girl," said the voice. "That's better." Not talking to me.

I took a breath and eased around the corner, the same corner I'd dashed around with a bucket of produce when I was trying to rescue Wallace. There was the bank of levers for operating the doors. And there was Nakri's butt pressed against the bars, shifting uneasily.

And Kayla.

I sighed, disappointed but not surprised, and eased back to where I could barely see. I would watch a few more seconds to confirm what she was doing, then tiptoe back the way I'd come. But Nakri whirled—Kayla snapping at her—and oriented toward me, ears out, trunk reaching through the bars, searching for my scent. Kayla turned and looked, then stepped swiftly toward me. I crouched and scuttled back, aiming for cover under the work table. She was on me like a serval on a mouse, yanking my sling. I stifled a scream and lunged toward her, staggering to my feet. She'd hooked the sling with an ankus. She disentangled it while I was standing up and grabbed the back of my neck, her hand sliding below the brace to grip my skin, the ankus half-raised in her other hand.

"Damn you, Iris," she hissed. "Why do you always have to screw things up? Why the hell can't you mind your own *business*." She shoved me toward Nakri, toward the bars. "Why do you make me do these things?"

I stumbled forward, propelled by her iron hand, knowing she would hit me with the ankus, knees failing me, my neck muscles spasming. Damrey trumpeted out of sight and then crowded into the back stall with Nakri. Nakri roared. They circled within the stall, big bodies brushing each other and the walls, big feet pacing fast, ears and trunks shifting and waving in the dim light.

Kayla pushed me half-upright to the bars and, out of the corner of my eye, I saw her raise the ankus. "Don't kill my baby," I gasped. "Don't."

Her face was frozen in rage and determination. "You'll tell Jean."

She would kill me with no more thought than she'd killed Wallace. I had no strength to fight, no place to escape to. An elephant collided with the bars and I felt them hum against my body. We were away from the narrowly spaced bars, away from safety, standing by bars spaced wide enough for keepers to slip through, bars where trunks could reach people. I lunged into them, jamming my thick body through, into the stall with the two elephants. Kayla shrieked and swung at me. The heavy stick came down on my shoulder, and I fell forward, into the melee of elephant feet. A leg brushed me and shoved me sideways. I caught myself with my good hand and was shoved again, pushed sprawling against the bars, my arm a searing agony. I twisted, desperate to get out of Kayla's reach, blank with terror and pain, the elephants or my own mind roaring. I looked up to see the ankus rising up again, aimed toward my face, no way to evade it.

A thick gray leg crammed me against the bars. A blur of elephant. Trunk reaching over me, circling Kayla's upraised arms, crushing her against the bars, then letting go and stepping back. Nakri, it was Nakri, with Damrey flapping her ears and trumpeting behind her.

Kayla crumpled next to me on the other side of the bars, her face two feet from mine, her eyes open and sightless, the ankus alongside her.

I lay paralyzed as the two elephants milled around, feet scuffling on the floor, squeaks and rumbles, Damrey's trunk fumbling at my legs and then my chest. After a minute or two, they hadn't stepped on me or grabbed me. I pulled myself up and squeezed out, dizzy and nauseated, half-tripping over Kayla.

I limped away and stopped to lean against the wall by the levers. Light switches. I turned them on. It made no difference. Still two elephants in the second stall. Still Kayla lying on the floor, her head at an impossible angle. I thought, I should pull her away from where the elephants can reach her. I couldn't do it. I made it to the work room and sat shuddering on one of the metal folding chairs, my hand trembling on my belly, until Denny and Linda found me.

Chapter Twenty-nine

My friends needed only a few words to understand what had happened. Denny checked Kayla. There were no surprises. The elephants had moved to the front stall and left her body alone. They were quiet. Linda made phone calls, then she found acetaminophen in the first aid box, a drug I was actually permitted to take, and gave me two with a mug of water. She handed me damp paper towels to clean my face and hands and pulled bits of straw out of my hair. My mind began to clear.

"Baby okay?" she asked.

I nodded. "Moving around a little. Seems good." Denny relaxed his hovering. "What happened at Reptiles?" I asked him.

"You gave me the idea, about those elephant collars texting the rangers. I bought a motion detector that does the same thing. Fifty dollars. I set it up at the door to Reptiles, and it texted me."

"I got that," I said. "Did she take the turtles? Where are they?"

Linda said, "They're fine. We didn't see a soul. I think Kayla assumed Denny was somewhere on the grounds and set off the motion detector to find out. Once we showed up, she knew we would be occupied at Reptiles and felt safe to come here. Probably never occurred to her that anyone else would be around, especially you."

"How did she know about the gizmo?"

Denny said, "I had trouble setting it up, and she helped me. She was really into it."

Of course. I sighed and said, "She wasn't all that reassured—she used a back door to the barn, and she was on me in a flash when Nakri noticed me."

I stood up shakily and rummaged in the work room until I found the bag of dried mango slices. I walked to the front stall, where the cows were hanging out, and said, "Nakri." She came right over and seemed unclear whether she should turn around or not. I held out a mango slice, and she reached for it with her trunk tip, breath going in and out of the two air holes, the moist little finger on the end grasping the treat and ferrying it to her mouth. Her dark little eye gleamed. "Thank you," I said. "Thank you." For saving me. For not killing me. For being who and what she was, even though I could never really know her. I fed her slice after slice, one at a time, until the bag was empty, then I walked back to the work room and sat down again.

The pain had subsided into a collection of sullen aches by the time the EMTs arrived. Ian walked in a minute later, eyes wide. I checked my watch and was surprised to find it was almost seven-thirty. Linda gave him the short version. Ian looked at me in deep dismay. "You shouldn't go in with them. Not safe. You were lucky." His tone implied that I should know better.

Detective Quintana arrived next. Neal showed up excited, spewing questions and orders, but Quintana got there first and was in charge. Neal caught on and sputtered to silence before the detective had to yank his chain. Quintana told us all to keep quiet, checked in with the EMTs, then said to a woman officer in uniform, "Office Kurtch, keep these people separate and silent."

Ian said, "I got work to do."

Quintana wasn't impressed. "Stay here with the others. Oakley, we'll start with you." He herded me out of the work room and into the keeper area by the front stall. Neal followed us. I leaned my back against the viewing window, the two men glowering at me. Quintana said, "What happened here?"

Neal said, "She looks like a train wreck." He stuck his head in the work room. "Denny, get her a damn chair."

I said, "I need to eat."

Neal said, "And a carrot or something."

Denny delivered. I sat down and handed back the carrot. "Wash it and peel it." Who knew whether it had elephant slobber on it?

"What's with all the bandages?" Quintana asked with no hint of sympathy.

"Car crash," Neal said. Quintana looked at him from under his eyebrows.

"Car crash a few days ago," I said.

Denny came back with a properly prepared carrot and a fossilized doughnut. "Coffee soon," he said, and retreated. The officer stuck her head out and pulled the door closed after him. Quintana and Neal turned to me.

Quintana said, "So. A woman is dead. And it better not be because you didn't mind your own business like I told you to. Start at the beginning."

Did Kayla die because I'd set this trap? All that impulsive vitality ended forever in one horrific instant. I searched for reflex guilt and didn't find any. She'd killed Wallace and was happy to let Damrey take the blame. She'd desecrated Rajah and abandoned Calvin behind bars. She'd done her best to kill me. "Sorry, what was the question?"

Quintana scowled. "What happened?"

I tried to pull myself together. "Kayla was selling zoo animals for traditional medicine, probably to people here in the U.S. She had connections in the Asian community from a previous job. I caught her in the act here at the barn, and she tried to kill me with the ankus. Nakri saw Kayla do that to Wallace. She stepped in and saved my life." Ian and Cheyenne worked within range of that deadly trunk every day, no matter what Mr. Crandall dictated. "I don't think Nakri meant to hurt her, just to stop her, so I wouldn't die like Wallace did." I had no idea what Nakri's intentions were, but I owed her big time. I would cut her all the slack I could.

Denny brought me coffee, black, and some packets of white powder. "Nothing real in the fridge," he said before I could ask for milk or cream, and left me to my suffering.

I took a sip for courage and said, "Kayla had expensive jewelry, with a story about how she got each piece for free since her pay wasn't much. She probably started with the elephant hair, clipping their tails. The elephants are trained to back up to the bars, so it was easy and safe. That's what she was doing when Wallace caught her and that's what she was doing this morning. Cambodians believe that an elephant-hair bracelet will protect their babies." There was some kind of irony in that, but I couldn't grasp it at the moment.

"And you knew she'd be here doing that?" Quintana looked at me in a way that made me wonder whether he could put handcuffs on a person with one arm in a sling.

"This week I told everyone that Ian was feeding the elephants red palm oil as a dietary supplement and that their tails had grown out again."

"Is this true?" Neal asked.

"Quiet," Quintana said.

"Yeah, it's true. Dr. Reynolds approved it. Then I told everyone that you were going to secretly ship out the elephants on Monday morning."

"Is this true?" Quintana asked.

"No," Neal said. He looked at me sidelong. "How did you manage all this communication from home?"

I chewed on the carrot stub. "Phone."

He and Quintana looked at each other.

I said, "The idea was to get word to the thief so he or she would come to clip the tails one last time before the elephants left. And she did. I wanted some back up—" I moved my sling in explanation "—so I made Linda and Denny help. We hid and waited to see who showed up. I thought she'd come over the back fence, but she probably didn't this time."

"Back fence?" Neal asked. "You can get in that way?"

I nodded, which made me wince. I looked toward Quintana. "He found it, too."

"Did you plan to tell me about this someday?" Neal's eyes did the laser beam thing, only with sparks.

"I was going to call you once we saw who it was. Both of you. This was all my plan, and Denny and Linda didn't want to do it, but I talked them into it." I tried dunking the ancient doughnut in the coffee. "We hid and watched, but Kayla set up a diversion at Reptiles. Linda and Denny went to check that out, and I stayed here."

"And you saw…?" Quintana said.

"Like I said, Kayla clipping Nakri's tail. You'll find scissors and the cut hairs by the back stall. Nakri scented me, and Kayla caught on in an instant. She was *so* fast. She pulled me out from where I was hiding. I went in with the elephants to get away from her and fell down. She was going to kill me with the ankus, but Nakri grabbed her and pulled her against the bars. It was so quick…" I slipped back into that moment and felt my head go light.

Quintana's deep voice brought me back. "This time you're trying to convince me that the elephant really did do it?"

I nodded and gnawed on the doughnut to ground myself. "Yeah, this time she did."

Neal said, "The missing tiger?"

I nodded. "Rajah's probably at her house in the freezer. Some of him, anyway. She knows, knew, how to dress out game. She took the dead cub and the turtles, too. All of them are used in traditional medicine. The real money was probably the tiger."

Quintana, as usual, looked disappointed by humanity, me in particular.

"Search her house," I said. "You can't dismember a tiger and not leave evidence. And look for that other turtle. Denny really, really wants it back. And please turn Calvin loose."

Quintana said, "Did that last night. His daughter showed up. She was in Seattle with her kids seeing some doc who says he can cure autism with a special pill. Then she went touristing with a friend. She says didn't know about her father."

Good news. "Calvin withdrew his confession."

"His daughter told him she was at a church retreat the night Wallace died."

She'd never mentioned that. Maybe she liked people thinking that she was a person who could settle a score for good. Maybe her alibi was totally phony. It didn't matter.

"More importantly," Quintana said, "Lorenz's neighbor finally noticed that he was gone, and his cat was hungry. Somebody gave him the story. He came in to tell us his emus got out the morning Wallace was attacked, and Lorenz helped him round them up. Couldn't have been at the zoo at the same time." He made a face. "*Emus.* What has happened to the American farm?"

Calvin was back home and in the clear. I felt a huge relief. Calvin behind bars was not the way the universe should operate.

Quintana said to me, "You go back there and wait with the others. Send out that other woman."

"Wait," I said. "I'm sure Kayla sent those letters to Dr. Reynolds to implicate Ian. Can you tell by looking at her printer? I read about that once…"

Quintana said, "Go back there and wait."

When Quintana was done with us, he issued various warnings and let us go. Denny said the detective needed to pay more attention to his spiritual side—he had way too much yang and not enough yin.

Neal followed us outside and told Denny and Linda to get to work. "You"—pointing to me—"come with me." He commandeered the security guard's electric cart, and we drove to the Administration building. While I was grateful for the ride, my body had forgotten the carrot and that doughnut. My neck and shoulders hurt, not to mention the arm, and I was filthy from sprawling in elephant dung. Neal said, "We need to talk, but it can wait until tomorrow if necessary."

"Might as well get it over with. Are you going to fire me?" I hoped that was a joke.

"Can't. Not while you're pregnant and disabled. You could sue the socks off the zoo."

"Nice to know." The implication about the future, after I healed up and gave birth and thereby lost my free pass, was not lost on me.

Somehow it was after eight o'clock. Jackie's eyes were huge as I slogged past her and into Neal's office. It still didn't seem right for him to settle into Wallace's chair behind Wallace's desk. I dropped into the guest chair. Neal looked at me and walked to the door. "Jackie, go get a sandwich or something and bring it here. Carton of milk and two cups of coffee."

"*Senior* Administrative Assistants do not go out for snacks," she said. "And the cafe doesn't open until eleven anyway."

Neal leaned his forehead against the door frame. "Jackie, a *Senior* Administrative Assistant knows how to make things happen. *Make it happen.*"

A sullen "yessir" came from the reception area.

I waited, mind going blank, while he messed with his fine new computer. "Where are those temps?" he muttered. "People think they can come in any time they want around here."

"They're on the bus," I said. "I stole their car."

He didn't lean his forehead on the monitor. He merely closed his eyes for a few seconds. "Right."

"You can tell when people clock in? From here?" That was a level of surveillance I hadn't expected.

"Only if you load the software that came with the time clocks."

My inhabitant woke up and did his own messing around inside me. Jackie came back with food much sooner than a trip to the nearest convenience store would require. She put an aromatic takeout bag and two mugs on Neal's desk without a word and returned to her desk. I heard the intern's voice outside as she closed the door. "Now what am I going to eat? You can't just take—"

I unearthed a breakfast sandwich—fried egg and sausage patty. "You want half?" I asked. He shook his head, and I consumed it all with excellent manners. Rapidly but delicately.

He said, "I used to have a wife with a metabolism like that. Reminds me of short-tailed weasels."

I sipped a little coffee. I'd barely touched the cup in the elephant barn, so I was still within my quota. "One of us has to tell Dr. Reynolds that her best friend killed Wallace and is dead now. And about the missing animals so no one else is blamed."

Neal said, "I'll take care of it."

"She'll take it hard, even if she doesn't show it." That was all I could think of to say, in hopes he would do it gently. As if there were any way to soften this. "Tell her those stalker letters came from Kayla and not Ian. She must have found out he had a crush on Dr. Reynolds and tried to implicate him."

He said, "If the police confirm the letters, I'll tell her. That will not let him entirely off the hook, however. I will deal with Ian later. You, I will deal with now. What, exactly, made you think setting up this scheme in secret was okay? One person's dead, and it's pure luck you aren't, too. This is *beyond* loose cannon. I'll be starting disciplinary action, and I am definitely putting you on office duty for as long as you work here."

Some internal compass needle quivered between tears and anger. As usual, I found out which way it settled when I opened my mouth. "You wouldn't be sitting in that chair if Kayla hadn't killed Kevin Wallace. Maybe that means squat to you, but it means a lot to the people who worked with him. It's not like you or the police were figuring this out. This could have gone on for *years,* and she was starting to take *live* animals. Of *course* I kept it secret. You'd never believe a word I said, anymore than that cop. She tried to kill me and my baby, and I sure couldn't count on *your* help." I managed to stop myself there and sat still, taking one shuddering breath after another.

Neal's face was cold and still.

I said in a near whisper, "It got personal, but I didn't think it would end like it did."

Neither one of us said anything for a little while.

I said, "I tried to work with Detective Quintana, but he wouldn't. He said I was trying to link too many things together, and that I should stick to my birdies. That made me mad so I tried to see if everything *could* be connected. The only link I could find for the missing animals was traditional Asian medicine. I looked it up on the Web, and they all had medicinal uses. I was amazed at the volume of animals and the billions of dollars."

Neal rubbed his nose and moved his jaw around. "Did you know it was Kayla?"

It seemed we'd agreed to a sort of truce. "It had to be someone at the zoo, even with the hidden way in. It didn't make sense that Damrey and Nakri were so upset when the NAZ committee was here. They were both in circuses. I saw a performance recently. It was incredibly noisy, with flashing lights and people doing all kinds of weird stuff. The elephants were steady as could be. Damrey and Nakri shouldn't have been so agitated by a bunch of people standing around at the barn. I figured that whoever killed their buddy Wallace must have been there."

"That was a stretch. They haven't been in any circus for years, either one of them." He was disagreeing, but without the arrogance that set my teeth on edge.

"The turtle in my car clinched it. How could anyone except a zoo person steal it and know where I was and which car was mine and what direction I would turn to go home? A bunch of us were at the Vulture's Roost Tavern, and I made it clear that I was still trying to figure it all out and that I was connecting Wallace's death to the stolen animals. She left before I did. She didn't live far away. She must have put the turtle in my car before she set up the zoo van and waited to t-bone me."

"The zoo van? You were hit by the zoo van?"

I realized too late that this was another item I'd kept secret. "Hap found the van in a parking lot all bashed up."

The phone rang, and he picked up, scowling at the interruption. His side of the conversation was mostly "uh-huhs", ending with "Thanks. Let me know." He tapped his fingers on his desk. "The police are at her house. They're hoping to bust her customers. We're to keep quiet about the traditional medicine angle."

I liked the idea. Her customers might be buying rare animals killed in Asian forests as well as the zoo animals.

He said, "She gets caught in the act with the elephants, kills a guy, and keeps on stealing animals. And she tried to kill you. That takes brass."

Neal was staying calm. I wasn't sure why or how long it would last. "She was tough, but she may have killed Wallace out of panic. She had lightning reflexes, and he might have surprised her. When I showed up, she knew I would cost her the income, her job, and her friendship with Dr. Reynolds, plus she might be tried for murder. She reacted really fast—impulsively."

The phone rang again. He muttered, "I told Jackie…" but answered. A lot of uh-huhs and thank-you-very-much's. He drummed his fingers on the desk and seemed to switch gears. He leaned toward me, compelling blue eyes in a tanned face. "Oakley, I will think about what happens next. You dealt with the problem, but you won ugly. No more Lone Ranger. I am responsible for this whacked-out institution. I am paid to make decisions and to take certain risks, and you are not. Not this kind of risk. Next time you get an inspiration or a suspicion, next time you learn something about this place that matters—"

"I talk to you," I said. I'm not stupid. He was rethinking firing me. And yet. "And you'll *listen* to me?"

His jaw clenched and relaxed. "I will listen. *However*, that's not the same as agreeing. If I do not agree, that is not a license for you to do whatever you feel like. Is that clear?"

"Yup."

He leaned back in the chair, appraising me. "You're pretty tough yourself."

I remembered that Jackie said he'd been in the military.

"You covered for your buddies. Sometimes that's admirable, sometimes it's stupid. You didn't fool that cop, but I don't think we'll have any trouble there. I said I was the new foreman and would keep you out of trouble. He said he'd send me a condolences card."

"I kind of liked him. He was a step ahead of me most of the way. I wish he'd have worked with me."

"Not in this life. That last call was to say Denny's going to get his turtle back. It was in her bathtub. And Quintana found a key and a receipt for a meat locker at Kayla's house, so the tiger is probably accounted for, too."

"Ask them to check her printer against those letters."

"I'll remind him." He tapped his fingers and straightened up. "I don't see how we can prove Kayla killed Wallace. Convicting her of violating the Endangered Species Act might not have worked either. The courts would struggle with selling parts of endangered species when they were captive bred. Nakri saved us a lot of legal hassle. Not that anyone wanted Kayla dead."

I nodded.

"But Nakri also created a lot of hassle." He was thinking out loud.

I made a concerned-and-listening face. Neal was swifter than I'd thought. I was having trouble keeping up.

"The elephant exhibit can't meet current requirements. They should be in herds of at least three animals, and it would be good to breed Nakri—cows love having a calf around. We won't meet optimum standards, regardless of investment, because the square footage potential is inadequate. Kevin Wallace and the Species Survival Plan coordinator made arrangements to ship them to a zoo that's expanding their elephant yard by several acres. They'll have state-of-the-art facilities for a big herd. It was a good solution. But they won't take a proven killer and an old blind cow."

Sam had been right about Wallace not being straight with him. But that plan was dead, and we were still stuck. "What can we do?"

He shrugged. "Wait until Damrey dies of natural causes. Then ship Nakri to any place decent and go out of the elephant business. In the meantime, hope Nakri doesn't blow away anyone else."

"She won't."

"Be nice if you're right. We're already short-handed." He glowered a little. "That was a joke."

"Um, I have a suggestion."

An unwelcoming stare.

"Okay. Never mind." So much for promises.

Neal rubbed his nose. "Let's hear it."

"Drive around behind the elephant barn, outside the perimeter. There's a big buffer zone between the zoo and the road. It would be interesting to know who owns that strip and whether the zoo could claim it. It looks like several acres, and there's more land adjoining that's not being used for much of anything."

"Already looked into it. The city owns it and wants to sell that land to balance the budget."

"You and Mr. Crandall are going to roll over and give up?"

"Oakley, you are not in a position to play hardball."

We glared at each other until the phone rang again.

After fielding the call, apparently from the mayor, Neal hung up and said, "I'll take another look at it. Beat it. Call me when you're ready to come back."

I beat it.

Chapter Thirty

It was Denny's day off, and he wasn't around. He didn't need to be part of this. I was still on the disabled list, still wearing the neck brace and sling. Linda was in uniform. We looked like "Wrong Way!" and "Right Way!" in an OSHA safety video. It was early in the day, the time before the zoo opens when keepers are scrambling to get as much done as possible before the crush of visitors begins. It was also the time when we were least likely to be observed or interrupted.

Linda unlocked the keeper door to the Reptile building. We walked into the center aisle, the back sides of exhibits to the right and left. Pumps hummed, reptile smells greeted us. The air was humid and a little warmer than outside. Arnie was standing on a stepstool leaning over an aquarium. He looked up, surprised at the intrusion. I watched him recognize us, watched a little fear cross his face. He was manipulating a suction tube that pulled crud out of the gravel in a frog exhibit. Arnie shut the little machine off.

"Good morning, ladies! What can I do for you?" His greeting was a little less perky than usual. He stepped down to solid ground.

We eased down the aisle toward him. I stood by his left side, Linda by his right side. I took the tube out of his unresisting hand and put it down on the lid of the frog exhibit. "Arnie, we need to talk."

"Sure! Any time. What about?"

Linda smiled with her teeth showing. "Arnie, you know and we know that Kayla took those turtles while you were working Reptiles when Denny was sick. You thought it wasn't important, right? No big deal if she wanted them for pets. I mean, they were pets before we got them, and we had four of them. Kayla was nice to you, and you decided not to notice."

"No, no, I wasn't here. It was news to me. It was all fine when I left that day."

Linda smiled again, and I was glad she was my friend and not my enemy. "Arnie, Arnie," she said, "what are we going to do with you? You saw how mad Dr. Reynolds was about that work order for the repairs next to the clouded leopards. And then you knew Kayla took those turtles, but you didn't say a word."

"I didn't take those turtles." A feral glint arose in his eyes. He would bite if we pushed him too far.

Linda didn't care. "What do you think, Arnie, that Neal would say if we told him you saw Kayla take those turtles? I mean, after the cub dying and all. How do you think he'd react?"

Arnie shook his head. "No. I didn't. He wouldn't like it. It's not true. I mean…"

I took over. "Arnie, I never saw you as a guy who wanted a lot of stress in his life. You're more laid back, right? Go home and sleep well at night?"

He knew it was a trap, but he couldn't figure out what to do about it. "Yeah, I try to be easygoing."

I laid a hand on his upper arm, a friendly grip. "This senior keeper gig, it's got to be wearing on your nerves. More pressure?" My grip tightened a little.

He looked at my hand. "No, it's fine. No, I mean, yeah, it's more pressure."

"You realize it's going to get worse. Right, Linda? I mean, Neal's going to kick ass about the work we do, and he's not easy to please. He'll pick on every little thing. Going to get rough."

Linda nodded brightly. "Neal's a mad dog. He'll go through this zoo like a chainsaw through butter. He's got big expectations for us all, especially senior keepers. Very demanding."

I said, "Arnie, we don't want to see you get hurt. We're think-ing that keeping your head down is the best thing for you. I mean, Wallace is gone, you have to start over with Neal. It won't be much fun. Maybe better to keep a low profile. Maybe better to go back to being a regular keeper, and let someone else take the hits."

Arnie got it. "Yeah, yeah. I see what you mean."

Linda and I smiled. I said, "We'd hate to see Neal come down on you like a ton of bricks." Linda squeezed his left arm, I patted his right arm. We closed the door behind us as we left.

On August 12, Mr. Crandall announced that the zoo had acquired "significant new acreage for an expanded, state-of-the-art elephant exhibit." By that he meant ten acres behind the existing zoo. This was after the city council held a week of public hearings. Bill "Thor" Thorson testified persuasively about the shortcomings of the old exhibit. Dale Baker spoke vehemently against zoos, comparing them to Nazi prison camps and Gitmo. This raised hackles and pretty much ruined his case for sending the elephants to a sanctuary. It also nearly got him punched out by a fan of Damrey's who wanted her to stay in Vancouver. Linda said that after the hearing, she saw Thor ripping Dale a new one, emphasizing something about "effective strategies."

On August 13, eight months and twenty-five days after Rick died, Robert Oakley Douglas was born. The birth was dramatic, terrifying, painful, and astonishing. In short, normal. My mother and Marcie served as birth coaches. Linda was out of town. Neal had sent her to a feline conference in the other Washington—the D.C. one. She was not yet a senior keeper, although Arnie had been reassigned as a regular keeper at his own request. Linda was in line for the job once the zoo's staffing settled down.

Robby emerged weighing eight pounds, three ounces, look-ing around in amazement. Denny examined his tiny palm and said he had a terrific life line.

Afterword

Biologists estimate that half of all wild mammal species are declining in the wild largely due to habitat destruction and overharvesting by our own species. For more information about the wild animals and issues mentioned in *Did Not Survive* and an opportunity to contribute to conservation, see the organizations listed below. Please do what you can to help.

- TRAFFIC, a wildlife-trade monitoring network with a fascinating website: http://www.traffic.org/
- International Elephant Foundation: http://www.elephantconservation.org/
- Association of Zoos and Aquariums Elephant TAG (Taxon Advisory Group/Species Survival Plan): http://www.elephanttag.org
- Clouded Leopard Project: http://cloudedleopard.org/

To receive a free catalog of Poisoned Pen Press titles, please contact us in one of the following ways:

Phone: 1-800-421-3976
Facsimile: 1-480-949-1707
Email: info@poisonedpenpress.com
Website: www.poisonedpenpress.com

Poisoned Pen Press
6962 E. First Ave. Ste. 103
Scottsdale, AZ 85251